weeping

weeping

A FRITILLARY QUILTER MYSTERY

SHELLY REUBEN

KATE'S MYSTERY BOOKS
JUSTIN, CHARLES & CO., PUBLISHERS
BOSTON

This is a work of fiction. All characters and events portrayed
in this work are either fictitious or are used fictitiously.

ISBN: 1-932112-20-0

Library of Congress Cataloging-in-Publication Data is available.

Published in the United States by Kate's Mystery Books,
an imprint of
Justin, Charles & Co., Publishers
20 Park Plaza, Boston, Massachusetts 02116
www.justincharlesbook.com

Distributed by National Book Network, Lanham, Maryland
www.nbnbooks.com

10 9 8 7 6 5 4 3 2 1

PRINTED IN THE UNITED STATES OF AMERICA

This book is for my husband, Charlie King.
Now and forever my hero.

And it's for Charlie's angels. Loyal, beautiful, funny, strong, and smart:
Jo Ann Davaris
Lucia Lilikakis
Mary Heaney

How lucky I am.

acknowledgments

Weeping was born in the mind of Susanne Kirk, who encouraged me for over a decade to write about a female fire investigator. Kicking and screaming all the way, I finally listened. After I wrote *Weeping* I turned it over, lumpy and misshapen to my literary agents, Bob Rosen, president of RLR Associates (who doesn't know I call him "my boss"), and Jennifer Unter, who was wonderfully gracious about more or less inheriting me. Between the two of them, they punched, kneaded, pinched, and prodded my book until, much to my surprise, it took on shape, form, and a delicious consistency.

Entirely because of Susanne Kirk, Bob Rosen, and Jennifer Unter, I fell in love with my own creation.

Then, my luck continuing, *Weeping* was delivered into the warmly receptive, kind, and capable hands of Stephen Hull, my publisher, and Carmen Mitchell, my editor, who at every turn, were sensitive to Fritillary and Ike, and did everything possible to assist them in investigating their first fire together.

My sweet and wonderful husband, Charlie King, as in the past, taught me everything I had to know about fire investigation, and will always be in my heart.

weeping

chapter one

I HAD ALWAYS BEEN ENVIOUS of creepy little geniuses who knew exactly what they wanted to do with their lives on their way out of the womb.

"Excuse me, Doctor, but could you disencumber me of this umbilical cord, clean up the mess, and give me a palette. I want to paint the Sistine Chapel."

Jealous. Jealous. Jealous.

That was me. Of them. All of them. The itty-bitty prodigies who plunk their chubby fingers down on the keys of a piano and Beethoven's Fifth comes out. The toothpicks in tutus who jut out an elbow or a hip on their way home from kindergarten, and next thing you know, they're dancing *Giselle*. The knobby-kneed brain children wearing bifocals and nerd shirts who beat everybody, including IBM computers, at chess.

What they had was what I had always considered to be the ultimate dream.

To know exactly . . . exactly what I wanted to do from day one. To look up into the sky and not to have seen a choo-choo train or a kangaroo but to have seen clouds as cumulus or stratocumulus entities. To know that they are not made out of cotton but out of water vapor. To know that they are formed when moist air rises and becomes cooler. To have become so fascinated by clouds that

I could have decided right there and then, with a cold clump of grass under my head and a few dandelions stuck between my toes, that I loved clouds and wanted to be a meteorologist when I grew up. To have been twelve years old, watching a blastoff to the moon, and know that I was going to be an astronaut, or to sit at my mother's feet in the kitchen and know that someday I would be a mother and have children of my own.

That would have been my definition of heaven.

All that I had ever, ever wanted was to know, keenly, purely, and with impeccable certitude, that this is the direction in which I'm going. This is what I want to do. This is who I am. This is what I want to be.

But that is the one thing I never had when growing up.

My love affairs with career options were so intense and of such short duration that if my work life had been my sex life, I would have been a nymphomaniac.

Suffice it to say, I was not a happy camper.

Once, only once, when I was fifteen years old, did I get a glimmer of what I probably should have been destined to be.

I was babysitting at the time, and very responsible. Then, as now, I loved to work, even if I didn't know what the elusive "work that I loved" was going to be. Despite my omnipresent career angst, I was not a particularly neurotic teenager. I was pretty normal in that I detested doing dishes, loved my parents but didn't care to admit it in public, and would have hated to do homework if I'd ever allowed such an option to intrude upon my consciousness.

The people I used to babysit for every Friday night were Mr. and Mrs. Borkin, who lived across the street in a big barn of a house. They had a child named Bradley, a tank of goldfish, one occupant of which was always dead, a turquoise parakeet named Pickle (I don't know why I remember that), and very little furniture.

They were an odd, unattractive couple, and this is a conclusion I had come to even before I almost burned down their house. She, Mrs. Borkin, had straight, blunt-cut hair, bangs, and an unattractive, angular face. I think she was a chemist or a pharmacist. If she had poisoned her husband or her child, I wouldn't have been surprised. She was also a compulsive talker. Just listening to her tell me what to feed her four-year-old, when he should go to bed, what he was or was not allowed to do, and where she and her husband could be reached in case of an emergency was a dizzying experience because every nugget of information was buried in an avalanche of words, between which not a breath was taken: "Mr. Borkin and I love the theater don't you when I was sixteen I starred in the school production of *Little Women* and I played Jo there are chocolate chip cookies in the cupboard but don't eat any of the apple pie when Mr. Borkin and I were dating we used to pick apples at a farm near the university my niece has been accepted at the state college in Albany we'll be back no later than eleven o'clock I think the new stoplight on Main Street is going to . . ."

And so on.

Mr. Borkin, as could be expected, rarely said a word, and he never smiled. I have no recollection of what he looked like, but I remember that even when he was paying me at the end of the evening, I could look right into his face and not be one hundred percent sure of what I was seeing, almost as if he was a Mr. Potato Head and someone kept switching the nose and ears on me.

Mrs. Borkin had told me enough, or I'd listened at enough keyholes, to know that the reason there was so little furniture in the house was that they had played a game of brinkmanship with their credit and almost lost.

Houses in Conversation, New York, where I grew up, are very expensive. Just think three-quarters of a million dollars as a starting point and you'll have the price of an average Tudor or Colonial on a quarter-acre lot. The only reason my parents could afford to live there was that they had bought their house years ago, when most of our neighbors were farmers and most of our best friends were cows.

And so the Borkins, after paying their mortgage, had little left over for incidentals like chairs, sofas, tables, lamps, heat, and electricity.

Bradley's room was a small rectangle at the top of the stairs. Honestly, I think it was once a walk-in closet. He had a bed, a chest of drawers, and so on, but looking at it made you wish for the fantasy days of the 1950s, when children had cowboy patterns on their bedspreads and Lincoln Logs sets on the floor. He had a computer, of course. But no stuffed animals. No comic books. No warms and fuzzies. And there was that omnipresent dead goldfish in the den.

The den, inanimate marine life notwithstanding, was the only room in the house I could tolerate, because it had real furniture, which included a beat-up sofa with maple-wood armrests and matching chairs, a coffee table on which were old issues of magazines about child rearing, the aforementioned fish tank, a television that didn't work, a very full bookshelf, probably left over from the previous owner of the house, and a table lamp.

Because I had just discovered Dostoevsky, I'd brought along a book to read after putting Bradley to bed. I was riveted by the intense characterization, the passionate interplay of personalities, and the involved plot. It wasn't until ten years later, last year, in fact, that I realized there was sex, too, in Dostoevsky. As with career choices, I am sometimes slow on the uptake.

So I had tucked myself into a corner of the sofa, turned on the table lamp, and bent my head over a particularly exciting scene where Prince Myshkin was about to have another attack of brain fever. That's when I realized that either I was going blind at an astonishingly rapid rate or the light in the room was inadequate to the task at hand.

I stood up and peered down into the lampshade.

What do you know? There was a measly forty-watt bulb inside.

So I did what any avid reader would do under similar circumstances. I removed the shade, put the lamp on the floor so that the bulb was level with the book on my lap, and continued to read.

I know, because I was told a thousand times, that I am very, very lucky to be alive, and I have no quarrel with that. I *am* very, very lucky. After I fell asleep, I must have moved a hand or a foot and somehow knocked over the lamp so that the bare bulb fell against a cushion of the sofa.

I'll never know what it was that woke me up in time. Maybe Bradley calling out in his sleep. Maybe headlights of a rare car passing by that reflected in the window of the den. Maybe a dog barking, or Pickle squawking in that particularly strident parakeet way. But something woke me up before the fumes could overtake me. Whatever that something was, it propelled me into a state of instant awareness, and I had time to save both Bradley and myself before the sofa burst into flames.

Obviously, the fire had been my fault.

I had taken the lampshade off the lamp.

I had fallen sleep

I had knocked the lamp over.

And I didn't lie about it either, which had been a great temptation after being excessively fussed over for having saved Bradley's life.

My parents were not angry. They'd almost had heart attacks when they saw the fire engines pulling up across the street, but their evaluation of the situation after the dust settled was that the Borkins, living in a house they couldn't afford and subjecting me, the babysitter, to a cheap forty-watt lightbulb, had brought the situation on themselves.

I, on the other hand, felt guilty.

I hadn't liked the Borkins, but it was their house, they had left me in charge of it, and I felt that I was ultimately responsible.

So, as I found out later, did their insurance company.

chapter two

I SHOULD HAVE FIGURED OUT what I wanted to be on the day that I first met Ike Blessing. *He w*as what I wanted to be. But more about that much, much later.

The aftermath of a fire is generally about as bewildering as surviving a car crash or witnessing the commotion of objects being hurled around with random violence during the tempest of a tornado. You're shocked. If you move at all, it's generally in response to something that somebody tells you to do ("Check her for bruises." "See if she needs oxygen." "Get that blanket and put it around her shoulders."). You aren't at all sure of what happened to precipitate the confusion, and you have no idea what's going on.

The fire engines arrive.

Your parents rush across the street.

Someone, maybe the fire chief, asks you questions.

Your mother brings Bradley to your home and puts him to bed.

Your father — or maybe it's Mr. Tallman from the corner house — extracts from you the location of Mr. and Mrs. Borkin, whose house, apparently, is on fire.

On fire? How can that be? Just a few minutes ago, you were reading Dostoevsky.

The Borkins return.

Mrs. Borkin, the compulsive talker, is now compulsively talking hysterically.

Mr. Borkin's face is deadpan. Possibly he's thinking that with the insurance money he'll receive, instead of repairing the damages to his house, he'll go out and buy a thick steak or a blonde with a pert nose and no vocal cords.

A man who writes for *The Conversation Bulletin,* our weekly newspaper, comes up and asks me questions. I recognize him from the last tennis match I won at school. He took my picture then, and he takes one now as I stand, huddled in a blanket I don't need, by the flashing lights of a police car.

And then, almost without transition, I wake up the next morning and it's over. How did I get from there to here? Was I really babysitting for the Borkins last night? Do they really live across the street? Did what I think happened really happen?

I got dressed, went downstairs, and reassured my parents that I was quite all right and definitely capable of going to school that morning, to which they responded, "There is no school, dear. It's Saturday." Then they proceeded to become involved with one or another of my multitude of siblings, and I went out the side door of our house.

I could have gone out the front and been instantly confronted by the sight of the Borkins' house across the street, but I wasn't ready for that yet. If reality had to be faced, I wanted to sneak up on it.

It's amazing how slowly I can walk when I try.

I'd slept late that morning, and it was almost noon before I left the kitchen. I had considered myself an ultra-mature fifteen-year-old until about midnight of the day before. Now I felt young, inept, useless, and as if I would spend the rest of my life being pummeled by an ego-deflating and arbitrary fate.

It's amazing how quickly a teenager can turn into a two-year-old when everything doesn't go her way.

It took me about three years to cross the street, because it's difficult to walk across a slate path, down a flight of garden steps, over a patch of grass, down a curb, across a street, up a curb, and over another patch of grass without once looking up.

When I finished performing this inefficient combination of somnambulism and trespassing, I found myself on the sidewalk that intersected with the brick path that led to the Borkins' front door. The configuration of the house where I had babysat the night before was not complicated. Think of a loaf of bread. Square off the corners. Put a row of windows on the top floor. Put a row of windows on the bottom floor. Put a roof on top and a door in the middle. The den in which the fire started was on the right side of the ground floor of the house.

I looked up.

I was very, very surprised.

What I had both dreaded and expected to see was a loaf of bread that had been in the oven *way* too long and had been burned, blackened, deformed, collapsed, and crisped. What I saw instead was the same big old barn of a Borkin house, pretty much as it had been yesterday morning, with the exception of a board covering a broken front window and a trail of soot discoloring the siding outside the den.

I don't know exactly what happened then, but the next thing I knew, I had crumpled and was sitting on the grass. I guess I'd collapsed from the strain of . . . of . . . relief? Could that be possible? I *hadn't* burned the Borkins' house down. I hadn't. I hadn't. I hadn't. And . . .

"Are you all right, sweetheart?"

Those were the first words that Ike Blessing ever said to me, and to me they symbolize everything that I later came to know about the man. Observation: He recognized that there was something wrong. Concern: He took it upon himself to intervene and see if he could help. Masculine indifference: If he knew that in contemporary society the revised and reconstituted male is no longer permitted to refer to a girl as "sweetheart," either he didn't care, or he made the unsubstantiated assumption that I really *was* a sweetheart, which had the same effect on me as a protective, avuncular arm around my shoulder would have.

I don't remember what I said in response.

I don't remember a single thing *I* said or did the rest of that day, except to follow Ike Blessing around outside the Borkins' house and then to tail after him inside, and listen to what he had to say.

What I learned or figured out later was that Ike was Isaac C. Blessing of Isaac C. Blessing Associates, Fire and Arson Investigations, New York City, New York.

I saw him only that one day, and then he disappeared from my life for ten years.

He was thirty-five at the time and had been a fireman for umpteen years before transferring to the Division of Fire Investigation, where his job was to investigate fires. He was in line to become a supervising fire marshal when a mayoral election brought a change of command to the fire department, and the new commissioner, appointed by the new mayor, who was decidedly *not* a law-and-order man, opted to take homicide investigations away from the fire marshal's office and give them to the police. Which, in effect, meant not to prosecute arson homicides at all, since New York City police officers were neither equipped nor trained to investigate them.

In frustration, Ike Blessing left the department that he loved and the job that he loved, set up an office in Brooklyn Heights, and put out his shingle. Shortly thereafter, the fire commissioner resigned at the pinnacle of an influence-peddling scandal. He was replaced by a former battalion chief who loved fire marshals and restored most of their powers. But it was too late for Ike. He had pushed the Down button on that elevator, and there was no going back.

What I know now but didn't know until much later was that *my* fire was Ike's first case as a self-employed arson investigator. There were many, many more things about Ike that I didn't know.

What observations I did make that fateful day were pretty much limited to the man himself. He was then and still is handsome. He has the kind of hair you expect to see only in a retouched photo, but it's real and it really is an Alpine yodeler shade of blond. His eyes are diamond shaped and crystal blue. You'd think they would be cold, but they're incredibly warm and friendly. At least they are when he isn't taking on the guise of Avenged Justice. He has a big nose, big ears, and a square, Joe Palooka jaw.

Very rarely in real life do you meet someone who looks like the movie version of the man who just got back on his horse after saving a whole western town, but Isaac Blessing looks like that. And acts like that. I was a puddle of exhausted, nervous imaginings, and he was the tall, laid-back intruder to my neighborhood. He held out his hand. I took it, and he hauled me to my feet.

"I'm Ike Blessing," he said. "The insurance company asked me to take a look at this fire. Who are you?"

I was glued to his blue eyes.

"I'm Fritillary Quilter," I said. "But my friends call me Tillary."

"Do you live here, Tilly?"

I didn't choose to correct him. "No. I'm the babysitter. But I started the fire."

Ike didn't do anything for a few seconds; he just stared at me. Then he said, "We'll see about that."

He went to his car, where he opened the trunk and took out a flashlight. He flung a camera bag over his shoulder, and obeying a jutting motion of his head, I followed him. First we circled the house. There was a pile of rubbish in the backyard, outside the den window, on top of which was a burned, deformed, fabric-covered rectangle. He picked it up and tucked it under his arm. Then he proceeded to take pictures of all four sides of the house. He took most of the pictures outside the den.

"See, Tilly," he said, "when you walk the exterior perimeter of the structure you're investigating, you can get a general idea of where the fire started even before you go inside."

I had a very specific idea of where the fire had started. But of course, I *had* been inside.

We approached the front door. Ike wiggled the doorknob. It was unlocked.

"May I go inside with you, Mr. Blessing?" I asked with unchar-acteristic meekness, since I had no intention of being left behind.

"Sure, sunshine. Come on in."

He turned on his flashlight, but the first thing he did once in-side the door was to flick the light switch. Nothing happened.

"It isn't hooked up to anything," I explained, and I walked to an arched doorway leading into the living room, where there was another wall plate. I pushed that switch, and a bulb in the ceiling sent out a dim yellow glow.

"That's odd," Ike said.

"What?"

"The electricity is still on. The fire department usually turns it off."

"Why?"

"So that if there are any downed electric cables or frayed wires, there's no chance of a rekindle, and nobody gets hurt."

He moved toward the den.

"It started here," he said. Then he stopped and again did nothing except stare, but this time he stared for about five minutes, and he wasn't staring at me.

I followed his eyes as they studied the various objects in the room. The fish tank. All of the goldfish were dead. The windows on the back and side of the house. Unlike those in front, these weren't covered with boards, and they hadn't been broken, but a thin layer of soot covered every pane and transformed the bright sunlight outside into a grim shade of gray. The walls, too, which yesterday had been dull beige, were now varying shades of black, darker on the bottom, lighter as the soot moved to the top.

Ike Blessing stared at two chairs that matched the sofa where I had been sitting. He walked to the corner of the room where someone had tossed the lamp, and he picked it up; he poked around a bit in the debris of wet magazines, pushing aside my sodden Dostoevsky, and he located a circular area on the carpet which, apparently, had not been subjected to fire. Then he positioned the base of the lamp over the bare space on the floor and set it down. It was a perfect fit.

I was dumbfounded. It was like magic to see him perform motions that, I didn't know until much later, were a reconstruction of the fire scene. There was more magic when he took the burned, fabric-covered foam rectangle that he'd found in the backyard and repositioned it on the sofa.

"You were sitting here," he said. But there was a question in his eyes.

I nodded and pointed to the right side of the sofa, near the armrest.

Ike picked up my Dostoevsky. It was literally dripping.

"You were reading but" — he looked around the room again— "there wasn't enough light, so you —" He again crossed the den, this time to the opposite corner, where in with old blankets, sweaters, and books, he found a crushed lampshade. The one I had taken off the lamp.

Ike held it up.

Again, I nodded. "It was so dark," I squeaked.

Ike returned to where he had positioned the lamp beside the sofa and tilted it forward so that the broken bulb rested in the exact spot on the cushion where there was now a crater of black foam.

"This was a smoldering fire," he said. "You must have gotten out before it was going very long or you'd be dead. No offense intended."

I started to cry.

"Oh, sweetheart. Sweetheart," Ike said. "I don't want you to be unhappy. I'm just trying to scare the hell out of you so that you never do it again."

I blubbered and nodded. Ike took out a fresh, white linen handkerchief — he still carries them — and he dabbed at my eyes. But he didn't give it to me yet. First, he cleaned up the wreckage of my tears; after that he pretended to wring out the handkerchief, as if it were soaking wet, and then he gave it to me.

I never returned it to him.

The telephone rang.

Ike strode out of the den and followed the sound to a wall phone still connected in the kitchen. He picked it up.

"Hello."

I heard only his part of the conversation, but it wasn't hard to figure out what was going on.

"Right," he said into the receiver. "I'm almost finished here. . . . Yes. Very little damage. . . . No. All of the furniture was destroyed in the den. Smoke damage throughout the house and water damage on the ground floor. That's right, the electricity is on. . . . Yep. Exactly where the chief said it started. Heat generated by contact of a lightbulb with a sofa cushion. . . . Uh-huh. The babysitter. . . . Hold on a second, I'll ask her."

He looked down at me.

"Sunshine. Where do you live?"

"Across the street."

"How old are you?"

"Fifteen."

He patted me on top of the head. If he'd had one, I swear he would have given me a lollipop. He turned back to the telephone.

"Did you hear that?"

There was a murmur from the other end of the receiver. It went on for a long time. Ike listened patiently, and then winked at me. Into the phone he said, "You're a nice guy, Cecil, and since you were a reasonably good fire investigator before your brains turned to mush at that cushy corporate job, I'm going to do you a favor, but first I'm going to tell you who's standing in front of me right now."

Another murmur from the phone.

"No. It's not the fire chief. It's a sweet little girl named Tipperary Filter."

"Fritillary Quilter," I whispered.

Ike put a significant finger over his lips, gave me a "hush" glance, and went on. "She looks like an angel, Cecil. She's got a pretty sprinkle of freckles over a pug nose, eyes like green tiddly-winks, and a smile that would melt the hardest heart of a hard-hearted juror. Are you listening, Cecil? Because the smile is nothing compared to the tears, and I can guarantee you, my friend, that if the home office insists on subrogating against her family, you're going to confront some very compelling tears from this very com-pelling child. And you're going to lose big-time. This was an acci-dental fire, Cecil. Leave it at that. A good lawyer could argue that subjecting a babysitter to a room with inadequate lighting was property owner neglect, to say nothing of improper hiring prac-tices and violation of a dozen workmen's compensation and child labor laws."

The murmured response from the telephone this time was less emphatic.

"That's a good boy, Cecil," Ike replied. "And if the home office balks, you just send them to me."

Then he hung up the phone.

"What happened?" I asked.

Ike smiled. It made such a pleasant change to his face that I realized he didn't smile often.

"That was my friend from the insurance company. The one who hired me to investigate this fire."

"What did he want?"

"His bosses want him to sue your parents for the cost of fixing this house."

My mouth dropped. I was horrified. I mean, I had an older sis-ter who was already in college, and assuming some university would be unwise enough to accept me, that would make a total of five tuitions my father would have to pay to get all of us through school, as well as every other expense associated with bringing up a mob of children. If, on top of all that, my parents were going to be *sued*. Oh my God. Oh my God, I thought, and I did what any dutiful daughter would do under the same set of circumstances; for the second time that day, I started to cry.

Ike unfolded the fingers of my hand, removed his handkerchief, and again dabbed at the leakage on my face

"Don't worry, sunshine," he said. "I explained to them the error of their ways."

chapter three

I QUICKLY FORGOT about the fire in the tumult of things that a fifteen-turning sixteen-year-old has to do, none of which, in my scheme of things, included homework.

That summer my father introduced me to *The Three Musketeers*, which had serious consequences for the rest of my life, including the beginning of a never-ending love affair with nineteenth-century French literature. Sometime between my junior year in high school and an abortive attempt to go to college, I read everything I could find by Alexandre Dumas, father and son, and to this day *The Count of Monte Cristo* remains my favorite book. I also discovered Victor Hugo and read most of his famous tomes, including *Les Misérables* and *The Hunchback of Notre Dame*. But what really intrigued me were his less well-known works, like *The Man Who Laughed* and *The Toilers of the Sea*. It was in drama class, though, that my supreme emotional upheaval occurred, because it was there that I discovered *Cyrano de Bergerac,* and promptly fell madly in love.

Cyrano became my ideal. The man I wanted to become, except that I wasn't a man and there was very little likelihood that I would grow up to be a Gallic poet, swordsman, or cavalier. Nevertheless, my indoctrination in French literature sealed my fate.

Even though I still didn't know specifically what profession I would embrace (Brain surgeon? Policewoman? Architect? Pilot? Belly dancer? Courtesan?), I finally knew that, whatever it was, I wouldn't let it detract from my ultimate purpose in life, which was to be an adventuress.

I tried to pattern myself after a few heroes more contemporary than Cyrano de Bergerac, just to prove that I could be practical as well as purposeful. One was Antoine de Saint-Exupéry, who admittedly is not all *that* contemporary but at least lived in the same century in which I was born, even if we'd never been alive at the same time.

Saint-Exupéry, whom most people know as the author of *The Little Prince*, wrote absorbing books about flying. Books with wonderful titles like *Wind, Sand and Stars* and *Night Flight* After reading him, I was ready to commit myself to a job that would not require my feet to touch the ground, and I decided to be a pilot. I rode my bicycle to this tiny airport about three miles north of Conversation and told the airport manager, whom everybody called Prop, either for *propeller* or for *proprietor*, that I would do whatever needed to be done in his office (answer phones, wash windows) in exchange for flying lessons. Prop was reluctant at first, but I pushed him out of his chair and organized his bills, receipts, weather reports, FAA notifications, and lesson schedules so perfectly and so quickly that, in short order, he agreed.

"One lesson," Prop said. "But fuel is expensive, so we go up when I have to fly somewhere anyway, and the lesson you get is what I have time to give. Agreed?"

"Agreed." I grinned and stuck out my hand.

He ignored it. "A man shakes hands with equals. You're just a kid. And I want a note from your parents."

I saluted.

"Skip the shenanigans and come into the Chart Room with me. I'm going to teach you how to read a weather report."

I worked at that airport for four and a half weeks, and developed very strong legs from bicycling six miles to and from our house. During that time I wheedled five flying lessons out of Prop. I kept my pilot's log; I studied high-pressure systems, warm fronts, air masses, and condensation. I finally learned everything I would ever want to know about clouds, and I made every effort to memorize the instrument panel of the venerable old Piper Super Cub in which I was training. And I really did try. Truly I did.

Unfortunately, it was obvious from the start that if I had been Amelia Earhart I would have gotten lost even before I'd found the plane. My first problem was with what's called "trimming." There's this little thing down around your knees that you are supposed to crank to trim the plane. No matter how many times it was explained to me, I couldn't grasp the concept. So I lied, and nodded, and pretended that I did. Then there was that damned instrument panel. Not too many dials, levers, and gizmos, I admit. After all, the Super Cub is a stick plane. (That was *another* problem. What genius decided that you can propel a zillion-pound object over a mountaintop by yanking back on a broomstick?) So it wasn't like flying a jet.

I could usually figure out where the artificial horizon was. And I rarely argued with the altimeter or the fuel gauge. My biggest challenge, and this indeed would be a serious problem for a potential pilot, occurred the day I was asked to determine where I was in the sky at any given point, in relationship to myself. I couldn't, for the life of me, decide when I had completed the arc of a turn. If my instructor said, "Do a forty-five-degree turn to your right," I didn't know if I had just gone forty-five-degrees or if I'd gone a hundred and eighty. He would have me use landmarks as reference points. He told me to check if my wingtip was *here* as opposed to *there*. He said to take it one arc at a time, or to try three hundred and sixty degrees in one fell swoop. Nothing worked.

That same day, Prop asked me to identify the round dial at the upper right-hand side of the instrument panel and tell him what its function was. I stared at it. I squinted at it. I fe-fi-fo-fummed at it. To no avail. Anguish as I might, I couldn't figure out what the damned dial was.

Finally, I turned to Prop and said, "I give up."

He sighed and said, "It's a clock."

Of course, from that time on we both knew that any pilot certification I would be getting would be in my dreams.

But we parted company amicably, and it was he who referred me to my next after-school job. The week before, a group of fraternity boys at Hudson University had chartered a plane to New Orleans, where one of them was being given a twentieth birthday party by his very, very, very wealthy parents. Not only did they bring their girlfriends along, but they also brought their own professional photographer. Walter Troska was his name.

Walt had an office and lab on the second floor of a drugstore only two blocks from my high school, and his bread-and-butter business was taking pictures at sorority and fraternity houses, including class photographs, yearbook photographs, formal photographs, and candid pictures at parties. He was very good at what he did, and since at least two parties were thrown each weekend, he wasn't losing money.

On that chartered flight to New Orleans, he had sat next to Prop, who was piloting the plane. Walt told my old boss something about his business and added that the girl who had been working for him for three years had just quit and he was looking for someone else.

Prop, in turn, told me.

I think that by then he was looking for a gentle way to get rid of the hopeless dodo who had come to him for flying lessons, and he thought if he could get me interested in something else, I wouldn't be too devastated by the reality of my own ineptitude.

The reason his plan worked was that another of my heroes was a photographer. I had fallen in love with *her* when I was thirteen years old and was watching an old movie with my mother. It was a "defining moment" of sorts, and I've never forgotten the spell that movie cast on me. It was a school day, but for some reason — maybe I had the flu — I'd stayed home from school and was keeping my mother company in the basement while she ironed in front of the television.

The movie classic that day was *The Margaret Bourke-White* story, staring Teresa Wright. I was stunned. I was shocked. I was agog with amazement that there could ever have existed a woman such as she. She was beautiful, Margaret Bourke-White was. She was talented. She had developed a passion for a profession, for a craft. And she was persistent. She took hundreds of pictures from dozens of angles or in dozens of different lights before she settled on the one that would be *the one* to which she would affix her name.

Her career achievements were as awesome as her courage. She had so compellingly photographed machinery and factories for *Fortune* magazine that she made smokestacks and molten steel look like works of art. She traveled with the Allied troops in Europe during World War II, taking combat photos for *Life* magazine and being Johnny on the spot to immortalize the prisoners, living and dead, with horrifying and memorable images of Nazi concentration camps. She was sassy, strong, independent, fiercely committed to her work, fearless, and — I used the word before — courageous. So courageous. Toward the end of her life, after she contracted Parkinson's disease, she told her editors at *Life* magazine that she wanted to educate their readers about the debilitating effects of the disease *by doing a photo essay on herself.*

I wouldn't have done that.

I would have hidden under a blanket eating praline ice cream and watching old movies for four years while I waited to die. But not her. Not Margaret Bourke-White. My hero. Almost as good as Cyrano de Bergerac (no one would ever be *that* good), she crumpled up hundreds, thousands of pieces of paper to maintain the flexibility in her fingers so that, despite the Parkinson's, she would be able to take pictures.

She didn't belong to clubs or groups or organizations. She didn't ask for help. She just did what had to be done, and did it better than anyone else. She was my kind of a woman. A do-it-yourself, antagonize everybody, and top it off with panache kind of a gal.

I decided to become Margaret Bourke-White the second the movie about her life was over, and when the opportunity arose, I looked up Walter Troska's telephone number, asked for a job interview, and lied about my age. I told him I was already sixteen, which I wouldn't be for twenty-two more days.

During the two and a half years that I worked for Walter, I went to a lot of fraternity parties, and I learned many things for which I will never have any use if I live to be two hundred years old. One experience I had was valuable, though. It touched on Dorsey Browning, and although I didn't know it at the time, that compelling and beautiful woman would have a cataclysmic impact on the way I would eventually choose to spend the rest of my life.

chapter four

EVEN THOUGH MY ACCOMPLISHMENTS as an employee of Walter Troska were uneven, overall I was more successful than not. For the first eight or nine months, I worked solely in Walt's lab, helping him to develop negatives, enlarge and print photographs, code them, and mount them on large sandwich boards, which Walt then delivered to the lobbies of the appropriate fraternity or sorority houses. We left them on display for about a week, after which we collected both the boards and the students' photo orders. I helped Walt to print and deliver the pictures, too.

It took me months to prove my *competence* (I never put the wrong code on a photo) and my *speed* (I was faster than anyone who had worked there before), followed by weeks of begging, pleading, and cajoling before Walt finally agreed to train me on his clunky old camera and to let me go to a party by myself.

I was sixteen at the time, and totally fearless. Double negative notwithstanding, I believed that there was nothing I couldn't do. This was probably true as it would have related to putting my head in a lion's mouth, doing acrobatic stunts on the wing of a biplane, or trekking into the Amazon forest with only a container of bug repellent and a copy of *Bartlett's Familiar Quotations*.

But the easy stuff has always eluded me, and easy stuff with numbers pushes me right over the edge. F-stops, for example, precipitated a crisis similar to that of flying arcs in an airplane. F-stops on a camera have been explained to me hundreds of times. Explained patiently, irritably, clearly, and meticulously, both by experts and by knowledgeable laymen. I still don't get it. Add a light meter to the mix, and my eyes and mind go into meltdown at the same time.

To me, f-stops are like blood pressure or the International Date Line. Things that I *say* I understand to get teachers and bosses off my back but that I really consider the obsessions of people talking in tongues. Although I'm a whiz at solving just about any conceivable puzzle or brainteaser, and I'm never tripped up by word games with answers like "That's because your grandfather is your mother's brother-in-law from a first marriage," this does nothing to make my other ineptitudes more palatable.

However, despite my problems with shutter speeds, light, shade, and shadow, it turns out that I have perfect eyesight and uncanny depth perception.

One of the things Walt taught me about taking candid pictures at social functions was how to estimate distances so that I could set my focus quick and dirty without having to fiddle with the lens. Are the girl and the guy beside the fireplace fifteen feet away? Twelve? Or more like ten? How about the idiot who grabbed the microphone from the band's singer and thinks he's Elvis Presley? He's at least thirty feet from the camera. Wrong or right?

This was terrific training for me, and I use it in my work today whenever I draw schematics of fire scenes, under which I modestly write the words "not to scale." Because I'm so good at it, it's actually closer to scale than anyone would think.

Walt trained me and then sent me out on my maiden voyage

with a camera, a high-power battery pack, and a strobe light, warning me not to step in a puddle or I'd get an electric shock. He also gave me a camera bag and extra film. The party I went to wasn't particularly rowdy by fraternity house standards. I shot ten rolls of film, and I drove to Walt's lab early the next morning to drop them off. I was convinced that I had done an exemplary job.

I hadn't.

There were two synchronizations on Walt's old black box of a camera, which is worth about five thousand dollars today, I might add. One was for flashbulbs and one was for the strobe. To the left of the lens was this wee, small lever. If the lever was up, the synchronization was for flashbulbs. If the lever was down, it was for the strobe.

The lever had been in the up position while I was at the party, but I didn't know it. Since I was using the strobe the entire time, the camera and the light source were out of sync.

I groan even now when I think of it, but all of my film came out black.

I was surprised that Walt didn't fire me on the spot. I don't remember exactly what he did or said in response to the catastrophe. I guess it was another one of those convenient memory blips I have, like the one after the fire. I do remember that my career as a photographer came to an abrupt halt, and I had to admit to myself that, along with Cyrano de Bergerac and Antoine de Saint-Exupéry, I would also not grow up to be Margaret Bourke-White.

Working for Walter Troska was a good way to make money, though, since I was saving for college, and as long as I kept my fingers off lens caps, I presented no danger to his livelihood. I stayed with Walt until the summer after my senior year in high school.

I do *not* want to talk about my college experiences. I will say just three things.

One. With the exception of *Beowulf*, which I could happily have lived without, I had read in high school every work of fiction that was required reading for freshman English, including all of the Great Books of the Western World. So I was bored, bored, bored.

Two. The quantum theory of mechanics is like f-stops and blood pressure, and despite Herculean efforts on my part, it steadfastly refused to drop anchor in my brain.

Three. I am not now nor have I ever been "college material."

My father's best friend, Jules Hornfinder, who is also his accountant, is a bit of a gossip and a very nice man. He told my father that he had a client named Oliver Wicks, whom Uncle Jules liked very much. He described Oliver as an honest man in a cutthroat industry and said that Oliver told him that Precaution Property and Liability Insurance Company, where he was a claims supervisor, was hiring new employees and that he was looking for two new claims representatives for his own department.

Claims representatives.

What was a claims representative?

My father then asked Uncle Jules to call Mr. Wicks (I know this is getting complicated, but you should have been there when Uncle Max was arranging for a discount with his landlord's brother-in-law so that Aunt Suzie could get a new stove) and tell him that I was a super-smart high school graduate from a good family ("Oh, Daddy. *Please!*") and that I was looking for a job.

I had no objection.

After all, it had become crystal clear to me that whatever my "calling" was, I was too deaf to hear it, and that if I was going to be able to get an apartment of my own so I could embark upon a life as an adventuress, I was going to have to find a job.

chapter five

EVERYONE WHO GOES TO WORK in the claims department of an insurance company should be required to watch *Double Indemnity* the minute they're hired. The movie is considered to be a classic, possibly because of the sexy way Barbara Stanwyck crosses her legs when she's seducing Fred MacMurray, or because of MacMurray's naïveté in believing that he could live happily ever after with a murderous vixen in a blonde wig, but the real value of *Double Indemnity* is as a primer on insurance fraud.

Stripped of its bells and whistles, this is the plot.

Insurance salesman Fred MacMurray meets the young, slutty wife of a mean-spirited older man. She wants Fred to sell her an insurance policy on her husband with a clause to pay double if he dies an accidental death.

Slut crosses her legs.

Just so.

The insurance salesman falls for the slut.

They decide to stage an accident in which the cheap, unlovable husband appears to have tumbled off a train.

Husband gets dead.

Wife files a claim with the insurance company for double indemnity.

Stanwyck and MacMurray think that now they can walk off into the sunset holding hands filled with thousand-dollar bills.

Not so fast.

Edward G. Robinson is the claims manager at the insurance company; when he is notified about the death, he tells MacMurrary (his best friend), that he smells a rat.

The plot thickens.

Stanwyck and MacMurray start to distrust each other.

Stanwyck shoots MacMurray.

MacMurray shoots Stanwyck.

Everybody dies or goes to prison, except Edward G. Robinson.

The insurance company keeps the money.

Justice prevails.

In real life as well as in fiction, there is a whole lot of insurance fraud. There are also a lot of legitimate claims filed by decent people who've just had a streak of bad luck.

Here's how it works.

To keep the math simple, we'll say that the house you're buying costs $100,000. You plunk down $25,000 in cash and take out a $75,000 mortgage. As soon as you take out that mortgage, property insurance is no longer a matter of choice. You *must* have it, because whether your house burns down, blows away, cracks in half, or gets swept off its foundation by the Wicked Witch of the West, the bank that lent you the money is going to want it back.

Let's say nothing catastrophic happens for years and years and years, and you've managed to pay off a third of your mortgage. Then a disaster occurs, and the house is demolished. Assuming that it's a legitimate claim and that the insurance company intends to pay the full value of the policy — all $100,000 — who gets the money?

First, the bank. It gets back the entire unpaid balance of the mortgage, in this case, $50,000.

You keep the rest.

If your house is paid in full and you have no mortgage, you get it all.

If the contents of your home are insured and paid for, depending on what type of a policy you took out, you will be reimbursed for that, too.

So, essentially, the less you need money, the more you stand to receive if you are the victim of a nasty and arbitrary twist of fate.

After an incident or an accident has occurred, the policyholder gets the money the insurance company owes him by calling the person who sold him the policy, usually his agent. The agent, in turn, calls the claims representative.

Claims representative is the job I applied for and got at Precaution Property and Liability Insurance Company.

My new boss, Oliver Wicks, was and is the sweetest, most fretful, least forceful, most honorable and anxiety-ridden man that I have ever met. If he were a dog, he would be Rin-Tin-Tin, nervously shredding napkins before leaping into the river to save a member of the Royal Canadian Mounted Police. Then, after making the rescue, he would be Monday-morning quarterbacking his actions until he had convinced himself that he could have done it better or faster, and that he had offended half of his bosses by being too good and the other half by not being good enough.

When I went to work for Ollie, he was about thirty years old, which seemed ancient to me at the time. He has the most endearing premature bald spot, surrounded by a halo of brown tufts, and honest but tentative eyes, as if he's embarrassed that he isn't a cad.

Ollie also has a mustache, which I consider very devil-may-care in a man reluctant to stand out. It is robust and shaped like the roof of a pole barn. The mustache caps a wonderful smile.

I liked Ollie the minute I met him, when he attempted to let me know right off who was the boss.

Ha!

If Ollie hadn't been in love with his wife, I'm sure that within three or four minutes he would have fallen madly in love with me, because . . . well, just because. His wife is six feet tall. Ollie is only five seven. She's big, self-confident, and a court reporter. With her dyed yellow hair, dark brown skin, and happy disposition, she very much resembles a giant sunflower. Ollie and Aurora have no children, so she babies Ollie, Ollie loves it, and they both love me.

Uncle Jules did me a favor when he found me the perfect job, even if I still didn't feel that I had found my true vocation. Did I like insurance work? Yes and no. What I *liked* about it were the insights it gave me into other people's lives. Who they were. How they lived. What they valued. What they possessed. How they reacted to their losses. Their honesty. Their covetousness. Their confusion. Their skullduggery. And, more often than I would have expected, their generosity and nobility.

My three favorite things about the job were

- Helping people who deserved to be helped, even if etiquette and professionalism dictated that I should have folded up my tent and gone home

- Figuring out what really happened when the incidents of a particular claim, for whatever reason, didn't add up

- Investigating fires

What I *disliked* was the bureaucracy, irrational and irate policy-holders, manipulative and dishonest lawyers (ours and "theirs"), report writing, and all the paperwork, paperwork, paperwork.

I also very much disliked helping people whom I considered obnoxious boors, even when their insurance policies indicated that they were entitled to my help.

Let me give you some examples.

In the dislike category, we had a hurricane on Long Island. In and of itself, this was not an unusual occurrence. One of the houses in the hurricane's path sustained some, but not very much damage. The homeowners, a couple named Schultz, put in a claim, and I went along to the loss with our adjuster, because I was being trained at the time.

A claims adjuster, by the way, is the person who evaluates the extent of the damage and how much of the claim we should pay. A professional in a related field is called a "public adjuster." Some policyholders hire public adjusters in exchange for a percentage of their insurance settlement. As a group, public adjusters are considered ambulance chasers. In the same way that it's a company adjuster's job to salvage as much and pay out as little as possible, it is the creed of *all* public adjusters to maximize their clients' losses and to account not only for the big stuff — like stoves, sofas, Steinway pianos, canopy beds, and the two Mercedes parked in the garage — but also for every sheet on every roll of toilet paper, every yogurt cup, every bobby pin, and every retractable ballpoint pen. They have to estimate the value of what has been destroyed and claim reimbursement from the insurance company on behalf of the policyholder.

To do this, they fill out a proof of loss.

Mr. and Mrs. Schultz were obviously not native to the United States. They were over insured and ran a computer software company out of the living room of their house. When I asked them questions about their claim, they formulated terse and offensive answers that marched in lockstep out of grim and unsmiling lips. They were aloof, superior, and contemptuous in their treatment of everyone, including the county disaster coordinator, who hadn't slept in three days. I overheard Mrs. Schultz threatening to sue that poor slob because the riverbank adjacent to *her* house wasn't sandbagged before her neighbors'. Although other families lost everything — house, furnishings, high school yearbooks, love letters, cars, and pets — the hurricane had practically tiptoed past the property of these whey-faced martinets. There was some water damage to the carpet in their den, and a branch torn from a tree in the backyard had cracked a sliding glass door. To hear them describe the damage, though, you would have thought it was Dresden after an Allied bombing attack.

What particularly stood out in my mind, then and now, was something that Mr. and Mrs. Schultz *didn't* do. For as long as I've been in the insurance business, every single uninjured homeowner whose house, car, apartment — whatever — was damaged always initiated a conversation with firefighters, police, Red Cross, or insurance guys like me in exactly the same way. They would say, "At least nobody got hurt."

That they did so reaffirmed my faith in humanity.

That the Schultzs never uttered those words made me pure and simple hate them, their smug indifference and the pale, beige sterility of their angular furniture and soulless lives.

When I got back to my office, I marched up to Oliver Wicks's desk and announced, "I'm denying the claim."

My boss started to blink uncontrollably. I sometimes bring that out in him. But his voice was steady enough when he asked, "On what basis?"

"Personality. I can't stand them."

Ollie stopped blinking. Then he opened his desk drawer, fiddled around with something wrapped in crinkly paper, held out a white wafer in my direction, and said, "Have a mint."

Suffice it to say, I was taken off the Schultz claim.

Of the kind of case I love to handle, there's one in particular I'll never forget. The policyholder's name was Ruth Epps (amazing the things we remember), and she was a real lady.

That's an old-fashioned term, isn't it?

But Mrs. Epps epitomized everything my mother hoped I would become when she nagged me to sit with my knees together on a bus, never put on makeup in public, not to smoke on the street, and let feeble old men carry my luggage because it makes them feel like Sir Water Raleigh doing the puddle thing with his cape.

Mrs. Epps lived in Palisades, New York, and was at church when the power in a three-block area went out. Since her church was on the other side of town, she didn't know about the blackout until she turned onto her block and saw fire apparatus parked outside Number Six Old Pine Road, where she had lived her entire married life. The sequence of events began with a car slamming into a utility pole across the street, the impact from which knocked out the neutral wire and caused the electricity in her house to lose its ground.

From the minute the loss was called in, there was never any question that the fire was accidental. At that time, I liked to respond to fire losses myself because . . . Well, I didn't really know *why* I liked to respond to them, I just did. Anyway, that day I went along with our insurance adjuster for the ride.

As soon as I got there, I realized that, even though the house was still structurally sound and could be repaired, the damage was pretty disheartening. The problem had originated at the step-down transformer on the utility pole where the crash occurred. This was where the electricity, carried by overhead power lines, was reduced from 440 volts to the voltage capacity of the wiring inside Mrs. Epps's house, which was 110 volts. It was also where the neutral or ground line returned the unbalanced power to the power plant.

If there is no backup ground inside a house when a neutral line goes out, all the unbalanced power pours into the residence through the circuit breakers in a power surge. First thing, the circuit breakers start to cook. Simultaneously, a lightning bolt of electricity heats up, fuses, or melts all the wires in the house — even wires way the hell and gone in the attic, the guest bedroom, the furnace room, the pantry, and the master bathroom on the second floor. Eventually, the power goes off, but when it's surging, not only is it frying the wires, the red-hot wires themselves are coming into contact with other combustibles.

Picture this: The house is the shell of a toaster.

The electrical wires inside the walls are the wire elements inside the toaster.

Imagine those wires glowing. Red hot.

The house's combustibles, including walls, floors, curtains, sofas, and chairs, are the toast.

Because Ruth Epps's house was built around 1920, most of the old-fashioned wiring was sheathed in cloth that had dried out and deteriorated.

Think kindling.

And so little fires, some of which self-extinguished, broke out here, there, and everywhere, and even though the Palisades Fire Department was quick to respond, there was no way to prevent excessive smoke, fire, water, and overhaul damage.

Overhaul, in this case, was particularly gruesome because

firemen had to poke holes in just about every wall and ceiling, looking for sparks or insulation that might be smoldering or burning even though the visible fire had been put out. When the firefighters took up their hoses and stowed their gear, they left behind a nightmare of sodden carpets, burned drapes, books, clothing, lamps, and pillows covered in soot.

Poor Ruth Epps. She was a wreck by the time we got there, and her insurance wasn't the issue.

I will always remember our tea party. Precaution Property and Liability Insurance Company provided the tea.

After we got to the house, our company adjuster, Paul Hollister, went down to the basement to take pictures. I stayed upstairs, because I was worried about Mrs. Epps. At that time, Ruth Epps was sixty-eight years old. She was slim and had the kind of face my grandmother's generation would have called "handsome". Her silver hair was beautifully coiffured in stylish, short curls, and pearl earrings perched prettily on her small ears; her makeup was flawless, and her lipstick was just the right understated shade of red.

She looked like a woman who liked herself and who had spent her whole life being loved.

Even though it was a warm, end-of-summer day, it's always dank and cold in a house right after a fire. Mrs. Epps was dressed for a morning at the country club, in a khaki skirt, a tailored white blouse, and smart shoes with highish heels.

How does someone dress to attend to the shambles of her life?

Poor Mrs. Epps. She couldn't have looked more lost.

When I interviewed her, she answered my initial questions — about where she had been at the time of the fire, how she had discovered it, and so on — with self-restraint and poise. We were standing in a breakfast nook off the kitchen. If its windows hadn't been covered with grime, and if the dead plants in the windows hadn't been trailing black leaves like ugly strands of witches' hair, the room would have been sunny, cheerful, and bright. Two cartons had been set on a small, octagonal table in the center of the room. As we spoke, Ruth Epps's eyes inadvertently drifted to her right or left, alighting on a curio, a knickknack, or an object of affection that she suddenly recognized with a pang.

There's the photo album of our trip to Canada; the cover and the top two pages are soaking wet, but do you think that we can . . . ?

Sure, we can save it, Mrs. Epps. Put it into the carton.

Oh, and look here! My Royal Doulton balloon lady. Mother gave it to me a year after I married Archie. One of the balloons is cracked, but maybe we can . . .

I don't see why not. Into the carton.

Aunt Vera's silver cigarette case, dented and covered with grime . . .

A crystal candlestick, one of a pair. The other . . . shattered. Gone.

My jewelry case. Where's my jewelry case? There was this one particular bracelet Archie gave me on our honeymoon. We were very poor then, so we could only afford to go to Atlantic City. It was alternating bands of jade and ivory. I don't expect it's worth all that much, but when Archie . . . Archie . . .

And then it all came pouring out. The words and the tears.

Ruth Epps was having a truly terrible year.

In February her mother, whom she adored, had died in her sleep.

In April her favorite brother, whose name I forgot, but I remember that he was a golf pro, had been fired from his job of thirty years and attempted suicide.

And just three weeks earlier, Archie, who had been on dialysis since he was fifty-nine years old but still managed to lead an active life and continue as president of the paper products plant that he founded . . . beloved Archie had experienced complete kidney failure and died.

Now, the fire.

Mrs. Ruth Epps sobbed. As she did, I realized that I was witnessing the breakdown of a woman who had been strong for her mother, strong for her brother, strong for her husband, and strong for herself.

But the fire had done her in.

That's why I decided that we should have tea.

There was no electricity in what was left of the house, and the water had been shut off, so I went downstairs to where Paul was opening and closing closets and drawers, whispered a few words in his ear, and asked him to drive to the local deli.

During the fifteen minutes that he was gone, I raided the cupboards for unopened packages of paper products, of which there were an abundance, since Archie's company had manufactured them. I took the cartons off the octagonal table, found a roll of paper towels and a bottle of household cleaner under what was left of the kitchen sink, and set about cleaning the table. As I fiddled and fussed, Mrs. Epps stood motionless, registering nothing of what was going on around her, tears streaming down her face.

I heard Paul's car pull into the driveway, went outside, and disencumbered him of his bags. When I returned to the kitchen, Ruth Epps allowed me to lead her to one of the cartons I had placed beside the octagonal table. I gently pushed her down. If I'd had my druthers, I would have served her tea in the elegant gold-and-ivory teapot her students gave her the year she retired from teaching high school, but I didn't, because it was broken.

So I gave her a white paper cup with a tea bag dangling over the edge like a sad flag of surrender, and I took one myself. My post-fire drug of choice being chocolate chip cookies, I put half a dozen on a paper plate in front of Mrs. Epps and said, "How long has it been since you ate?"

That was my icebreaker.

She never did eat any of those chocolate chip cookies, but she did drink the tea, and she did stop crying. And start crying. And stop again. And start again. The way you do when your whole life has capsized and you're telling a complete stranger your story. From prom night, to the birth of your daughter to her wedding to the last trip you went on with your darling, wise mother and with Archie, the love of your life.

By the time Ruth Epps left her house that morning, I had helped her save a few more bits and pieces of her life. She was a little stronger, a little weaker, and all cried out.

Then she went her way, and I went mine.

When I got back to the office, I told Ollie about her, and he told me a few stories too. There was one about a fourteen-year-old boy, a pet turtle, and a flood. There was another about an elderly baker and an out-of-control bus that crashed through his shop window on the day his son graduated from medical school.

I guess every claims representative at every insurance company has his or her Mrs. Epps.

Anyway, she was one of the reasons why I loved my job.

chapter six

IT'S A FUNNY THING about Conversation, New York. In a sense, it was a very stratified community, even though I never particularly felt that way growing up. When I was a child, my life was defined by three things: my bicycle, my library, and my school. In and of itself, I guess that just shrieks out the word *privilege*.

Privilege. Privilege. Privilege.

That was me, in pigtails.

Let's face it; I didn't have to lose sleep over drive-by shootings or thugs selling drugs on street corners. Other than an occasional classmate who got pregnant or landed up in a drug rehab, all I had to worry about was whether or not my bike got a flat, or if my tennis balls went flat.

We were not a great town of cops or firemen, either. Not one of my friends' fathers had ever run into a burning building to save an old lady or a kitten. They didn't leap out of squad cars to arrest opium dealers; they didn't raid the houses of importers of illegal elephant tusks. Every one of my buddies, except me, had conventional parents who were doctors, engineers, lawyers, or business executives. They carried briefcases, had insurance coverage, and got great benefits packages at work.

Not my parents, though. My father didn't have a college diploma, and he worked in our basement. What he did for a living was invent, patent, and develop prototypes of things with wheels. Folding bicycles. Racing wheelchairs. Rolling weed whackers. Portable ramps. Self-propelled luggage. Things like that. I don't know how many of these devices he had to dream up before he accumulated enough money to pay for even one year of one of his children's tuitions, but somehow he did the job.

My mother was my father's assistant. She helped him by holding knobs and gizmos when he said, "Hold this" (something his children were also able to do). Mom typed his correspondence, did his bookkeeping, and got wheeled around in things a lot. We all did.

And she raised a brood of kids.

It's because of my solid, middle-class, no-commotion childhood, including Girl Scouts, where I got badges for making beanbag dolls and growing stunted cucumbers, that it took me so long to figure out what I wanted to be when I grew up.

Had I been raised in the city, taken public transportation to school, and seen recruitment posters every day for the police and fire departments on the subway, I probably would have tried to become a homicide detective. Doubtless I would have mouthed off to a boss and been fired within the first year, but that's beside the point, because I would have found my *direction* sooner.

I would still have become what I finally became, but I would have made a few less wrong turns along the way.

Or . . . I wouldn't have.

I don't know, but it's fun to fantasize.

Anyway, in the town of Conversation, all the cops and firemen are snobs. My theory is that they think we residents are rich, arrogant, self-important, and spoiled, so in order to avoid being snubbed by us, they snub us first. I'm pretty sure I'm right about this, because in all the years I lived in Conversation it has never dawned on any of our police chiefs to send an officer to the high school on Career Day to tell us about his job. The firemen were kind when I was a fifteen-year-old inadvertent fire setter, but they were also aloof and didn't mingle beyond what was necessary to put out the fire, untangle their hoses, and go home. Despite which, the memory of that small conflagration stayed with me, albeit unconsciously, for years and years and years.

Why am I certain that this tiny, incendiary incident in my life held so much meaning?

Because of my continued fascination with fire investigation.

After I was trained as a claims representative, it was obvious to others, long before I figured it out, that I was drawn to fire cases, and over the years I seemed to have developed an instinct for the right questions to ask, the right documents to request, the right rooms to look in, and even the best lawyers to hire. I was also good at smelling out fraud, particularly when it involved arson; it was something I just plain loved to do. I enjoyed it so much that I never applied for a promotion and I didn't accept one that was offered to me, because if I had been stuck in a managerial role, I would be distanced from my fire claims.

Yes, this was an unorthodox way to work, since most claims reps just sit at their desks and fiddle with computers, forms, and telephones. But I was allowed a lot of latitude, because I got results.

My one area of weakness, and I attribute this to my happily over-privileged childhood, is that I did not think of myself as an investigator *per se;* so it took me *forever* to realize that the frustration I felt with the cause and origin experts I hired was more than justified.

Let me back up a little and put what I just said in context.

When an insured calls us with a claim on a house, a car, a factory, a boat, whatever, we make a few phone calls, do a little paperwork, and send an adjuster to the loss to estimate the damages and give us an overview of what happened and what *has to happen* from that point forward.

Let's say a hurricane rips into a residence. Our adjuster will advise us to contact a company to board up the broken windows to protect the house against further weather damage and vandalism, he'll tell us to hire a cleanup crew, and so on.

In a sense, not only does he estimate the loss, the company adjuster is also our advance scout for detecting foul play. He lets us know if he suspects that something isn't on the up-and-up, and he turns on the light bulbs in our heads that say "arson" or "fraud."

The company I work for employs some very good insurance adjusters. My favorite is Paul Hollister, a tall, thin, nice guy with very white skin, very light eyes, and a disconcerting lack of eyebrows and eyelashes. Since he also has narrow shoulders and sandy hair, he looks exactly like a filter-tipped cigarette. Paul's the adjuster I was with the day we brought Ruth Epps her sympathy tea, and because he knew I liked to do fires, he often suggested that I meet him at a loss when an interesting claim came in.

Once an adjuster has decided that something fishy is going on, he advises the claims rep, me, of his suspicions. For example, the chief of the fire department that fought the fire in question might have told Paul that one of his men smelled kerosene, or that a neighbor saw someone with a gas can running away from the premises before the fire, or that all the doors to the house were open when the apparatus arrived. Any of a number of scenarios.

After Paul, or some other adjuster, relates his suspicions to

me, I call a cause and origin investigator, which is actually a mis-
nomer because you have to figure out the origin of a fire before
you can determine the cause. But that's another story.

It's at this point in the process that I'd been having problems,
because the fire investigators we'd been hiring didn't have a clue
about what they were supposed to be doing. They would arrive on
our doorstep with certificates and diplomas from this authority
or that, smugly self-assured that, having passed a few tests and
learned a few formulae, they could descend upon a fire scene and
do the job. The worst were engineers, who knew nothing about
fire *except* for what they had learned in a classroom, and they
looked about as comfortable at a fire scene as debutantes at a
demolition derby.

When I started at Precaution Property and Liability, the old-
time investigators were still working, and it was from them that I
gleaned whatever bits and pieces I had come to know about fire.
Most had been firemen, and except for the odd course they had
taken to get away from their wives, everything they knew about
fire, they had learned on the job. These guys, none of whom were
Rhodes scholars, had fire savvy and knew what to do at a fire
scene. They were like aged prospectors. Not necessarily dainty
enough to bring home to Mother but with a nose for gold.

My old-timers had a nose for fire.

They knew all the ins and outs of fire investigation. Knew
where the fire started. How and why. They even knew when they
didn't know, and they weren't afraid to say so. But they are a van-
ishing breed, being pushed out by engineers, and engineers *always* know where a fire started. They *always* know why and how
it started. They're adept at going into convoluted and incomprehensible explanations involving chimney effects, inversions, up-

drafts, downdrafts, backdrafts, and flashovers, none of which they have experienced in real life or at a fire since they never go to fires, but all of which they have "modeled" on computers in the sterile safety of their homes.

On three separate occasions I caught three of these geniuses at fire losses with checklists clutched in their hands, as if they wouldn't know what to look for unless they had found "TRIPPED CIRCUIT BREAKER" or "LOW BURNING" or "V-PATTERN" written down on a little itemized sheet.

Frankly, I was sick of them.

They thought they knew everything; they never admitted when they were wrong; they never, *never* asked questions, and they made mistakes. Mistakes are unacceptable in my line of work. Too many people can get hurt. If you say that a fire is incendiary when it isn't, you've branded someone an arsonist for life. If you let an arsonist slip through your fingers, you're ignoring criminal activity, endangering human life, and paying claims that should not be paid.

I admit that engineers do look good on paper. They have six-page résumés with lots of impressive letters behind their names. Criminal and civil court judges love them, because they make fire investigation look scientific, and they can quote equations to substantiate what they say.

But does what they're saying make any sense?

Is any of it true?

Not many people seem to care. All that matters to the Powers That Be is that their opinions *sound* scientific.

I still care, though.

So does my boss, Oliver Wicks.

We just weren't sure what to do about it. In fact, we were having one of our "heated discussions" (meaning I was shouting, and

Ollie was now-nowing me to death) when, almost overnight, our fire investigation situation drastically changed.

"No, Ollie. I will *not* call Terry Mickelman. He's an arrogant, repressed asshole. His collars and cuffs are never clean, he overcharges, and I'm tired of looking at the Phi Beta Kappa pin he wears on his mustard-stained tie. Terry Mickelman is a jerk."

"But he's a Ph.D."

"He's a *jerk* with a Ph.D. He's —"

The telephone rang.

Ollie picked up the receiver, mouthed, "It's the . . ." and shooed me out the door. Then he pulled a legal pad forward and began to write.

About twenty minutes later, he called me back to his office. Apparently the rumors we'd heard about the Westchester office were true, and for a variety of reasons that nobody bothered to explain, the home office had decided to shut it down and give us all their work. Ollie was told that he could hire anyone he wanted to compensate for the extra caseload. New employees would have to be trained, though, and training took months. All of which meant that, in the meantime, he and I were going to be doing a whole lot more work.

"Like what?" I asked.

"For starters, I'm giving you a five-hundred-thousand-dollar loss in the Bronx."

"I don't want it. Give it to Marlene. I'm bigger than she is. I can push her around."

"It's a fire loss, Tillary."

"Fire?"

"That's what I said."

"Where?"

"In Riverdale."

"Riverdale? House? Apartment? Embassy? What?"

"Private home. A big old Victorian sitting on two and three-quarters acres of land ten blocks from Embassy Row."

"When was the fire?

"Three weeks ago. On the Fourth of July."

"What's the Westchester office done so far, Ollie?"

"Nowhere near enough."

chapter seven

RIVERDALE, WHERE ISABELLE and Dortimer Browning had lived in a large Victorian, is a hoity-toity section of the Bronx. Originally, their house was in an area so rural that letters addressed to "Mr. and Mrs. Browning, intersection of Grumbaker and Fenton Roads" always arrived safe and sound. Over time the area built up, streetlights were installed, and the distance between their residence and the street became the exception rather than the rule. To comply with new regulations of the emergency services, and to get their mail delivered properly, it became necessary for the Brownings to name the long and circuitous driveway that they shared with the people next door.

Dortimer fancifully decided upon Labyrinth Lane. Number One Labyrinth Lane. The McDevitts, the neighbors on the other side of the driveway, lived at Number Two.

The Brownings, Dortimer and Isabelle, had three children. Faith was the oldest, Hope was the middle child, and Dorsey was the baby. By the time Dorsey came along, Isabelle had grown strong enough in their marriage to put her foot down about some of her husband's more accessible eccentricities, and she told Dortimer that she categorically refused to name their last child Charity.

So Dorsey it was.

Hope died in infancy, and Isabelle, who if her photographs

didn't lie was an enchanting creature more like a wood sprite than like a mother of three, died of spinal meningitis when her surviving daughters were thirteen and two.

Dortimer, an odd grab bag of gentle paranoia and whimsy, proceeded to raise his children alone. In many ways, Dortimer Browning was a nice old thing, and marvelously creative in his lunacy. He had never been physically attractive, with his crooked, bowed legs and ears that looked like butterflies resting on either side of a milk jug, but there was something sweet about him, and more than a few people agreed that if Snow White had ever advertised for a publicity shy eighth dwarf, Dortimer would have gotten the job.

He was said to be brilliant and worked as a mathematician at Corwyn Marks, in the department where they make measuring devices for the aerospace industry. At home, he built things, wonderful, enchanting, magical things for his two daughters and himself.

Because of his paranoia, which was confined within very specific and hard-edged boundaries, Dortimer had installed a new roof on his house. The roof looked as if it had been laid with regular asbestos shingles. Only Dortimer and the roofer knew that underneath the asbestos shingles was a layer of sheet metal, and only Dortimer knew that before it had been nailed to the framing, he had dabbed dots of candy apple red nail polish on the corners of each sheet.

Although he never explained it to the roofer, Dortimer was certain that everybody of relevance to the survival of this planet knew that Tyrangeans loathe the color red, and that even a thousand years after it has been applied, they still find the smell of nail polish sufficiently repellent to drive them away.

Tyrangea is an elusive planet. So elusive that only Dortimer knew of its existence. He had charted its orbit, which because of a rare confluence of magnetic fields, gravitational pulls, and solar gases, is so elliptical that, were it reproduced on a computer, it would look like one of those long balloons that clowns twist into animal shapes at parties.

It had not been difficult for Dortimer to conclude that Tyrangea was inhabited, and by his calculations, which fluctuated wildly each time he redid them, he was reasonably certain that the planet would be in the neighborhood of Earth in approximately eighteen to twenty years.

If, when she was alive, Isabelle believed that the planet Tyrangea was recurring specks of dirt on her husband's telescope, dirt that had a tendency to shift from place to place, thus accounting for the unusual orbit, she never told Dortimer, and she lovingly and constantly replenished her bottles of candy apple red nail polish without comment or complaint.

We know these things because Isabelle, Dortimer, and their two daughters kept detailed and voluminous journals, all of which survived the fire.

Dortimer's reinforcement and pretreatment of his roof were what he considered "extraordinary precautions," ones he felt compelled to take because he was a conscientious father, he had two daughters, and it was his responsibility to protect them. This is why Dortimer also had several concealed closets and passageways constructed in his home. Nooks and crannies where he and his children could hide or hide things from the Tyrangeans should they come, and should they prove hostile.

Personally, Dortimer believed that Tyrangeans were friendly souls, and that they were only visiting Earth to acquire cuttings from food-producing trees and shrubs, not excluding cherry, blueberry, pear, chestnut, fig, and mango. He was quite certain that the planet of Tyrangea was diminutive (another reason for its elusiveness), and that with its burgeoning population (they hadn't discovered birth control yet), small, fruitful plants would be in great demand.

Dortimer never speculated about what Tyrangeans looked like, and other than shielding his house against danger and putting four dots of candy apple red nail polish on either side of the front and rear fenders of his car, he rarely spoke of them. Both of his daughters believed Tyrangea to be a fairy-tale place he had made up rather than a threat to their lives or his sanity.

Their father, after all, was a purveyor of fabulous things. He built Faith an elaborate tree house tucked in the arms of a sturdy chestnut tree. Its steps were made out of rulers, its side walls were park benches, and chairs jerry-rigged from chimney caps and painted to look like toadstools sat on either side of a little multi-colored table made out of an abandoned wagon wheel.

On the day Dortimer presented it to her, Faith followed her father into her tree house and politely listened to him expostulating on the fun she and her friends would have there. She briefly studied the colorful amalgamation of park benches, toadstools, and wagon wheels, looked up at him, and with no discernible expression on her face, said, "Thank you, Father." And that was all she said. Then she went to her room to play by herself, without toadstools and without friends.

From his youngest daughter, a happy little exhibitionist who loved to sing and dance, Dortimer received a much more ebullient response. Dorsey was the delight of meter readers, UPS drivers, and mailmen, for whom she performed a special skit that started with a tap dance and ended with the presentation of pieces of gravel from the driveway, which she claimed to be emeralds from King Solomon's mines. For Dorsey, Dortimer had built a small stage at the back of his vast Victorian garage, complete with a plywood proscenium arch and shower curtains on which he had glued glitter-covered stars.

Dorsey's delight inspired Dortimer to create even more objects of whimsy for her, ultimately resulting in a house and grounds that looked like a cross between a miniature golf course and Disneyland.

There were arched bridges over man-made brooks that led to playhouses with turrets, drawbridges, and moats. There was a little brick path called the Rue de Nowhere, where Dorsey walked hand in hand with imaginary beggars, soldiers, and kings. There were ropes that dangled from trees, perfect for swinging and belting out Tarzan-like yells. And there was a tiny, dainty lily pond, in the center of which was a rock where Dorsey often pretended to be a water nymph or a shipwrecked countess waiting to be rescued by Sir Somebody, who was in hot pursuit of a treasure chest drawn on his half of a parchment map.

Other toys and objects had also been built for his two girls by their gentle parent who loved them dearly, despite his conviction that we were to be visited shortly by probably harmless but possibly dangerous invaders from outer space.

Despite my overall fascination with Dortimer Browning and his family, many years after the fire, three things were of particular interest to me. One, that Faith never moved out of the house. Two, that when Dorsey was eighteen years old she went to Hudson University to attend its School of Dramatic Arts. And three, that the big, beautiful white elephant of a Victorian house where they had lived was insured by Precaution Property and Liability Insurance Company, the company for which I eventually went to work.

chapter eight

THE SKELETON STAFF INVOLVED IN CLOSING the Westchester office sent us the Browning file by overnight mail.

On my first, haphazard glance through the pages, I gleaned that fourteen days ago, on July 4, a fire broke out at Number One Labyrinth Lane in the Riverdale section of the Bronx. A twenty-one-year-old woman, alone in the house at the time, died in the fire. The residence was co-owned by this woman and her sister. The victim's name was Dorsey Browning.

There were no official fire reports in the folder I'd been sent. No newspaper articles. No interior photographs. No schematics. No interviews. No witness statements. But there were a raft of internal memoranda, all of which made it clear that this case was going to take me by the hand and lead me to the Land of Pull Out Your Hair.

According to the report filled out by the inept claims representative of the now defunct Westchester office, Alistair McDevitt, his wife, Beatrice, and a few of their friends were sitting on the terrace behind their house on the Fourth of July. They were having drinks and watching firecrackers go off at a nearby golf course. One of the people at that party was Faith Browning, sister of the deceased.

The report didn't specify who first noticed that the house

across the street (actually, the shared driveway) was on fire, but at 11:30 P.M. someone dialed 911. At 8:00 the next morning, Faith Browning called Precaution Property and Liability's claims department. Two hours later, Vincent Mendloop, an adjuster from the Westchester office, went to the fire scene.

This is where it got tricky.

New York State law requires that any death unattended by a physician has to be treated as a potential homicide. In the Bronx, those vested with the authority to investigate fire deaths are New York City fire marshals. By the time Vinny Mendloop arrived at the loss, the fire had already been extinguished, and there was an official fire marshal car parked outside, which meant that the fire department was still in possession of the scene and no one, including the property owner, would be allowed inside. Excluded, our adjuster took only exterior photographs of the house.

When he returned to the loss two days later, he encountered our policyholder on the front porch. According to Vinny's notes, Faith Browning was a woman in her early thirties and attractively dressed in a couture black sheath. She had a strand of real pearls — adjusters notice that sort of thing — around her neck.

"Yes?" she said, her voice haughty, her body blocking his entrance.

Vinny introduced himself, explained who he was, apologized for intruding, and said, "Your broker suggested that I stop by since we weren't able to contact you by phone. I need to take interior photographs of your home to document the loss."

Miss Browning's face was expressionless. "My sister died in that terrible fire," she said. "The funeral is today, and I am in mourning. You certainly may *not* come inside."

Then, according to Vinny's notes, Faith Browning went inside and closed the door in his face.

Despite his emphatic ouster, Vinny did walk the outside perimeter of the property. He didn't take any pictures, but he peeked through an opening in the dingy lace curtain over the glass panel in the front door, and he noted that the furniture in the front hall appeared to be intact. He continued to reconnoiter, peering through windows to the living room, library, kitchen, breakfast nook, dining room, parlor, and the enclosed back porch. He wrote in his report that although the rooms upstairs appeared to be heavily damaged, other than a layer of smoke and soot covering everything, the first floor of the Browning residence was in relatively good shape.

Vinny continued to poke around at the scene until Faith caught him looking through the dining room window, at which time she jerked it open and screamed, "Go away!"

For the following five days, internal memos flew back and forth as Vinny kept trying to set up appointments with our policyholder to get inside the house. Finally, on Friday, July 14, he negotiated the lengthy driveway to One Labyrinth Lane on the off chance that he might get lucky. The front door was open; after knocking loudly for a minute or two and getting no response, he walked inside.

According to Vinny's report, he was stunned by what he saw. Or, to be more accurate, by what he *didn't* see, because none of what had been in the house when he'd come before was there now. He wandered from room to room. All were stripped bare; the only things left were the light fixtures and the dust.

The piano in the parlor . . . gone. The Oriental carpets, Victorian lady's chairs and settees, dining room table and chairs, desks, china cabinets, sofa, drapes, end tables, lamps, tapestries, landscapes, prints and paintings, stereo, record collection, telephones, knickknacks, books and bookshelves . . . gone. All gone.

Confronted with a situation the likes of which he had never before encountered, Vinny Mendloop drifted aimlessly toward the stairs and was about to put his foot on the first step when he heard a rustling noise coming from above.

"What are *you* doing here?" Faith Browning demanded as she descended from the second floor landing.

"I . . . I'm . . ."

"You're from the insurance company. What do you want?"

"I came to . . . to document the loss, but —"

"Well, it's a *total* loss. I expect to be reimbursed for the full policy limit."

With a sweep of his hand, Vinny indicated the rooms at the bottom of the stairs. "But where . . . where *is* everything?"

"I threw it out."

"You . . . you . . ."

"That is correct. Everything was destroyed in the fire. *Everything.* So I brought it out to the curb on garbage pickup day. I disposed of it. And now that you've had your jollies invading my privacy, please telephone my broker and tell him I want to pick up my check."

"But . . ."

"No buts," Faith Browning said, once again slamming the door in his face. Vinny went back to the Westchester office, scrawled out everything he remembered about the encounter, and added that the household furnishings from Faith Browning's first-floor had been essentially intact and that, in his professional opinion, she had removed them to an unspecified location where they were being stored. He believed she was putting in a claim for valuable items that had *not* been destroyed in the fire, and that she was attempting to perpetrate a fraud against the insurance company.

He recommended that we deny the claim.

Good advice. Unfortunately, it stopped there; no follow-through was done. That was going to be my job. First and foremost, I wanted to get our legal department involved, to have them issue subpoenas to the fire department for their fire incident reports, fire marshal reports, and every photograph that had been taken.

I wanted to contact Faith Browning through her broker and request that a signed, sworn proof of loss be submitted to my office within sixty days of the loss. Also on my to do list were checking back issues of newspapers to see if anyone had written about the fire and calling the Department of Sanitation to see if they'd made any bulk pickups on Labyrinth Lane during the ten-day period before July 14, by which time all of the furniture had disappeared. I was also going to ask for a roster of sanitation men who worked that route in Riverdale. I wanted to talk to them about the quality and quantity of items picked up at the Browning residence after the fire. I wanted to do a property check on One Labyrinth Lane to see if previous fires had occurred at that address; I wanted to interview Faith Browning's neighbors. Had they seen anything suspicious with regard to the removal of her household furnishings? And all of this had to be done posthaste, because if we were going to deny the claim, and it looked like we were, we had to be sure of our facts or we'd be hit with penalties so severe they'd make being slapped around by the Internal Revenue Service look like fun.

By law, if an insurance company has not paid a properly submitted claim in a timely fashion, the policy owner can sue for triple damages. Let's say the value of the policy is $500,000. If a jury finds in the plaintiff's favor, he can walk out of the courtroom a million and a half dollars richer, plus interest from the date the claim should have been paid.

This law was passed to dissuade insurance companies from arbitrarily denying legitimate claims. When it's not being abused, it's a good law, and it puts the onus on the insurer to be careful, to be honest, and to be right.

As far as the Browning residence went, I thought Vinny Mendloop had stated our case clearly, but we didn't have anywhere near enough evidence to support it. Worse than that, we had never called a fire investigator to the scene.

I had just finished my first go-through of the Browning file when Oliver rapped his knuckles on my desktop and said, "Can I come in?"

I looked up. "Hi, Ollie."

"Find anything interesting?"

"It's *all* interesting. Our policyholder is a real piece of work."

"Oh," Ollie said softly. He looked worried, but he usually looks worried. "Bosley just faxed this to me, Tillary. He wants to know what we think."

My boss handed me a memo from Bosley Kellogg, one of the nicer attorneys in our legal department.

Dear Ollie:

I am in receipt of a letter from the law firm of Spenser and Knowes. Dottie Knowes, who has worked for us in the past, is representing Hercules Electric in a lawsuit being brought against their radio division by Faith Browning. Miss Browning is also a Precaution Property and Liability policyholder. It is my understanding that we are paying the full replacement value for the structural damage to the house but that our adjuster deems her personal property claim suspicious. In her lawsuit against Hercules, Miss Browning states that a clock radio manufactured by Hercules Electric that had been located on the night table beside Dorsey Browning's bed was defective and caused a fire, the result of which was the destruction of her house and the death of her sister.

Dottie Knowes has advised me that Hercules Electric always vigorously defends itself against lawsuits, and that it is determined to fight this one. Under no circumstances will the company settle. They've hired a fire investigator who has worked for them before and whom they say is "the best in the business." Since Faith Browning is involved with us on the same loss, Hercules wants to know if we would like to share his services and split his fee.

Your office has an exemplary record on fire claims. Since you and Fritillary Quilter have done a terrific job in the past, I would appreciate your input on this difficult and potentially damaging case.

Please get back to me on this immediately, Ollie.

The name of the investigator they're recommending is Isaac Blessing.

I've never heard of him.

Have you?

chapter nine

I'M NOT GOING TO SAY THAT BELLS and whistles went off in my head when I read the name Isaac Blessing. Nor did I have a quick flashback to little old fifteen-year-old me. If anything, I may have experienced the tiniest wisp of a tickle. A sort of an "Isaac who?" of the brain. But as fast as the tickle tickled, it was replaced by the greater need to determine if we wanted to position ourselves on the same side of the defense table as Hercules Electric.

As far as I was concerned, our first and only objective was to protect the interests of Precaution Property and Liability, and the way I saw it, we had two means of achieving that objective.

The first was adversarial. The "us" versus "them" road to victory or defeat. This involved subrogation.

Subrogation. Subrogation. How best to explain subrogation?

Think of an automobile owner. Let's call him Marvin Kaplan. Marvin owns a red Jeep Grand Cherokee. He's driving it to his golf lesson at the Chelsea Piers when he loses control and crashes into the front of The Friendly Bakery Shop on West Twenty-first Street. Marvin claims that even though he stepped on the brake, the car went into drive, which is why he slammed through the plate-glass window.

Nobody was hurt, the police arrived, an accident report was filed, and all of the insurance companies were notified.

Marvin's insurance company paid for the bodywork that had to be done on his car, and The Friendly Bakery's insurance company paid for the repair of the plate-glass window, the new window framing, a new sign, a new door, a display case, and assorted pastries.

Enter: Subrogation.

The Friendly Bakery's insurance company, now out of pocket for a bunch of thousands of dollars, *wants its money back.* So it takes out its roller skate key, winds up the lawyers in its legal department, and tells them to subrogate against (i.e., sue) the company that insured Marvin Kaplan's Jeep, because Marvin's driving created all the damages and expenses in the first place.

The legal fees involved in retrieving this money inevitably exceed the total sum of the dollars paid out, and subrogation, stripped of legalese and elocution, is really just a way of taking money out of one insurance company's pocket and putting it into another's. And since the insurance company being subrogated against is often subrogating against someone else (the manufacturer of the Jeep), who is subrogating against somebody else (the manufacturer of the brakes), and so on, nobody benefits except the lawyers. The bad news is that, in the long run, it is always, always, always the regular old middle-class policyholder who pays the lawyers' fees by way of higher premiums — whether he has ever filed an insurance claim or not.

The situation with the Browning claim started with a loss. In this instance caused by fire. Precaution Property and Liability insured Faith Browning's dwelling (the actual structure of the house) as well as the contents. *Contents* means personal property and household possessions.

Because our adjusters had been unable to get inside our policyholder's house, my company hadn't yet evaluated the structural damage or cleanup costs. From the few exterior photos Vinny

Mendloop had taken, it looked as if most of the fire had burned through the residence's top two floors and roof. Detailed estimate notwithstanding, repairing it would be expensive.

All of which meant that our first order of business would be to determine what actually caused the fire. Had it been started by a faulty clock radio, as Faith Browning was alleging? Or had the fire been caused by something else? And what *was* that something else? Inquiries were going to have to be made, and money was going to have to be spent.

Among the questions we had to answer were these:

Did we want to subrogate against Hercules Electric for the $200,000 plus what it would cost to repair Faith Browning's house? Or should we hook up with Hercules, as our house counsel had suggested, split the fire investigator's fees, and see what Isaac Blessing had to say?

For me it was a no-brainer. I agreed with Vinny Mendloop. I didn't trust Faith Browning and thought her personal property claim was bogus. As to the fire, it had occurred on the Fourth of July. Parties. Booze. Combustibles. A crazy night. Could a firecracker have gone wild? Could the house have been victimized by an act of vandalism? Had someone had too much to drink and carelessly discarded a cigarette?

Since our Westchester office hadn't called in an investigator, we didn't have a clue. We had to go back to square one, and square one was the fire.

So *no*, we would not subrogate against Hercules Electric, and *yes*, we did want to work with their fire investigator and split his fee.

Ollie had been waiting patiently as I went through all of this in my mind. Finally, I looked up from the fax and said, "You call Bosley, boss. I'll give Isaac whoever-he-is a call. Then, we shall see what we shall see."

chapter ten

BY THE TIME OUR LAWYER TALKED to the Hercules Electric lawyer, and their lawyer did the back-and-forth routine with Faith Browning's attorneys, five weeks had gone by. It wasn't until August 29, almost two months *after* the fire, that our new fire investigator and I finally met. I took the subway to Brooklyn Heights, where Isaac C. Blessing Associates was located on the top floor of a beautiful old limestone building overlooking the Promenade. It wasn't a doorman building, so I pressed the button next to Blesssing's name, shouted my name into the intercom, and was buzzed inside.

As soon as Isaac C. Blessing opened the door to his office, I realized who he was. Once I'd made that connection, I remembered everything else about him, too. Ike Blessing at forty-five was a slightly older and craggier version of the man I had met ten years earlier. A few more lines shot out of the corners of his eyes, but those eyes were still diamond shaped and still dazzlingly blue, and his hair was still the silky color of corn tassels.

Another thing. Ike smiled at me. I'd forgotten that smile. It was just about the nicest damned smile that I had ever seen.

Simultaneous with my figuring out who Ike was, I snapped my fingers, peered right into his eyes, and said, "I'll be damned."

"Excuse me?" Ike said, looking down at me as if I were a neighbor's curious but harmless pet.

I peeked my head inside his door and smelled coffee. Coffee and chocolate. I don't know what I expected to smell. Char-broiled upholstery and wet ashes, like the last time?

Ike grabbed me by the elbow and led me down a short corridor to his office. He drew me to a chair across from his desk, pointed, and said, "Sit." I sat. But I was still gaping at him openly. He leaned casually against the corner of the desk and crossed his arms over his chest.

He smiled again. I kept staring. Then I said, "My name is Tillary Quilter."

"You called. We have an appointment. I'm a trained investigator, so I figured that one out."

I couldn't stop staring.

"Sweetheart," he said, "is my slip showing or something?"

I should have laughed, but my mind was too boggled to think. "I . . . I . . . ," I stammered. "Just now, when you opened the door, I . . . I figured it out."

"Figured what out?"

"Figured out my whole life."

"Glad to be of service."

"You don't remember me, do you?"

Ike leaned over my chair, dropped one hand to each of my armrests, and this time *he* stared at *me*. I mean *really* stared. He was uncomfortably masculine and uncomfortably close.

"You have eyes like green tiddlywinks," he said, as though he were evaluating the paint job on a car. "You've got about as many freckles as you used to have, and you've been in the same room with me for five minutes without fainting, crying, or borrowing my handkerchief, which by the way, you never returned. You're right, sunshine. I don't recognize you."

He pulled away and resumed his comfortable slouch against the edge of his desk.

I started to say something, anything, but he put a finger over his lips in the same gesture he'd used a decade before. Then he looked up at the ceiling for a few seconds. "There are two things a fire marshal always remembers," Ike finally said. "One is the first fire he ever investigated. The other is the last. The first fire I did as a marshal was in a Dempsey Dumpster outside a strip joint on Tenth Avenue, a few blocks from Times Square. The last was an arson at the Nogales Social Club on 137th Street in Spanish Harlem. I can remember every detail about each of them. After I quit the fire department, the first fire I did as a private investigator was important to me too. The name of the homeowners was Borkin. They lived in a single-family home on Jefferson Avenue in Conversation, New York. The key witness to the fire, who was also instrumental in its ignition, was a cute little pug-nosed girl named Fritillary Quilter." He paused. "Fritillary. What kind of a name is that?"

"A fritillary is a kind of a butterfly," I responded automatically. I was used to the question.

"Butterfly," Ike muttered. Then he walked behind his desk and lowered himself into a high-backed swivel chair.

"Well, *I* recognized *you*, too," I suddenly burst out. I couldn't resist myself, and even I could hear the you-think-you're-so-smart undercurrent in my voice. In short order, though, my smugness dissipated and my tone changed to one of awe.

"All these years." My voice dropped meditatively. Ike was obviously listening to every word I said, but in an important sense I was really talking to myself. "All these years, I've been gravitating toward what you do . . . what I *saw* you do ten years ago in the Borkins' house. At every loss I go to, I compare what I see and do *now* with what I watched *you* do then. I try to move the way you moved, think the way you thought, and look at a fire scene through your eyes. But I didn't realize until *just this minute* that I was doing it. Somehow, over time, I had completely lost the memory of you. You personally. I never forgot what you *did*, though. And I'm fully aware of how good you are at doing it. You're the best, Ike Blessing, and the best is what I want to be. *You* are what I want to be."

The object of my adoration, at that moment, had every right to laugh out loud or pick up a broom and sweep me out of his office. Instead, he said solemnly, "You can't be me, Tilly."

I blinked a few times. Then I cocked my head to one side — (I learned how to do that from a dog I'd once had) — and I smiled.

"Okay," I responded cheerfully. "Then can I just follow you around?"

chapter eleven

HERO WORSHIP, I SUPPOSE, can be a little bit unnerving. Or a lot, depending on who is doing the worshiping and who has been plopped on top of the pedestal to be adored.

Years ago, when I was young and impressionable, I had watched Ike Blessing reconstruct a fire scene. The surgical intensity of his powers of observation and deduction had so impressed me that, even though I hadn't realized it at the time, I'd embarked upon a parallel career.

Ike was the Pied Piper of fire investigation, and I was trailing along behind him like a kid trying to fit her feet in her father's footprints in the snow. Or sand. Or ashes.

But I still had a lot to learn, and I still knew very little about the case I had come to his office to discuss.

I looked at the heaps of official documents and photographs spread out on Ike's conference table and said, "Where do we start?"

"There's always only one place to start when you're dealing with fire," Ike answered.

"At the fire scene?"

"Right. We have an appointment this morning to inspect the Browning residence. Eleven A.M. Faith Browning's lawyers are acting like a bunch of pissy broads that don't want to invite us to their tea party. Unless we can obtain a court order, today is the only bite of the apple we're going to get. I've got extra boots and flashlights for you in my car. After we're done in Riverdale, we'll come back here, and I'll show you the fire reports and photographs. It's going to be a long day, freckle-face. Are you up to it?"

Was I *up* to it?

I *lived* for it!

I grinned and mixed every metaphor, allusion, or whatever it's called that I could think of when I answered, "You, Lone Ranger. Me, Tonto. Lead on, Macduff."

chapter twelve

MY FIRST IMPRESSION of the Browning residence did not earn me high marks as a realist, but if imagination is the springboard for inspired guesses, I'm not sure it did me any harm, either.

There's an idea I learned in my abbreviated exposure to Aristotle in high school that stuck with me. I've always felt like a philosophical slacker for not reading more, but this one concept — it referred to fiction but I like to think it's applicable to all art forms — was something to the effect that art depicts life "not as it is, but as it might and ought to be."

Ike Blessing stopped at the end of the long driveway called Labyrinth Lane, and what I saw when I looked through the windshield was the dream house that I never knew I had dreamed. It was love at first sight. Or love at second sight, as I later came to believe. I turned to Ike to see if he was feeling the same thing, but all I saw in those bottomless blues was the mind behind them, observing, calculating, and already engaged in the process of making distinctions and evaluations.

Let *him* work, I said to myself. I'll just sit here and worship an edifice that was obviously built to bask in the sun of my soul.

I slowly got out of Ike Blessing's car, my eyes never leaving the house's white clapboards and glossy green shutters, neither knowing nor caring if what I was looking at was a Gothic Revival, a Queen Anne, or Hansel and Gretel's Gingerbread House. When I got home, I dug out a few architectural books and discovered that my dream house was styled after an Italian villa, with tall windows, an expansive porch, a low-pitched roof, and a cupola located at roof level. I also read that between 1850 and 1890 dozens of exactly the same houses had been built, using blueprints from George Jackson Jefferson's book, *Country House Architecture, Including Blueprints for Cottages, Farm Houses, and Villas,* and that this house was probably built in 1885.

But I found out all of that later. What I knew then and there, and I knew it with the stunned certainty of a time traveler who suddenly finds herself flung smack-dab in the middle of her own past, is that in every way except for time and place I was standing in front of Meg Nelligan's childhood home.

Although at the time I wouldn't have known a Victorian from a Colonial from a tent, I did know that Meg and her family had lived in a house just like this one on Orchard Hill Road in Conversation, New York. Meg's mother, Mrs. Nelligan, was a romantic soul, pretty, petite, dynamic, and great with children. She ran our summer theater. Meg's dad was probably her stepfather, because she called him Jolly instead of Dad. He was also unbelievably nice, and acted as if it were a great privilege to have his daughter's friends wandering around the house with our bicycles dumped on his front lawn like leftovers from a yard sale.

We kids called him Jolly, too.

He was a big, rumpled man with a sunburned bald spot, a gruff voice, and a sweet disposition. He never interfered with his wife's management of our theater group, and his one great love, other than making money, was tennis.

When I didn't have to move props or paint sets, Jolly and I played tennis on their court behind the house. He liked playing with me because I have such a wicked backhand. My serve is only so-so, but when I reach across my body and my racket slams into that fluffy little ball, I am the Goddess of Swing.

I admit that I led Jolly on by implying that someday I just *might* go professional, which was his dream for me, and I was willing to perpetrate that small fraud because I loved hearing him shout out "nice shot" or "put a little more spin on it," and I got free tennis lessons.

The best thing about the Nelligans, though, was their house. The porch was wide and wrapped around the first floor like the brim of a Mexican hat. In the summertime, they kept all the windows open, and none of us ever bothered to walk the extra few feet to the front or back doors when we could just walk through a window to get in the library, living room, or den. After rehearsals, Mrs. Nelligan used to give lemonade and cookies to her sweaty cast and crew, and since we little thespians had the run of the place, I often wandered from room to room in search of an annotated script, a pair of misplaced eyeglasses, a costume someone had left in the hall closet, or the bathroom.

That house on Orchard Hill Road was the brightest, most cheerful and haphazard collection of rooms that I'd ever seen. The furniture was comfy, overstuffed, and old. Long voile curtains over the library windows fluttered in the breeze, while beams of sunlight illuminated dust motes that looked like fairy souls playing bumper cars in the sun. There were huge, worn Persian carpets stopping just short of the wrought-iron registers that added decorative touches to the parquet floors.

People lived, laughed, and had pillow fights in the Nelligan house. Water balloons were tossed from attic windows, and you could sprawl on the floor in the den, taking turns reading aloud from *Alice's Adventures in Wonderland*, or listening to your friends rehearsing their lines for the summer play. The Nelligans lived in the kind of a fantasy house that everyone should be lucky enough to brush up against at least once in a childhood, if for no other reason than just to experience life "not as it is, but as it might and ought to be."

And so, with the memory of comfortable rooms and Jolly's tennis lessons fluffing up the cushions in my brain, I approached the stairs leading to Faith Browning's house with a beatific look on my face, predisposed to like anything and anyone I encountered there.

"Wake up, butterfly," I suddenly heard Isaac Blessing say.

I looked at him. "Huh?"

"We have work to do."

Ike took his camera bag out of the car trunk, flung it over a shoulder, and said, "We won't need boots or helmets." He stuck one flashlight into the back pocket of his jeans, handed me another one, and slammed the trunk.

When I looked up again at the house, I got a glimpse of bright blue tarp, and I realized for the first time, identical blueprints notwithstanding, I was *not* standing in front of Meg Nelligan's Victorian. The house I was about to enter had experienced a fire. It was a house in which a young woman had died. No theater group. No lemonade and cookies. No Jolly. Just a fire loss and a fire investigation. And so I shook the memories out of my head, sighed, and followed Ike Blessing onto the lawn.

I had done it only once before, but I remembered the routine. Walk around the outside of the structure; analyze the fire damage; look for evidence.

Hey. You never know when you're going to trip over a fire-cracker . . . or a carelessly discarded lampshade.

And we would take pictures, of course.

Ike always worked a fire scene counterclockwise, for no particular reason as far as I could discern, and it took us about ten minutes to get behind the house. That's where most of the fire occurred. The back of the second-floor roof was covered with the blue tarp I had seen from the driveway; plywood sheets were nailed over the rear windows on the third floor, and more sheets of plywood covered the windows of the cupola. All of the clapboard and trim, including the areas around the kitchen, the back porch, and the second-floor bedrooms, was heavily stained with smoke and soot.

Humph. Some dream house.

After Ike shot two rolls of film, he and I returned to the front of the house.

A slim, fair-haired woman was waiting for us on the porch.

"Isacc Blessing?" she asked from the top step.

She had an attractive smile, a three-hundred-dollar briefcase, and shrewd eyes.

"Himself," Ike said. He indicated me. "Fritillary Quilter. Precaution Property and Liability."

We all nodded and smiled.

The lawyer said that her name was Colleen or Celine or Clarissa something or another, and then she unlocked the front door.

"I don't know what good it's going to do you." She looked over her shoulder and grinned. "Most of the repairs have already been made. There's not much to see."

Ike stopped. He looked at me. Hell, I was as shocked as he was. When someone puts in a claim for property damage, the insurance company gets to evaluate the damage before it has to pay the claim. That's what the policy says, and that's the way it's supposed to be. I didn't know much about civil suits like the one Faith Browning had initiated against Hercules Electric, but I *did* know that there's such a thing as spoliation of evidence, and I knew that if what Colleen, Celine, or Clarissa was telling us was true, she knew it too. Which is probably why she was so eager to leave.

She pushed open the door.

"Make yourselves at home," she said. "Don't take anything. Don't break anything. Don't alter anything. And don't let the bedbugs bite. I've got another appointment. The electricity is on, so you won't need those flashlights, and the door locks itself, so just pull it shut when you leave. Ta ta. See you in court."

She hurried down the porch steps, slipped behind the wheel of a shiny black Mercedes, and was out of sight faster than you could say, "Wait a second. You can't *do* that."

Obviously, she could.

Ike was standing halfway between the living room and foyer, photographing rooms at odd angles, when I caught up with him, and damn it, there I was, déjà-vuing all over again. Here, and in who knows how many other George Jackson Jefferson houses, was the same living room, with the same magnificent parquet floors, tall windows, recessed window seats, and engraved fireplace mantel that, because I spent so much time in Meg Nelligan's house, had been such a big part of my childhood. Even though I had never been in it before, the house was as familiar to me as that of a favorite movie star. One whom I *think* I know intimately, because I've seen her so often on the television set, but who, like the house I was standing in, I don't really know at all.

Ike lowered his camera and turned to me. "Can you draw?"

I reached for my bag. It usually hangs from my shoulder like an affectionate chimp and is about the size of Lake Michigan. I whipped out a pencil and a legal pad.

"I do really good elephant faces, but my favorite is Elvis Presley with the pouty lower lip."

"Can you draw a schematic of a room?"

"Yes indeed-y. Straight lines with openings for doorways and windows are a particular specialty of mine."

Ike flipped open his camera bag and pulled out a tape measure. "Draw a floor plan of the house. Put in everything. Windows. Built-in bookcases. Radiators. Closets. Electrical outlets."

"Okay. But you can put away the tape measure. I don't want it."

"You may not want it, but you need it."

"No, I don't. Test me."

"All right. How big is this room?"

I looked to my right and left. I looked up and down. I pretended I was back in Conversation, working for Walter Troska and taking pictures at fraternity parties. I stood against one wall, estimated the distance to the wall opposite, made like I was a camera, and clicked my eyes. I did the same in the opposite direction. Then I announced, "Fifteen by twenty-six. The window seat with the cushions is six and a half feet long."

Ike pushed the tape measure at me and said, "Hold this end."

I did.

He made me follow him around while he measured the room.

"I'm right, aren't I?" I said when we were finished.

He looked me dead in the eye. "I'm impressed."

"I'm impressive."

Hey, cocky is as cocky does.

Ike tossed the tape measure back to me. "Get me the dimensions of the outside perimeter of the house while I finish up in here. When you're done, we'll go upstairs together."

"You mean you'll wait for me?"

"Sure, sunshine. You still want to learn how to investigate fires, don't you?"

"Passionately."

"Well, that's the place to start."

chapter thirteen

WHEN YOU'RE GROWING UP, one of the things your parents never tell you about is balloon construction. They tell you about birds, bees, and how to tie your shoclaces. They tell you to look both ways before you cross the street. But they never warn you about the absolutely and positively most dangerous way to build a house.

Balloon construction.

It *sounds* harmless enough, doesn't it? Almost whimsical. As if a balloon construction house would be light and airy and need to be moored like a blimp so that it won't float away. But that's not what it means. It took me a long time to finally understand balloon construction, and then it was only because Ike made it impossible for me *not* to understand.

Ike Blessing is an interesting man. He doesn't move around much at a fire scene, and it's obvious that most of the activity is going on inside his head. He's not one of those brooding geniuses, though, and if you interrupt him to ask a question or because you need another roll of film, he doesn't go all snarly and get a you've-just-ruined-my-train-of-thought expression on his face. Instead his big old blues just slide over to where you're standing, and even though he looks at you more as if you're an interesting burn pattern than as if you're a human being, he gives you what you need to have or tells you what you need to know.

I try not to interrupt him often, because it's a strange and wonderful thing actually to be able to *see* someone thinking, and when Isaac Blessing is in a room where a fire has occurred, his thought process is visible, like one of those transparent body kits for children, where you can see through the clear plastic skin to the arteries, organs, and bones inside.

All in all, after watching him work, I'm not convinced that Ike Blessing *investigates* a fire scene as much as that he *processes* it. I don't really know what I mean by that, except that *investigation* implies conscious activity, and when Ike's at a fire, not only are his eyes, ears, and mind at work, but I could swear the pores of his skin are thinking, too.

Not that thinking was going to do him much good here. Colleen, Celine, or Clarissa hadn't been kidding when she said that most of the repair work had already been done, and as I followed Ike from room to room, everything was so sparklingly unlived in and disconcertingly clean that I felt more like a prospective home buyer than a claims representative. There's something just plain weird about a house over one hundred and fifteen years old that has absolutely nothing in the way of atmosphere. It's like granny going in for a face-lift and coming out so sleek and polished there's nowhere for her past to get a foothold for a pleasant reminiscence about days gone by.

All the walls in the recently reconstituted Browning house had been Sheetrocked, plastered, and painted. The carved oak moldings had been so beautifully varnished that the wood glowed instead of shined. New floors had been put in with tongue-and-groove boards as icily perfect as the brand-new floor in a high school gym.

The first floor in Faith Browning's house smelled of varnish and smoke and had no furniture. Otherwise, it was exactly the same as in Meg Nelligan's house. The front door led to a large foyer, with a library to the left and a den off the library. The living room was to the right of the foyer, and like the library it was at the front of the house. An oak staircase with an ornate balustrade swept around the main vestibule between the living and the dining rooms to a wide hallway on the second floor. The first bedroom on the second floor was enormous and had its own bathroom. It and a smaller bedroom across the landing overlooked the driveway.

There were two more bedrooms on the second floor: a big brown one over the dining room, in the northeast corner of the house, and a small one with coral walls on the northwest side, over the den. Both had their own bathrooms and faced the backyard. Each was a perfect box with the requisite openings for doors, windows, electric outlets, and switches. I knew a woman had died in the coral bedroom, but I couldn't see any indication in either room that a fire had ever occurred.

The big, brown bedroom looked out on the kitchen roof. Ike led me to a window, opened it, and told me to follow him out on to the roof. Someone had left an aluminum ladder propped against the side of the house. Ike steadied it and went up. When his boots were level with my head, he grabbed a corner of the blue tarp we'd seen from the lawn, yanked hard, and flipped the tarp away from the board to which it had been nailed. Then he descended the ladder and pulled me over. "Your turn, Tilly."

I climbed the ladder and peered inside.

"Holy shit," I said.

What had seemed from the ground to be a neat package that, at worst, had been subjected to smoke and char was in fact

Diablo's House of Horrors, enclosed in a blue Tiffany box and positioned on top of the perfect dream house.

On top of *my* perfect dream house.

I'd never seen anything like it.

Everything above the two back bedrooms was a chaos of collapsed beams.

"Come with me," Ike commanded.

I went down the ladder, and back through the window. I followed him to the center stairwell and up the last flight of stairs to the tarp-wrapped wreckage of the attic and what was left of the cupola.

What a mess.

Timber jutted out at all angles like deranged pick-up sticks. Rusty nails menaced the air like piranha teeth, and warped flaps of sheet metal hung from ceiling beams. There was nothing left of what had once been a roof, and every charred surface exhibited the unmistakable burn pattern that mimics an alligator's back and is called "alligatoring."

Ike gazed at the incinerated wasteland of rafters, insulation, and roofing material, the gears of his thinking machine in rapid motion and no expression at all on his face. He had led me to the cupola, three stories above the entrance door. He took a step toward the front wall, the one that overlooked the driveway, reached into his pocket, and removed a shiny silver dollar and a one-dollar bill. Ike folded the dollar bill around the coin and looked up at me briefly. "That's so it won't roll," he said. Then he crouched down to a crevice between the floor and the wall and dropped that money missile right into the hole.

"Huh?" I said.

Ike crooked his finger at me.

I followed him again, this time down the stairs, past the second floor, to a door in the kitchen that led to the cellar. Once we'd gone down the cellar stairs, it took Ike only a few seconds to orient himself, and after he'd figured out north from south, he strode forward, looking for something on the concrete floor. Looking. Looking. When he got to the foundation wall at the front of the house, Ike began to move more slowly. More carefully. Another few seconds and he motioned me over and kneeled. He picked up the silver dollar.

Then he looked up at me.

"*That's* balloon construction," he said.

chapter fourteen

I'M NOT A STUDENT TYPE. I never have been. At least a thousand times I've promised myself that I would read everything Thomas Jefferson ever wrote. That, along with all the writings of John Locke, Thomas Paine, and Benjamin Franklin. I want to read the Magna Carta, too. But I never have. I have no problem racing through my nineteenth-century French novels or autobiographies of my heroes, but as for the rest, there's a whole lot about the exhilaration of learning that just never clicked in my brain.

A lot of people thrive on a university campus. I know that. For them, sheepskin is an aphrodisiac; being near ivy-covered walls makes their hearts beat faster and their knees go all wobbly. Like being in love. If I even get *near* a college, I want to hyperventilate.

The minute Ike Blessing held up that silver dollar, though, I was hooked. I felt euphoric at having acquired specialized knowledge. I wanted to grab it and hold it tight, like a relative I'd loved and lost who had suddenly come back to life.

When I got my first glimmer of what Ike was trying to convey to me with his demonstration of balloon construction, I don't know why, but I got all wishy-washy and wanted to cry. In fact, I did cry. I know this, because when I opened my purse at home that night, right on top of my wallet I found a handkerchief.

Ike Blessing's handkerchief.

I guess some things never change.

On the way back to Ike's office, we grabbed a few sandwiches from a deli on Montague Street and went inside. I don't remember eating, but the sandwiches disappeared, and at some point Ike must have set up a pot to percolate, because we were drinking coffee all afternoon.

The conference table.

What a nightmare of heartache. What a treasure trove of information.

Everything we needed to know about what happened in the house on Labyrinth Lane was there. Piles of reports. Stacks of photographs. Insurance records. Statements under oath. Requests for production of documents. Inventories of personal property. Repair bills. Autopsy report. . . . The complaint:

> **PLAINTIFF**, FAITH BROWNING, IS AN ADULT CITIZEN OF THE STATE OF NEW YORK, WHO RESIDES AT ONE LABYRINTH LANE, RIVERDALE, NEW YORK.
>
> **DEFENDANT,** HERCULES ELECTRIC, IS A PRIVATE CORPORATION, ORGANIZED AND EXISTING UNDER THE LAWS OF NEW YORK FOR THE PURPOSES OF MANUFACTURING, SELLING, AND DISTRIBUTING ELECTRIC AND ELECTRONIC PRODUCTS FOR COMMERCIAL AND PRIVATE USE.
>
> **PLEASE TAKE NOTICE** THAT THE PLAINTIFF, FAITH BROWNING, DEMANDS OF THE DEFENDANT, HERCULES ELECTRIC, UPON INFORMATION AND BELIEF AS FOLLOWS:
>
> 1. THE FIRE STARTED IN A HERCULES CLOCK RADIO LOCATED IN A SECOND-FLOOR REAR BEDROOM OF THE PREMISES.
> 2. DEFENDANT AND/OR THEIR EMPLOYEES, SERVANTS, OR AGENTS NEGLIGENTLY DESIGNED AND/OR MANUFACTURED THE SUBJECT CLOCK RADIO; FAILED TO WARN PLAINTIFF OF DANGER OR ELECTRICAL SHORT CIRCUIT . . .

And so on.

Plunging into the jumble of documents would have been a nightmare of incomprehensibility, except for two things: One, I had Isaac C. Blessing to lead me past each "Wherefore" and "Hereby stipulated" and help me distinguish what was and what wasn't important — "Don't even bother to figure out those wiring diagrams, Tilly. That's what electrical engineers are for."

And two, there were photographs.

The photos in the matter of *Faith Browning v. Hercules Electric* (and *Faith Browning v. Precaution Property and Liability*) affected me the same way as did my cup of tea with Mrs. Ruth Epps that fateful morning in Palisades, New York. The same, but magnified a thousandfold. Just as Mrs. Epps's tea made the grief of loss at a fire real to me, the photographs made the deadly aftermath of the fire at One Labyrinth Lane real to me. Or at least they made one death much too real.

We were very, very lucky that so many pictures had been taken the day of the fire. The day Vinny Mendloop, our company adjuster, had been turned away for the first time.

"Where's the fire marshal's report?" I asked.

Ike stuck his hand into a stack of documents and plucked it out.

I read it quickly, and didn't slow down until I got to the section labeled "Cause of Fire":

> The fire started in the northwest bedroom, where a Hercules clock radio was located on top of a night table adjacent to the deceased's bed. The cause of the fire was irregular electrical activity occurring in the clock radio, which acted as an ignition source.

"What's irregular electrical activity?"

"A meaningless, catchall phrase that sounds good," Ike said.

I raised an eyebrow. "Catchall or not, it seems to be an unequivocal conclusion."

"It sure does."

I looked at the signature at the bottom of the report. "Who's Jeremy Fry?"

"A fire marshal I worked with a long time ago."

"Is he any good?"

"He's the worst fire investigator I ever met."

"Aw. Come on. Don't hold back. Tell me what you really think."

"Let me put it this way, Tilly, if it would take a really bad fire marshal an hour to screw up a fire investigation, Fry could do it ten times worse in half the time."

"He's lazy. Right?"

"On a good day, he's lazy. This fire was on the Fourth of July."

"Which means?"

"That he was lazy and busy. Not a good combination. Particularly on an active night."

I looked down again at the stack of photos.

"He can't be that bad if he took all of these fire scene pictures."

"He didn't take them. Captain Burchfield is responsible for the photos."

"Who is —"

"Captain Burchfield is a great fireman. Years ago, Tilly, fire hydrants used to be made of wood, and we had an expression: Iron men and wooden hydrants. Captain Burchfield is an iron man. We worked together for a year in Ladder 105, and there was nothing he hated more than losing someone in a fire. He considers it a personal affront to God. So he fights back with photos. If there's a death at one of his fires, he calls in the photo unit to document it."

"I would have thought that was the fire marshal's job."

"It is."

"Doesn't he trust the marshals?"

"Captain Burchfield doesn't trust the pope, and he's a good Catholic."

I shuffled through a few more papers. "Is there a police report in here somewhere?"

Ike found it, passed it over to me, and watched while I read it.

"It says here that the police didn't investigate because the fire marshals deemed the fire accidental."

Ike's light blue eyes darkened. Uh-oh. Storm warnings.

"I gather this sort of workmanship doesn't thrill you," I said.

"Do I look thrilled?"

"Didn't somebody tell me that you stopped being a marshal when the fire department gave arson investigation to the police?"

"I did, and they did. A year later the marshals got some of their powers back, but they still can't make arrests at a homicide."

I frowned down at Jeremy Fry's fire report. "Maybe that's a *good* thing."

Ike shook his head.

"I'd put New York City fire investigators up against any marshals, anywhere in the world. Jerry Fry is a freak of nature. Like sinkholes and slugs. He's no more the fire department's fault than sewer explosions. You hate them, but they just keep happening."

I let the police report drop to the table.

"Ike. What *did* happen at Faith Browning house?"

Instead of answering the president of Isaac C. Blessing Associates motioned me over to the window behind his desk.

"Come here, sunshine."

I joined him at the window. Ike's office overlooks the most beautiful view in New York City. To my left I could see the New

York Harbor, lights twinkling on the water surrounding the Statue of Liberty and Governors Island. The navy yard, the magnificent, *magnificent* Brooklyn Bridge, and all of lower Manhattan, with its towers and spires, were in front of me. Twilight had just descended. Skyscrapers nuzzled the skyline across the river, their windows alive with light against a dramatically darkening sky.

"Jesus," I gasped. "That's unholy awesome gorgeous beautiful."

Ike smiled.

"But it's *dark* out." I looked at my watch. "And it's late. I've got to go." I turned regretfully to the conference table. "And we haven't even looked at the photographs."

"You haven't," Ike said. "I have."

"I want to look at them, study them, and extract every last little bit of information out of them, Ike. I want to learn everything there is to learn about this fire."

"I know you do, sunshine. But Rome wasn't built in a day."

"No. But Rome was burned in a day. Ask Nero."

Ike leaned back against his desk, winked, and said, "Now *that's* a fire I would have liked to do."

chapter fifteen

ON WEDNESDAY MORNING, Bosley Kellogg, the Precaution Property and Liability lawyer who had dumped the Browning case in my lap, scheduled an examination under oath for Faith Browning at her attorney's office on Third Avenue. Bosley said I could tag along if I carried a briefcase, didn't smile, and kept my mouth shut.

"Try to look like a second-seat lawyer," he said.

I promised I would try.

Normally, I have a fairly wild mass of curly brown hair that surrounds my head like swarming gnats, but in the spirit of the day, I took out my rubber cement, thumbtacks, and axle grease, slicked it back, and managed to twist it into a nonevent at the back of my head.

I put on the "severe" suit my sister gave me after she'd worn it once to take the orals for her Ph.D. (Everybody in my family is brainy except me. I'm the exploding sewer cap.) It was a gray pinstripe with narrow lapels. I'm capable of behaving, but only minimally, so I couldn't resist adding red shoes and a red silk shirt to the mix. But the skirt was tailored, and I felt that I was still functioning well within the parameters of "sedate."

Bosley Kellogg and I announced ourselves to the receptionist at Prado & Blatt, and after a short wait we were greeted by either Mrs. Prado or Miss Blatt, I don't remember which because they both had small heads, round bellies, and stood with arms akimbo on waists, looking very much like teapots. Whoever it was, Prado or Blatt, was pleasant enough. She led us into the conference room, where a court stenographer was waiting to record every word of Faith Browning's statement.

Faith arrived late and last.

To say that she had a presence would be an understatement.

Faith Browning looked like someone going all out to convince the world that she *was* somebody, and that you, you poor misguided fool, just weren't cognoscenti enough to know who she had the skill, common sense, glamour (ha!), and good sense to be.

Since Faith Browning had put in a personal property claim of over a quarter of a million dollars, to which I did not think she was entitled, I admit that I was prejudiced even before I got there. Anyway, I have a natural aversion to females who look as if they're wearing industrial-strength bras, by which I don't mean to imply that Faith was unattractive. She's just not my 1950s sex goddess cup of arrogant, pretentious creep.

Faith wore her dark, stylish brown hair in a severe cut, had good skin, a blah, do-nothing nose, and a nice arch to her eyebrows. Her large, dark eyes were attractive and compelling, but that she looked at everything as if she were estimating its resale value, markedly diminished their allure.

The entire time that we were in her lawyer's office, Faith Browning didn't smile once. I did see a flicker of some unidentifiable emotion draw her lips tightly over her jaw when Prado or Blatt referred to property values in Riverdale, a response I wasn't supposed to see to a conversation I wasn't intended to overhear, so of course, I made a mental note of it. Other than that, waiting for an emotional response from Faith was like clocking time on a line to nowhere.

As to Faith's examination under oath, instead of describing what she said, I'll crack open a door to the Prado & Blatt conference room and present an excerpt, complete with all appropriate nouns, verbs, and adjectives. The person asking the questions was our attorney, Bosley Kellogg.

> Question: Now, in the column headed Attic Closet, the first of many items you list as having been destroyed in the fire is a blue silk purse with a beaded peacock design. When did you acquire that?
>
> Answer: That purse was said to have belonged to the original Mrs. Andrew Carnegie. I purchased it, as well as many other items of clothing, at auction houses in New York City, at consignment shops, or from individuals, of whom I have not the faintest recollection now. Aside from my bead and tapestry bags, I also had a museum-quality collection of antique hats, gloves, and jewelry, many of which are on the list you're holding in your hand. Since I have always enjoyed generous discretionary income, it really was not outrageous for me to purchase twenty to thirty vintage handbags, each of which was valued at over five hundred dollars. As a matter of fact, doing so was well within my means.

I had no inside knowledge of what Faith could or couldn't afford, but I did have personal experience with people who acquire outrageously expensive doodads, since my Uncle Al collects bottle caps and would happily trade his firstborn child for a mint condition, postwar, hand-crimped Mountain Dew, and my cousin Joe drives his wife crazy because he just *has* to have the next limited-edition miniature Model A Ford with honest to goodness hinges that open and shut over the engine compartment. So it wasn't Faith's acquisitive mind-set that pissed me off, it was her attitude, of which she had enough to frost the nose hairs on a penguin.

Again, from her sworn statement:

Question: Did your sister have a life insurance policy?

Answer: I doubt it.

Question: Did you check?

Answer: With whom?

Question: How about the agent who got you your Precaution Property and Liability homeowner's policy?

Answer: The man to whom you are referring was a fairly recent addition to our stable of lackeys, and would be of no use whatsoever.

Question: Do you consider everyone who works for you to be a lackey?

Answer: Of course. Don't you?

If I'd been Faith Browning's lawyer, I would have torn the five-hundred-dollar Gucci bag right off her lap and smacked her on the head with it. But Prado . . . or Blatt didn't wince. Not once.

Which brings me, without a plausible segue, to why we were in those law offices that morning, listening to Faith's pretrial drivel. According to the insurance policy we sold her, if Faith Browning wanted us to pay her claim, she was obliged to produce a signed, sworn, dated proof of loss, which despite repeated requests from our office, she had failed to do. She was trying to get around the proof of loss requirement by submitting what she called an "inventory of destroyed personal property," a fifty-nine-page, single-spaced opus, each page of which listed about one hundred items, the values of which were grossly inflated, if she had ever, indeed, owned them in the first place.

Among these items were Royal Crescent place settings for twelve, with matching demitasse cups and saucers, value: $40,000; Louis XIV mirror with violins and lutes carved into the frame, value: $8,000; ten embroidered linen table napkins, value: $1,000; Koos van den Akker designer suit, value: $3,000; Givenchy blue-leaf-patterned silk crepe cocktail dress from Paris, value: $5,500; fifty-eight back issues of *Country Life* magazine, value: $1,000.

Twenty single-spaced pages of Faith's list itemized over five hundred records and compact discs that she claimed had been destroyed in the fire, including titles, performers, labels, and so on, which begged the question if they had all been destroyed in the fire, how had this woman, who seemed to be incapable of retaining invoices or receipts for anything else, managed to acquire such detailed information about each label?

How indeed!

We believed that, at most, five percent of the CDs and records actually *had* perished in the fire — I love that word — *perish*, and that, after writing down their titles, et cetera, she had retrieved, boxed, and saved the rest.

Question: In the spare bedroom closet, you listed a Christian Dior evening gown from Paris.

Answer: That is correct.

Question: Will you please describe it?

Answer: It was a gift from an old boyfriend. Silk chiffon with little rosettes woven into the bodice.

Question: What was your boyfriend's name?

Answer: Philippe. French, and charming, of course. The accent is on the last syllable.

Question: And what is Philippe's surname?

Answer: Cotieu . . . Cotieux . . . something like that.

Question: Do you know where he currently resides?

Answer: In heaven, one would hope. He's dead.

All of Faith's ex-boyfriends were dead or had moved and left no forwarding address. All of her expensive china or one-of-a-kind designer cashmere coats or floral Staffordshire pitchers were gifts from (also dead) relatives or had been purchased from stores she couldn't remember or that had gone out of business. And, of course, she had no receipts, credit card records, or canceled checks for anything.

Fantasy. Fantasy. Fantasy.

As for the other things she claimed to have lost in the fire, including the furniture, carpets, paintings, piano, books, CD players, stereos, appliances, and crystal that Vinny Mendloop had seen when he looked through the windows of her house, we believed that she was storing them at some undisclosed location until after we paid her claim, at which time she would feel that it was safe to bring them home.

And that would be never, if I had anything to say about it.

Bosley Kellogg's purpose in taking Faith Browning's examination under oath was to get *on record* every single item she had listed on her "inventory of destroyed personal property."

> Question: Next on your list is four Ralph Lauren guest towels. Who purchased them?
>
> Answer: I did.
>
> Question: Where?
>
> Answer: In Bloomingdale's on Lexington Avenue. But it may have been at Saks or Lord & Taylor.
>
> Question: Do you remember how much you paid for them?
>
> Answer: No.

On her list, she had estimated their value as four hundred dollars. At one hundred dollars a towel, Midas must have dried his hands on them before she brought them home.

Question. Answer.

Question. Answer.

When it was all over, a fifteen-hundred-page, typed transcript of the interrogatory was prepared, one copy of which was given to Faith Browning for her signature.

> I, the undersigned, do hereby certify that I have read the forgoing examination under oath, and that to the best of my knowledge, recollection, and belief said deposition is true and correct.

Which is why we did it in the first place.

If our policyholder was going to lie to us about her loss and then sue us for treble damages if we didn't pay, it seemed both wise and prudent to encourage her to lie to us under oath.

chapter sixteen

ON FRIDAY MORNING, after Ike Blessing picked me up at my office so that we could drive back to Riverdale and nose around, I besieged him with questions.

I know. I know. I had the guru of fire investigation in a rare state of captivity and should have been ransacking his brain for important forensics, like what's the difference between paper oxidizing and wood pyrolyzing, or does crazing on concrete really indicate that a flammable liquid was used?

That's what I *should* have been asking.

Instead, before we even got to the FDR Drive, I said, "Ike, are you married?"

"No, sunshine. Are you?"

"Hell, no. I'm barely out of knee pants. This is the time of my life when I should be making foolish choices that will someday hinder my bid to become the President of the United States. Are you divorced?"

"No, I'm not."

"Interesting. I'm surprised that, at your age, you haven't taken the plunge."

"I never said that."

"Well, if you aren't married and you aren't divorced, what —"

My hand flew to my mouth. I looked sideways at Ike and got a quick, inadvertent lesson in what the word *chagrined* really means.

"Oh, my God, Ike. I'm sorry."

"Don't be sorry."

"I didn't mean to —"

"Calm down, sunshine. I'm not upset."

And he didn't look upset. Not in the least.

Ike rolled down his window. His left elbow rested on the window ledge and his right hand marked twelve o'clock on the steering wheel. He looked relaxed, sure of himself, and comfortable in his own skin.

So, Ike was a widower. Once he had been married. Now his wife was dead, *and* he didn't seem to care.

What kind of a man isn't grief-stricken after his wife dies?

Hmm . . . interesting. But not so interesting that I didn't notice it was a beautiful late summer day, we had a fire to investigate, the sun was shining, and . . . What the hell. Dead is dead.

"What are we doing today?" I asked.

Ike smiled. Instead of answering me he said, "When I left the fire marshal's office, Tilly, you know what my biggest worry was?"

I pondered the question. What would *my* biggest worry be if I'd quit a secure job with a pension and benefits to start up a company of my own?

"That you wouldn't have any clients?"

"No."

"That you'd miss the camaraderie of your fire marshal friends?"

"There wasn't any camaraderie. Fire marshals aren't firemen."

"That you would have to testify in court?"

"I like testifying. No. I was afraid that nobody would talk to me."

"Huh?"

"Without a badge. That I would introduce myself. Knock. Knock. Hello, Mrs. Homeowner. My name is Isaac Blessing, and Empire State Insurance Company asked me to come here to figure out where and how your fire started. Can I ask you a few questions about . . . and slam. She'd shut the door in my face."

"But if the homeowner —"

"Or factory owner, or car dealership, or hotel manager, or —"

"Whoever. If they put in a claim for something, don't they *have* to talk to you?"

"They have to let me in to inspect the fire scene. Sometimes we need a court order, but they do have to let me in. What they don't have to do is tell me anything."

"So if you want to ask Mrs. Homeowner —"

"If she smokes, or if the candles were lit at the time of the fire, or if she used her toaster to dry her socks, or her oven to dry her hair, she doesn't have to say 'Boo.' That's what I was afraid of."

Ike drove with a lazy confidence that reinforced my earlier cowboy image of him. Home on the highway. Home on the range.

"But you know what, Tilly?"

"What?"

"People tell me more without the badge than they did when I carried one. Why do you think that is?"

I considered his question for a few seconds and then said, "I haven't got a clue."

"Neither have I, sunshine. Neither have I."

We drove a half dozen miles without saying anything. I enjoyed looking out the window and relinquishing control to a trustworthy driver as I watched Roosevelt Island, the Hell Gate, and Randalls Island glide past. By the time we got to Riverdale, instead of thinking about reluctant witnesses, badges, and stupid policyholders who considered themselves ingenious when they stuck their heads in ovens to dry their hair, I was thinking about Ike up in the attic of Faith Browning's house and how he dropped that coin through a hole in the floor and it fell to the basement, three stories below. Balloon construction. What did it mean in the cosmic scheme of things? Why had he made such a point of it to me? And what did it have to do with the fire?

I was so caught up in my thoughts about floors and walls and descending projectiles that I didn't realize we had arrived in Riverdale until Ike stopped his car at a fork in the road on Labyrinth Lane. Faith Browning's house was four hundred feet to the left. Thirty-five feet to the right was a narrow gravel driveway that deadended at a classic English garden, looking so perky and serene with its population of phlox, hollyhocks, asters, lilies, and roses that I thought I had wandered into a late Edwardian painting.

Ike followed the road to the right. At the end of the driveway behind the fantasy garden, was a pretty little white house. I stuck my head out the window and read the name off the mailbox.

"McDevitt."

"I want to interview them," Ike said. He pulled up to the garden, shut off the engine, and turned to look at me.

"Did I ever tell you about a fire marshal I once knew named Ernie Fernandez?"

"Ike. I just met you. You've never told me anything."

"He had a gruff style, sunshine," Ike continued as if he hadn't heard me, "but he was a good investigator. Ernie understood fire, and he had a good conviction rate, one reason being that people talked to him. His partner used to say that bad guys would line up in front of him to confess."

"Bad guys, is that the technical term?"

"My second week on the job, I asked Ernie how he did it, and he said, 'Ike. It's like this. The dispatcher tells you to respond to a fire on Nostram Avenue in Flatbush. You get out of the car, walk toward the building, and see a guy standing on the corner with a swastika tattooed to his forehead. You ask him what he knows about the fire. He says, "All cops are pigs, and your mother is a whore." At that point, you got two choices. You can punch him in the mouth, and the interview is over. Or you can say, "That's right, sir. Now, about the fire on the top floor," and maybe you'll get some answers.'"

"Is that what you do?" I asked.

"Uh-huh. After he answers all of my questions, *then* I punch him in the mouth."

We got out of the car.

"Are you trying to tell me something, Ike?"

"Just be polite, Tilly."

"I will."

We walked up the path and rang the bell. Through the window, I saw a sweet-faced, elderly lady approach the door.

Before she opened it, though, I turned to Ike and said, "Do *I* have to punch her out before we leave? Or do *you?*"

chapter seventeen

I WAS ON MY THIRD CUP OF TEA and Ike had consumed half a plate of shortbread before Mrs. McDevitt seemed satisfied that we had answered all of her questions.

To Ike:

"I've heard only splendid things about firehouse cooking. Is it true that . . ."

"How gratifying that you actually saved people's lives. Was there one particular rescue . . ."

"I shall always perceive a fire scene to be both undecipherable and black. How is it that you are able to . . ."

To me:

"Where did you go to school, dear?"

"And before you worked as a photographer, you . . ."

"What was the subject matter of your sister's Ph.D.?"

The McDevitts are a charming elderly couple in a world that badly needs charm. Beatrice McDevitt's cheekbones are pronounced, her forehead is high, her jaw is wedge-shaped, and her eyes are piercingly intelligent. White hair frames her narrow face in well-disciplined curls, and her tight mouth is as quick to form a smile as the smile is of short duration. When she's sitting, her knees are pressed tightly together, and her legs are daintily crossed at the ankles, like a lady who has been invited to tea.

Beatrice McDevitt looked very much like a duchess dining with a queen. Any queen. Of anything.

After we explained why we'd come, she disappeared down the hall and reappeared about ten minutes later with a prettily arranged serving tray, tea, and biscuits.

Maybe that's what graciousness is. To act, when confronted by the inevitable, as if what you are being forced to do is what you had intended to do all along.

Alistair McDevitt, who oozed gallantry, was much more reserved and inherently quieter than his wife. After only a few minutes, I could imagine a scene early in their marriage where the two of them had sat down with a calculator, divvying up their lifetime allotment of words, with Alistair graciously saying, "You take eighty-five percent of them, dear. I shall be adequately provisioned with fifteen."

Alistair was one of those overly tall, gangly, distinguished Brits I associate with the kinds of private men's clubs that no longer exist. He'd be the man sitting by a fireplace, about whom old-timers told tales of daring exploits in the OSS during World War II. He was neatly dressed in an ancient lounge-about sweater over a crisply ironed button-down shirt. I guess his concession to informality was that he wasn't wearing an old school tie, if there really is such a thing. He had an aesthetic face, like that of a martyred saint, and his conversational contributions were generally limited to "More tea?" or "I'm afraid that's so" or "Quite a tragedy. Quite. Quite."

Yet there was obviously much more to him than a drawing room Englishman, for he had the most noticing eyes I'd ever seen. Without seeming to make moral judgments, they appeared to be evaluating every word we said and following the circuitous route of our conversation like an air traffic controller tracking blips on a radar screen.

Ike put me in charge of the first half of our interview, so I let the conversation ramble for a while, because I wanted to get a feel for Faith's neighbors before asking the sorts of questions that might scare them away. We learned, for example, that Alistair was actually Dr. McDevitt, with a Ph.D. in Elizabethan literature. Until their marriage (I was taking notes), Beatrice had been an actress. She took a twenty-year hiatus to raise two sons, then gravitated right back to the theater and taught high school drama until Alistair retired.

The McDevitts met at Eton, got married the day after graduating, and immediately crossed the Atlantic so that Alistair could do postdoctoral work with an Elizabethan scholar at Princeton University. Dr. McDevitt taught literature in New Jersey for five years before he went to the Purchase campus of the State University of New York as head of their English Department. He ended a long and successful career in Purchase as Professor of Literature Emeritus.

The McDevitts had been living on Labyrinth Lane for twenty-two years when Ike and I met them. Their house was an enchanted cottage, surrounded by flowers and filled with sink-into chairs and a scattering of museum-quality pieces that looked as if they'd probably once belonged to the Marquis de Oops There Goes My Head. On the walls were a pleasant hodgepodge of beautifully framed photographs of Beatrice costumed in a variety of roles, of which I recognized Lady Macbeth, Camille, and Hedda Gabler, and on just about every end table, piano top, and fireplace mantel were snapshots of children, grandchildren, and great-grandchildren, all of whom looked appropriately adorable, even though I, personally, cannot stand kids.

Neither, apparently, could Beatrice.

"I was an excellent drama teacher," she said. "But other than my own, I've never been particularly fond of children. There are exceptions, of course. Both Alistair and I were extremely close to the Browning girls. One doesn't like to admit it, but one does have one's favorites. Mine is Faith. I've always felt as if destiny gave me Faith because I never had a daughter. On the other hand, Alistair doted on Dorsey. He's still too upset over her death to talk about it. Aren't you, darling?"

Beatrice turned her arresting silver-gray eyes to Alistair for confirmation, but her husband remained mute, although I think I caught a barely perceptible nod of his head.

Then Beatrice abruptly changed the subject. "Dortimer was a mathematician, and he believed in creatures from outer space," she said.

I jerked up my head and studied her face to see if she was smiling, but I perceived not a shred of humor.

"Excuse me?" I said, not sure I'd heard her right.

"Even though he was slightly daft," she went on imperturbably, "it was impossible not to love him, and his girls adored him, despite his unusual ideas on child rearing."

"Unusual in what way?"

"Well, he never allowed a television set in his house, because he wanted his daughters to read the classics and to take notes on what they had read. He believed that, in doing so, they would develop their intellects and imaginations. Dortimer was quite firm about this, although he in no way demonized television, and he permitted Faith and Dorsey to watch whatever they wanted to when they visited friends. He simply felt that the constant presence of a television stunted intellectual growth, a point of view with which I agree. As a substitute, perhaps, they all became inveterate journal keepers and letter writers."

"Faith and Dorsey, too?"

"Oh, yes. I remember walking in on the family one Sunday morning, and they were sitting around the kitchen table, pens in hand, looking very much as I've always imagined the Brontë clan must have looked. 'Goodness me,' I said. 'What *are* you writing?' Each one's answer, I recall, was so in keeping with his or her personality that I had to laugh. 'Scientific notes,' Dortimer responded. Dearest Faith said, 'My diary,' and Dorsey replied, 'A new play in which I shall star!'

"They were lovely children, and Dortimer was as perfect as a neighbor could be. He was kindly, nonintrusive, and invariably interesting. I suppose it was inevitable that our lives should intertwine, and without really intending to do so, Alistair and I became something of an extra set of parents to Dorsey and Faith. Since they lacked a mother, I believe we cast ourselves unofficially in the role of aiding and abetting their dreams."

After four more cups of tea, Ike and I had learned even more about the girls who'd lived across the lane. Dorsey had been the ebullient and affectionate one. Up until sixth grade, she was still doing song-and-dance routines for meter readers, mailmen, and the occasional parcel post or Federal Express driver who delivered telescopes and optical equipment to their home. The McDevitts, too, were a target audience and, unless they were out of town, could be found front and center at every one of Dorsey's opening nights, whether it occurred on the stage Dortimer built at the back of his garage, in a school auditorium, or in a theater on West Forty-fifth Street.

According to Beatrice, Dorsey Browning had an idyllic childhood with a father who was willing to be Hans Christian Andersen to every fairy princess, little match girl, or dispossessed mermaid she ever wanted to play.

"When Dorsey was seven years old" — Alistair McDevitt committed himself to a rare full sentence — "I introduced her to Shakespeare." His voice, which before had been only crisply polite, now projected an appealing resonance. "I taught her to say, 'The gaudy, blabbing, and remorseful day is crept into the bosom of the sea,' and when she enunciated those somber syllables in her dulcet, childlike voice" — Alistair's large eyes misted over — "it was most endearing."

Endearing to Alistair. Inspirational to Dorsey, because next thing you know, the diminutive Shakespearean had grown up and enrolled in the School of Dramatic Arts at Hudson University, my old photo proving ground. There was little that Beatrice McDevitt could tell us about Dorsey's college years, other than a recitation of the parts she had in the plays in which she'd performed, but she did know that after sharing a cinder-block dorm room for three months with a piccolo player who didn't understand the meaning of the word *deodorant*, Dorsey joined the Gamma Phi Beta sorority. There, she was able to live on campus in a comfortable stone house, concentrate on her studies, and aside from a few brief social forays to keep up appearances, be alone.

According to Beatrice, the move turned out to be a success, and Dorsey stayed at Gamma Phi Beta until her graduation, a happy event immediately followed by the announcement to her father, sister, and the McDevitts that she was auditioning for the role of Emily in a revival of Thornton Wilder's play *Our Town*. Dorsey desperately wanted to play Emily Webb, that innocent, ordinary small-town girl who, unlike the rest of us, is given the opportunity to come back to the world and revisit her past after she dies.

With the guileless bravado of youth, Dorsey passionately believed that no actress who had ever lived understood Emily as she did, and that the part had been written exclusively for her. Either in spite of or because of her audacity, the director let her audition, and as Dorsey could have predicted, she got the job.

In a letter the young actress wrote to the McDevitts over a year earlier, she said that performing her favorite part in her favorite play was becoming the happiest experience of her life. Beatrice read us that letter aloud.

> It's like going home,

Dorsey wrote.

> As if the protected universe Daddy created for me in Riverdale has been transposed to this cozy little theater on West Forty-fifth Street and his spirit is touching . . . no not touching, blessing everybody who comes anywhere near the stage.

I asked Beatrice if I could see Dorsey's letter, since I've always taken a romantic view of letter writing and think the choices a correspondent makes are revealing of bits and pieces of his or her soul. What stationery did she use? Did she write with a ballpoint pen, a typewriter, or a pencil? Did she write on one side of a sheet of paper or use both sides?

Dorsey's letter had been written in beautiful cursive on a single sheet of narrow-ruled, white, foolscap with a fountain pen filled with turquoise ink.

It was a gorgeous letter, and that cheerful, bright blue ink really got to me.

The McDevitts told us that *Our Town* ran for thirteen months; they had gone to four performances and had met everyone involved in the production. All were seasoned veterans with huge talent and bigger egos. But egos notwithstanding, the entire cast and crew, including the producers and director, were at a stage of

life where, susceptible to the quality of the material being presented, they experienced one of those rarest of rare theatrical oc-
currences, a happy set.

Dorsey wrote in another letter to the McDevitts,

*I think that we are becoming the characters in Thornton Wilder's
lovely play. Daniel Burroughs, our stage manager, started out a
pompous caricature of himself, but during the past few weeks
has become the guy we all depend on when we need a hold-me-
over loan or a shoulder to cry on. Lillian Mayhugh is hysterically
funny without meaning to be. She's very much like the character
she used to play on TV, which means that it really is possible to
be an egomaniac with a heart of gold. She's much more attractive in real life than on the stage, because she has to be frumpy
to play my mother, and believe it or not, has more than one
stage-door Johnny, all quite handsome, and all half her age! She
says she doesn't mind, as long as they're twice as rich. Lillian is
very protective, very demonstrative, and very demanding. She
seems to have taken a particular fancy to me, and buys me gifts
all the time. Once it was a flamingo pink feather boa, and another time she bought me a first-edition copy of* Our Town,
*which I shall cherish until my dying day. What she usually gives
me, though, is lottery tickets; she made me promise that if I ever
win the Big One, I'll give her a million dollars to start a small theater company committed to the greater glorification and pros-
perity of Lillian Mayhugh, of course. Lillian is from England, like
you, and when she isn't playing my mother with a decidedly
American accent, she is imparting the Wisdom of the Veteran
Actress to me, such as "Always cash your paycheck right away,
darling. One never wants to assign too much credibility to the
solvency of one's producers." This, by the way, is a song I've
heard before. Mrs. Gibbs, I mean Beth Meyers, who plays Mrs.
Gibbs, has also warned me about producers' checks, but in less*

refined language. Beth smokes unfiltered cigarettes, swears like a street thug, and has the soul of an angel. You should see the beatific look on her face when Arthur and I are doing our love scenes. You'd think he truly is her son, that Grovers Corners exists, and that we belong here more than we do in the real world outside. Then, of course, there's Arthur.

Arthur was Arthur Dawes, the good-natured young man who played George Gibbs, the boy in *Our Town* who marries Emily. In a rare burst of garrulousness, Alistair the Silent said that, before coming to the United States, if he'd been asked to describe how all Americans look, he would have conjured up an image of Arthur as a twenty-first-century Huckleberry Finn, floating down the Mississippi River on a raft. Beatrice added that Arthur's hair is pumpkin red and he has more freckles than I do, a comparison I could have lived without. Then she went on to describe what Faith wore to the opening night of *Our Town*, which I had no desire to know, before she got down to the nitty-gritty of the story:

Beautiful young actress. Handsome young actor.

Romance.

She refilled the teapot and resettled herself opposite us in a faded chintz armchair. "I suppose it was inevitable that Dorsey and Arthur would fall in love," she said, pensively stirring sugar into her cup.

Now we were getting somewhere.

"Did the affair last?" I asked.

"Actually, my dear, I'm not even sure there was an affair. At least not as we use the word today. When I was a girl, if one was being pursued, it wasn't necessary to exchange bodily fluids or risk sexually transmitted diseases for us to call it a love affair."

Beatrice tilted her head deferentially toward her husband. "Isn't that right, dear?"

Alistair smiled at her sweetly, then added with what I thought a hint of mischief, "I don't recall it being quite as glisteningly chaste as you do, Bea. But if that's the way you want to remember it . . ."

Beatrice lowered her eyes, and I was surprised to detect on her cheeks a genuine, all-purpose blush. She did return her husband's smile, though, and it occurred to me that, despite being well into their eighties, the two of them were still in love.

That was so cute.

Beatrice reached for another of Dorsey's letters, perused a few turquoise lines, and read aloud.

> I think that ever since Arthur and I started to play George and Emily, in some magical way we've become those two honest and innocent, small-town folk. In that context, a hop-into-bed relationship would be unseemly and not at all in keeping with Grover's Corners. So if you can believe it, Aunt Bea, what I truly think that Arthur and I are doing is . . . I think that we're courting.

"Aunt Bea" repeated the word *courting* dolefully, sighed, and returned the letter to its envelope. Then she leaned against the back of her armchair, wearily closed her eyes, and seemed to forget that the rest of us were in the room.

Reading from Dorsey's letters had taken its toll; muscles on Beatrice McDevitt's face that had been taut only seconds before went slack, leaving behind an expression of ragged despair. Alistair, less circumspect about his emotions, just let the tears that suddenly started stream down his face.

I stared at my knuckles, wishing I were somewhere else, and for about five minutes I couldn't think of anything to say. Then my curiosity overcame my good manners, and I blurted out, "What about Faith?"

Beatrice McDevitt jolted forward in her chair, reasserted control over her emotions and her facial muscles, and said, "Alistair and I called her Counselor for the first two years after she graduated from law school." Her eyes were tearless and cool. "But Faith soon put a stop to that."

I grabbed the sugar tongs and transferred cubes from the sugar bowl to my cup.

"If I had ever graduated from anything," I said — one sugar cube, two sugar cubes, three cubes. Four — "I would consider being called counselor or doctor or Indian Chief a compliment."

"We meant it as one, dear. But Faith preferred not to be referred to as an attorney until she had passed the bar."

"Passing the bar is like taking the road test for your driver's license," I said. "Everybody flunks the first time."

Beatrice smoothed a pleat on her skirt. "I didn't mean to imply that she had *failed* the bar examination. I meant that she never took it."

I stopped playing with the sugar.

"Why?"

Beatrice turned to Ike. "More biscuits, dear?"

Ike patted his stomach in the universal I'm full sign, and Beatrice explained, "Faith is a good girl, a devoted daughter, and as it turned out, quite a good nurse. When Dortimer's health began to fail, she devoted herself entirely to helping her father ease, as it were, the burden of his years."

"Did Faith live at home?"

"Yes, she did. Initially, Dortimer protested mightily, saying that it wasn't normal for a pretty young girl to be burdened with the care of an able-bodied adult who, he insisted, was perfectly capable of caring for himself, and —"

"And —" Alistair interrupted, "Faith turned Dortimer into an old man. She never gave him a moment's peace. She never let him be."

Beatrice gave her husband one of those wife-type looks.

Alistair ignored her.

"Dortimer had angina," he said stiffly. "Otherwise, he was in perfect health."

"Well, dear," Beatrice responded, "angina is a serious condition if left unattended."

"Nonsense. Dortimer ate well, exercised moderately, and visited his doctor every six months. He played the stock market, had a comfortable bank account, and was blessed with two daughters, who once grown, should have had the sense to do what our boys did. Love us. Stay in touch. Get a job. And go away."

Beatrice let out a ladylike snort of disapproval.

Alistair grumbled audibly. "None of my business, really. I just felt sorry for Dortimer. Grown man with a daughter always underfoot. No wonder he was over here all the time."

Beatrice patted her husband's hand. "You're right, dear. Faith *can* be trying at times. But she's a good girl, and her heart is in the right place."

Alistair reached over to pat the hand that was patting his. I'd have to remember that pat-pat technique if I ever got married. It was awfully sweet.

"Did Faith have a job?" I asked.

"Every now and then, she worked as a paralegal in Manhattan, but after Dortimer retired, she did it less and less."

"What did she *do?*"

"Well" — Beatrice tapped a fingernail thoughtfully against her teacup — "Dortimer thought it would make her happy to redecorate the house, assert her individuality and start off fresh. He offered her an unlimited budget to do anything she wanted, but she said that she liked continuity and preferred to keep the rooms exactly as they had always been."

"Did she garden?"

"Good heavens, no." Alistair looked appalled by the thought. "Faith was as the lilies of the field. 'They toil not, neither do they spin.'"

"Well, what *did* she do?"

"She took very, very good care of Dortimer," Beatrice insisted. "She carried an extra bottle of nitroglycerin for him in her purse, and since he spent so much time here, she gave us a small bottle for our powder room as well."

"Did she do anything else?"

"She's on the board of directors of the Lighthouse for the Blind and the Riverdale Junior League. She goes to the theater. To the ballet. To the opera. She's a frequent visitor to auctions and antiques shows. She cooked three meals a day for Dortimer, did his bookkeeping, and paid his bills. Even without practicing law, Faith had quite enough to do, and let's not forget that, being so much older than Dorsey —"

"How much older?"

"Eleven years. Faith practically raised her little sister. I won't say that she was a mother to Dorsey. Dortimer never would have laid such a burden on a child, but Faith was very attentive and protective, even though the girls were different in so many ways."

"How different?"

"Dorsey was a wood nymph. Frolicsome, enchanting, and gregarious. Had she lived, she would have been a great actress. It's tragic beyond measure that she died so young."

"She was my favorite," Alistair said softly.

Beatrice gave her husband's hand another pat and continued. "Faith was the serious and responsible sibling, the one who would be there for her family before a crisis reached emergency proportions. She's a discerning collector of antique clothing and accessories, a great one for keeping up her diary, and a real lover of the arts. It's less obvious with her than with Dorsey, but Faith has her gay, if one can use that word nowadays, or shall we say her *festive* side, too. She likes to go to parties, and she likes to give them. After *Our Town* closed, she threw a beautiful catered affair for the cast and crew. A heated tent was erected in the backyard and decorated to look like the interior of a barn, with old-fashioned kerosene lanterns, bales of straw, wildflowers, and a trio of fiddlers. It was lovely. Lovely. Even though Dorsey had a wonderful time, she was dead-set against the party at first, because like all younger sisters, she resented her older sibling's interference. Alistair is quite right, however, that Faith does meddle in other people's lives. It was Faith who sat beside me every day when Alistair went to the hospital for his triple bypass. And after Dorsey's nervous breakdown, Faith was so solicitous of her health and well-being, Dorsey could have been a newborn baby just home from the hospital. Interfering? If you call that interfering, then I would have to agree. Faith *does* interfere."

I expected Alistair to protest against the pedestal on which his less favorite of the two sisters was being positioned, but he just nodded his melancholy old head and left me with the new notion of cranky, superior, pretentious Faith, as a guardian angel.

While I was fidgeting around mentally with those drastically incompatible images, wondering if "guardian angel" equaled "control freak," Ike leaned forward in his chair and asked, "What nervous breakdown?" picking up on the one thing in our conversation that I had completely missed.

Beatrice McDevitt turned to him. "Have another cookie, dear."

Ike took a cookie.

"Four or five months ago, in late March or early April . . ." She turned to her husband. "When did Dorsey come home, Alistair?"

"Good Friday. April twenty-first. "

"That's right. It was a little over six weeks after her father's funeral. We were all shocked by Dortimer's death, because he had never really been sickly, but Dorsey was affected the most. That poor child was utterly devastated. For weeks she wandered around the backyard like a wraith. I could see her from our bedroom window. She would drift aimlessly between the bridge and the castle, looking very much like a lost Ophelia. Alistair felt so helpless, it almost broke his heart."

Ike ignored the broken heart.

"Bridge and castle?" he said.

"Oh, yes. Dortimer built them for Dorsey years ago. They were most imaginative, and really quite pretty. After her breakdown, she pulled weeds, planted bulbs, and hired Frank Gruber to restore the island and repair the bridge. When Faith told me what Dorsey was doing, we both thought it sheer lunacy, but we were wrong. It was therapy. Dorsey brought her childhood back to life, and Frank did a wonderful job. You have seen them; haven't you?"

Ike admitted that we hadn't.

"You must. Today. Before you leave. The island is north of the house, behind the hedgerow, and the bridge is thirty feet west of the island."

It was clear to me that Ike couldn't care less about islands or bridges.

"Mrs. McDevitt," he said, "it's important that I get ahold of a picture of Dorsey Browning. The sooner the better. Do you have one?"

Beatrice didn't respond at first, and her face assumed such a distracted expression, I was tempted to snap my fingers in front of her eyes to jolt her back to reality. But after about twenty seconds she said, "I beg your pardon. I was trying to remember where I put it." She turned to her husband. "The photo album, Alistair?"

"Bottom drawer. Right-hand side."

"Of course."

Less than three minutes later, Beatrice returned with a large, old-fashioned album containing sheets of thick, black paper to which the photographs had been affixed with tiny, gummed triangles that looked like little black dunce hats. She put the album on the coffee table in front of the sofa, and Ike and I hunched forward to look at jelly-faced ragamuffins with big smiles and dour teenagers wearing braces and looking put upon by the world.

"These are mine," Beatrice said, leafing rapidly past all of the children resembling her and Alistair. Then she dropped her finger to a snapshot of two laughing girls in the lower left-hand corner of the very last page.

"Dorsey was six at the time," she said. "Faith was seventeen."

The six-year-old had big doe eyes, long, dark braids, and a gamine smile as warm as a fresh-baked chocolate chip cookie. Her arms were thrown around the neck of her older sister, who was tumbling off balance as a result. There was a vaguely annoyed look on Faith's face, but no more than that of any older sister with an imp hanging on her back. In fact, both she and Dorsey looked completely normal, and the young Faith's eyes in no way resembled the two cash registers they had become by the time we met.

On a whim, I asked Beatrice, "Did Faith ever date?"

The elderly actress looked up from the photo album. "You mean did she have boyfriends?"

I nodded.

"Oh, yes."

Thinking back to the Christian Dior gown on one of her infamous lists, I persisted.

"Did she dress well?"

"She certainly did. You'd think it would be the other way around, that Dorsey would be the clotheshorse, but Dorsey was always happiest puttering around in a pair of blue jeans. It's Faith who loves clothes."

Ike took the photo album away from the old lady and weighed it heavily in his hands. "This is it?" His disappointment was obvious. "One picture of Dorsey when she was six years old?"

"I'm afraid so. Except. Wait a second. I think I still have . . ."

Beatrice walked to an ornate desk in the center hall and pulled something out of the center drawer. When she came back, she gave Ike the *Playbill* for *Our Town*, first opening it to the page with a small picture of Dorsey over a brief synopsis of her career. It was a dramatic head shot with one cheekbone, a stylized jaw, and her expressive, dark eyes highlighted. The rest of her face was in shadow.

"Can I borrow this for a few weeks?"

"You may have it. However, I have a request to make as well."

"Name it."

Beatrice reached over to take Alistair's hand. Her voice was brisk, but her eyes were sad when she said, "If in your travels you should come upon a photograph of Dorsey that captures her . . . for lack of a better word, shall we say her *essence*, will you make a copy of it for my husband, please?"

Ike said that he would, refused another cup of tea, and then asked the McDevitts to describe the sequence of events that had occurred at the party they'd thrown on the Fourth of July.

Who did what on the night of the fire? When? Where? Why? And to whom?

chapter eighteen

"IT WAS VERY HOT THAT NIGHT, and we don't have air-conditioning, so we spent the entire time outside. I can show you where we were, if you like." Beatrice put the lid on the sugar bowl and stood up. "Just give me a minute to clean up the tea things. Alistair, take Mr. Blessing and Miss Quilter out back. I'll join you in a minute."

I grabbed for a few plates and some spoons. "I'm helping you."

"Really, dear. It isn't necessary."

"Don't argue, Mrs. McDevitt. If I didn't and my mother ever found out, she'd use my head as a doorstop."

Beatrice gave me one of her revolving door smiles, and I followed her into the kitchen, scooting back and forth with empty cups, saucers, and cake plates while she did the dishes, which is just as well, because I've been known to break the expensive and irreplaceable ones.

When she was putting away the last of the tea things, I excused myself to go to the powder room down the hall. Since I was stuck there for a few minutes anyway, I amused myself by studying the decor. The walls of the small room were covered with a pattern of pink ribbons and pale pink roses, evocative of a gentler era, and appropriate to the gentle people who inhabited the house. There was a minuscule sink under a mirrored cabinet that had been painted pink to match the walls. Since I'm nosy and I have no shame, I opened the cabinet, looked inside, and inventoried a Plexiglas unit holding Q-tips, cotton balls, emery boards, and a tube of cranberry dream lipstick. There were also a bottle of aspirin with a do-not-use-after date of seven years earlier, a bottle of eyedrops, unopened but similarly expired, a small jar of Vaseline that belonged in a museum, and an antiquated tin of bandages, which made me feel nostalgic as I hadn't seen bandages in a *tin* in years.

On a narrow corner shelf opposite the sink was a collection of delicate old perfume bottles. I turned one over and read the label on the bottom: "Lalique." Next to the perfume bottles was a single silk orchid arranged daintily in an Art Nouveau vase.

Altogether, it was a most satisfactory room. The guest towels finished it off nicely, with pretty little pink appliqué roses that I didn't want to soil, so in true barbarian style, I dried my hands on my shirt. Then I closed the door behind me and went into the hall.

The hall was narrow and served two purposes. One was to be a display area for photographs of Beatrice in various costumed roles. The other was to connect the living room to the kitchen. The powder room, which was about four feet from the kitchen, was opposite two French doors that led to a large, screened-in porch. The porch was cluttered with cardboard boxes, dilapidated wicker furniture, a wrought-iron floor lamp with a broken bulb, and a relatively intact pinball machine. It wasn't the kind of room in which the McDevitts would be serving Sunday brunch.

I followed familiar voices to a screen door, which I let slam behind me — a bad habit of mine — walked a few more feet, and there they were.

"Oh. Hello, dear," Beatrice said, looking over her shoulder as she and Alistair folded the plastic covers they had removed from the chairs. Ike was already sitting on a chair with his back to the house. He had one of his omnipresent handkerchiefs in his hand and was reaching down for something stuck between two pieces of patio slate, but before I could ask what it was, Alistair dropped a chair cushion, so I hurried over to help him.

It was a really gorgeous day. The sun was bright, the sky was impeccably blue, and the air was filled with those swoony autumn leaf smells that just make you want to die of happiness. I plumped up a cushion next to Ike, sat down, and looked around to get my bearings. The patio, if you could call it that, was composed of hundreds of irregularly shaped slate slabs that fit together like a gigantic jigsaw puzzle, with thick clumps of clover growing between the slabs.

From the glass-topped table where Ike, the McDevitts, and I were sitting, Faith Browning's house was in plain view. Labyrinth Lane was to our left; after about four hundred feet, the road turned right into Faith's driveway. One branch of the driveway ran along the side of the house, past a wide stretch of yard to a free-standing garage. The other curved into a turnaround in front of Faith's house.

As I settled in to listen to the conversation that had started without me, I realized that the McDevitts had been sitting in this exact spot during their Fourth of July party, with their view of the Browning place unimpaired. Beatrice had taken a chair opposite me, and a gentle but persistent breeze rustled the leaves of the trees overhead and seemed to wash the last traces of tragedy from her face as she drew us into her memories of the night that Dorsey Browning died.

"Arthur Dawes arrived early in the evening," she recalled. "I don't know if Dorsey invited him or if he came of his own accord,

but if I were that boy's mother, I would have told him that he
wasn't doing himself any favors to come courting with a dooms-
day look on his face. Women like a man with backbone."

"Did Arthur join the festivities, or did he just stand there like
a slug?"

"He very much did not participate at first, but after we got a
few drinks in him, he cheered up considerably. Then he cheered
Dorsey up with his good news."

"What good news?"

"That Dorsey was being cast opposite Arthur in a very popular
soap opera on television."

"I thought Dorsey wanted to do theater?"

"Of course she did. We all did. She wanted a previously undis-
covered playwright to write a Pulitzer Prize-winning drama in
which she would star, and for which she would win a Tony, but
Dorsey had been out of work since *Our Town* closed, and a job is
a job, so the news thrilled her to the core. After Arthur left, the
child was positively fey."

"When did he leave?"

"At about six P.M."

"What happened after that?"

"I served hors d'oeuvres; we talked."

"What did you talk about?"

"Is it relevant?"

"It could be."

"Very well. Faith wanted to discuss their house. The kitchen,
to be exact. Dorsey had always hated the linoleum, the cumber-
some cabinets, and the lack of counter space, so Faith wanted to
talk about redecorating, hiring contractors, and the like. Dorsey,
however, couldn't be bothered with kitchens. Kitchens be damned,
she was in another world. The world of the theater. So as Faith

chatted away about chrome faucets and ceramic tiles, Dorsey kept after me to talk of 'Life' as we both referred to it 'upon the wicked stage.' What was Alfred Drake like? Did I ever do a show with Lunt and Fontanne? What did I think of Helen Hayes? Had I ever met Noël Coward?"

"And you answered her?"

"Of course. I love to talk about myself. I'm afraid it bored Faith to tears, though."

"Did she leave?"

"No. We stayed right here at this table for about an hour after Arthur left. That's when the green Jeep turned into the lane. Labyrinth Lane, you know. That's what we call our driveway. The driver stopped, got out of the car, and started towards us. But Dorsey left the table and went to him instead."

"Did you know who it was?"

"I'd seen him before when Dortimer was alive. A tall, handsome Negro gentleman. But I didn't know his name."

"Then what happened?"

"He and Dorsey went back to his Jeep and talked for about fifteen minutes. After that, Dorsey rejoined us, and he drove away."

"When?"

"Immediately."

"How did she behave when she came back?"

"What do you mean?"

"Was she happy? Was she sad? Was she angry? Was she excited? Was she depressed?"

"Dorsey was radiant."

"Did you see the man in the Jeep drive away?"

"I saw him continue up Labyrinth Lane. Most people use the turnaround in front of the Browning house so they don't have to back their cars into the main road."

"And you actually saw the Jeep go past your house again?"

"I assumed it had, but I didn't notice one way or the other."

"How about Arthur Dawes? Are you certain that he left Labyrinth Lane?"

"He took the path from the patio to the front of the house and probably walked to the subway. Most young actors can't afford a car."

"Do you think it's possible that the man in the Jeep never left?"

"Is there a point to these highly speculative questions?" Beatrice asked irritably.

Ike persisted. "Could Arthur Dawes have stayed in the area, too?"

Beatrice didn't deign to respond, so he changed the subject. "What did you do for the rest of the evening?"

"We ate hors d'oeuvres, drank champagne, and gossiped about mutual friends."

"Can you remember anything out of the ordinary happening that night, even if it seemed to be trivial and unimportant at the time?"

"You mean like getting a call from a wrong number, or being bitten by a wasp?"

"Exactly."

Beatrice raised an eyebrow and said archly, "Other than my next-door neighbor's house burning down and a child that I loved dying a horrible death?"

Ike smiled sheepishly. "Sorry, but yes. Other than that."

At first the elderly woman shook her head. Then, unconsciously, her hand fluttered up the front of her dress, and she clutched at her throat.

"Are you all right?" I asked.

She looked at me.

"Oh. Yes. Fine, dear. I just . . . remembered that . . . Alistair?" She turned to her husband. "Wasn't that the night I gave Dorsey my brooch?"

The old man thought for a moment.

"Yes, dear. I believe that it was."

"Brooch?" I asked. "What brooch?"

Beatrice flicked her fingers dismissively. "Just a pin I had. It was a turquoise stone surrounded by gold twists, pearls, and diamonds."

"It sounds pretty."

"It was *very* pretty."

"What about the brooch?"

"Nothing important."

"That's what I want to hear," Ike said. "Things that aren't important."

"Very well." Beatrice folded her hands primly on her lap. "Before the fireworks started, Dorsey dropped her napkin. She had been wearing a scoop-neck summer frock with spaghetti straps. When she leaned down to pick up the napkin, one of the straps broke. I took off my pin and reattached the strap with it. That's all."

"Was it a valuable pin?"

"It had been in the family for years, but I doubt if it was worth more that forty dollars. The diamonds and pearls were fake, of course."

"Did Dorsey give it back to you?"

"She tried to. She even protested that if I didn't want it anymore she was sure her sister would want it. But I'm always giving things to Faith, and I knew Dorsey liked it, so I insisted that she keep it."

"Where on the dress did you put the pin?" Ike said. "Show me on Fritillary."

With the forefinger of her right hand, Beatrice touched my left shoulder, about two inches below the collarbone.

"What else happened that night?"

"Nothing. It was all very bland. We watched the fireworks over the golf course, and Faith went into the kitchen to bring back some paper fans, because the heat was bothering her. I always keep three or four of them on top of the refrigerator. Then we opened a bottle of champagne, Faith toasted Dorsey's new job, and we sat around fanning ourselves like a bunch of drunken geisha girls. We must have been quite a sight." Beatrice tilted her head questioningly toward her husband.

"Au contraire," Alistair responded on cue. "You were quite lovely. I shall always hold the memory of that evening in my heart." And he said it in such a gallant way that I couldn't help feeling he really meant it, too.

Sweet guy.

"At about eight-fifteen . . . perhaps a bit later," Beatrice went on, "Dorsey began to fan herself fiercely and said, 'Wow. I just got so hot!' She laughingly complained that so many good things were happening to her so quickly, she was having a royal flush."

"Then what?"

"Then she got to her feet, a bit unsteadily, I'm sorry to say, announced that she had a splitting headache, and said she was leaving."

"Did she?"

"Did she leave? Yes, she did. Faith stood up at the same time. She grabbed Dorsey to steady her, surmised that the champagne had gone to Dorsey's head, and told us she would bring her little sister home. Then both girls left."

"And that was it for the night?"

"No. Faith came back a few minutes later."

"How much later?"

"Really, Mr. Blessing. I have no idea. Ten, fifteen minutes. No more than that."

"Was she with you for the rest of the evening? Until you discovered the fire?"

"Yes. Faith was with us the whole time."

"The *whole* time?"

"Yes . . ."

"No, dear." Alistair put his hand over his wife's hand. Such a gentle way of interrupting. Such a gentle, gentle man. "Shortly after the fireworks stopped, we ran out of vermouth, and Faith suggested that I accompany her home to retrieve a bottle from the den."

"Oh. Yes," Beatrice said. "I had forgotten."

"What time was that?"

Alistair thought for a moment. "The display always starts punctually at nine o'clock and lasts for exactly thirty minutes, so I would estimate that we left at about nine-thirty."

"Which door did you go in?"

"The side door. You can see it from here. It leads directly to the kitchen."

"Was it locked?"

"Not with so much going to and fro. We were having a party, you know."

"Did you accompany Faith when she got the bottle of vermouth, Dr. McDevitt?"

"I was looking through the bookshelves in the library at the time, as there was an early Tennyson I wanted to borrow."

"How many doors are there to this den?"

"Just the one from the library. There's a bathroom off the den, but that doesn't go anywhere."

"How close were you to the den?"

"Only three or four feet from the door, and you didn't ask, but the door was opened, and Faith was within earshot the entire time."

"How long before she came back?"

"A minute or two."

"And you're sure she never left the den before then?"

"I'm positive."

"What did you do after Faith found the bottle of vermouth?"

"We returned to our little party."

"When? What time?"

"I suspect nine forty-five or later. A little before ten."

"A little before ten," Ike repeated in a less confrontational tone. Then he paused and scrutinized the old man's face. "I'm sorry if this has been hard for you, Dr. McDevitt." His eyes moved to Beatrice. "Mrs. McDevitt. I just have a few more questions; then Fritillary and I will go away."

"It hasn't been hard," Alistair responded. "Actually, talking about it has been something of a relief."

"Good," Ike said. Then he turned away from all of us and once again fell silent as he appraised the surrounding area. I saw him studying the massive maple trees that lined either side of Labyrinth Lane and the border of mature lilacs separating the Browning property from the far perimeter of the McDevitts' lawn. Magnolia and dogwood trees peppered the yard of the massive Victorian, and as I stared at the turnaround in front of the house, I wondered if Ike was thinking what I was thinking. That it would be relatively easy for someone to drive or walk to or from the house without being seen.

Ike returned his attention to Beatrice, and there was a look of kindliness in those incredible diamond blue eyes I'd never seen before, as if he understood that the gentle relics he was interviewing really were giving him everything they had.

"When did you notice that the house was on fire?" he asked.

"The Fourth of July was such a hot night," Beatrice replied, "that none of us were in any hurry to get inside. I had a portable radio out here on the table because one of the FM stations was doing a broadcast of patriotic songs. The show was called *Songs That Got Us Through World War II*, and I was hoping they'd play some of my favorites by Vera Lynn. So we talked, drank champagne, and listened to the radio."

"And you noticed the fire . . . ?" Ike urged her back on course.

"At eleven-thirty, when the station broke in with the news. I stood up and reached over to swat at a moth. That was when I saw a flash of orange."

"Where?"

"At the back of Faith's house, over the kitchen. At first, I thought it was a rogue firecracker. When I realized that the light was continuous, I knew it was a flame."

"What did you do?"

"I hurried into my kitchen and dialed 911 while Alistair and Faith started across the yard toward her house. Faith was running, because she knew that Dorsey was inside. Alistair, of course, moves more slowly because of his age."

Ike turned to the elderly scholar.

"We were too late" was all that dear, heartbroken old man had to say.

"I drove over in my car," Beatrice continued. "And it's a good thing that I did. The fire engines had already arrived, but Faith was hysterical and had to be restrained from running into the house; Alistair was distraught. They both needed taking care of, and I'm good at that."

Ike Blessing stood up.

"I bet you're good at whatever you set your mind to, Mrs. McDevitt," he said. He turned to Alistair and added, "Thank you both very much."

The McDevitts also got to their feet. Beatrice started to walk back to the house, but Alistair bestowed on Ike that same quiet and penetrating stare I'd noticed when we first arrived. Finally, he said, "Exactly by whom are you employed, Mr. Blessing?"

Ike met the old man's eyes unflinchingly, even though *I* was totally taken aback by the question.

"My client is Hercules Electric. Faith Browning is suing them. She claims that a clock radio they manufactured was defective and caused Dorsey Browning's death. Fritillary here works for Miss Browning's insurance company. She's investigating the insurance claim."

"May I then assume that you disagree with our dear neighbor as to the cause of the fire?"

"Right now, Dr. McDevitt, you could say we're on a fact-finding mission. We don't know what caused the fire."

"Speaking of facts," I interjected, "do either of you remember any big vans or moving trucks being parked outside the Brownings' house after the fire?"

Both the McDevitt's turned to me. They looked so down and out. So tired and browbeaten that, as soon as I'd said it, I wished I had just kept my mouth shut.

Sometimes, I guess I hate my job.

"Why are you asking that, dear?"

"I wish I didn't *have* to ask it."

The old lady nodded. "So do I."

But she didn't answer. Instead, she turned to Ike, whom she obviously liked better than me, and said, "Did they ever find the will?"

Will?

What will?

Beatrice explained.

"After Dorsey had recovered from her breakdown, she entered our kitchen one morning carrying a handwritten document. She was really quite chipper when she said, 'Remember how a few years ago you asked me to witness your wills? Well, darlings, turn-around is fair play, because I've written a will too, and I want you to witness it.' Of course, we were shocked to hear her ask, because . . . well, because she was so young. Alistair said to her, 'Why, dear girl, *why?* Surely you can't be thinking of dying!' Dorsey answered, 'Hardly, darlings. I'm thinking of going back to work, becoming wildly successful, and getting astronomically rich. Rich people always have wills.' When we looked at her uncomprehendingly, she laughed. 'It's like an umbrella. If you have one, it never rains. I'll have a will, so I'll never die.'"

"Did you witness the will?"

"Oh yes. We both did; that's how we know that she left one."

"When did this happen?"

"A few weeks before the fire."

"Have you mentioned the will to anyone else?"

"No. I had completely forgotten about it until this moment."

"Interesting," Ike said. But that was all he said.

Later on, when we'd gotten back to Brooklyn and the Mc-Devitts were safely rid of us, Ike privately gave them his highest accolade. He told me that they were good witnesses.

Now we followed the elderly couple up the path that led around to the front of the house, where we had left Ike's car. Before he could reach for his keys, though, Beatrice put a restraining hand on his arm.

"You *will* try to find a photograph of Dorsey for Alistair. Won't you?"

"Yes. I will."

"Why don't you ask Faith?" I burst in, wanting to do *something* to be of help. "I bet *she* has dozens of pictures she can give you."

But the elegant old lady shook her head. "Faith told me that she has nothing left. Every photo album, every snapshot, and every picture of Dorsey was utterly and completely destroyed in the fire."

chapter nineteen

ONE OF THE THINGS ABOUT A LAWSUIT that always confounds me is that, after it has been initiated, nobody is allowed to talk to anybody else. For example, if we have a case that could be resolved by me picking up the telephone, dialing John Doe's phone number, and saying, "Mr. Doe, all I need from you is a handwriting sample" or "Did you ever own a white 1956 Thunderbird convertible with red leather seats?" I am not allowed to make that call.

In other words, in the world of lawyers, if the shortest distance to the truth is a direct line, no one is allowed to walk, talk, or dial it.

You can send smoke signals to the plaintiff's next-door neighbors and ask them whatever you like. You can waylay her cleaning lady at the bus stop and batter her with questions. You can organize a séance and try to interrogate her dead relatives. But woe to you if you dare to approach the repository of simple answers to simple questions, for you will get in deep shit with the court.

Guaranteed.

So I was heavy-duty frustrated, because the niceties of all this judicial mumbo jumbo made my eyes cross.

I tried not to think about it.

Instead, I tried to concentrate on what Ike was telling me as we drove back to his office. It had to do with case development. This included, among other things that I probably missed because I was replaying our interview with the McDevitts in my head, somebody (meaning me) calling up theatrical agents and asking about Dorsey; that same somebody going to the Lincoln Center Library for the Performing Arts and looking up whatever I could find out about her; and me also going through all of Faith Browning's construction receipts and doing an analysis of her expenses.

It wasn't until we were back at Ike's office and seated at his conference table that he really got my attention, though, when he asked, "How squeamish are you?"

"What kind of a question is that?"

"I thought it was an easy one."

"Well, it isn't. I'm squeamish around worms and slugs. I don't like them."

"Neither do I."

"And in biology class, I had no problem dissecting the starfish, but don't even *ask* me about the frogs."

"No frogs. I'll make a note of that."

"On the other hand, if you cut yourself on a piece of broken glass, I'd be perfectly capable of stanching the blood, cleaning the wound, applying antiseptic, and bandaging you, before I passed out."

Ike laughed. "I'd pass out first." Then he got serious. "I have some pretty grim pictures of the fire scene. Can you handle it?"

Could I handle it?

Who knew? I certainly didn't, so I lied. "Sure. Hand them over."

That was how I got my first intimate look at Dorsey Browning. Not in the gossip columns on Hot New Actresses. Not by reading a rave review of her performance in *Our Town*, or seeing a poster for the play in front of the theater on West Forty-fifth Street. These pictures were of a young woman who had been robbed of life but not of beauty, and they were sad, sad, sad. They were even harder to look at because the fact of her beauty created the illusion of life. Dorsey Browning, dead, was Sleeping Beauty on a bed of char.

I couldn't imagine being shown those pictures if I'd been someone who loved her.

There were dozens of post-fire photos. Only three of them were of Dorsey. The first was a close-up of her face; the other two showed her lying on a mattress. The rest of the photographs focused on various angles of her bedroom. These included the bed, after the body had been removed; the night table with the clock radio; and the floor.

But it was the pictures of Dorsey's face that haunted me. Them, along with something else I couldn't grab ahold of. Something maddeningly elusive that kept dive-bombing for attention in my head.

I know now that Dorsey's brown hair was styled in a halo of soft curls, but all the black-and-white photographs showed me was that it had been singed off below her left ear. What remained of her left shoulder revealed a delicate, ballerina-like collarbone that looked pathetically vulnerable in death. Her left hand was gone; the fire had consumed the fingers and the bones. Her left foot, which had been in the center of the bed, was burned off entirely.

The rest of her body, however, was practically pristine.

Sad, sad, sad.

Dorsey's eyes were mercifully closed, creating the impression that she had died in her sleep. She had a high forehead, a well-defined jaw, and expressive lips. Her dark eyebrows moved away from her nose in a straight line and dipped dramatically at the far corner of each eye, giving her an almost Oriental look. Her eyelashes were exotically long and cast heavy shadows against her pale cheeks.

I leaned closer and studied the photograph. I lifted it up, drew back from it, and held it as far away from myself as I could. Then I dropped it on the table between my elbows, dug my fingers into my hair, hunched over it, stared and thought. Staring and thinking. Staring and thinking. I wasn't even aware that Isaac C. Blessing of Isaac C. Blessing Associates had come over and was standing right next to me.

Finally, I looked up.

"What?" I demanded.

Ike pointed a finger at the photograph. "You tell me."

"Tell you. Tell you what? I'm frustrated, Ike, because there's something wrong here. Something wrong with Dorsey Browning's face. And I'm not sure what it is. It has to do with composition, like in a painting. Most of the time when you fool around with somebody's bone structure, you're destroying the natural symmetry of their face." I turned back to the picture. "I'm not saying that Dorsey had a nose job, but something about her nose bothers me."

"What?"

"It doesn't fit her face. It's . . . off kilter. I wish . . ."

"What do you wish, Tilly?"

"I wish we had another photograph of her so that we could compare —"

Then I snapped my fingers and spun around. "Well, Ike Blessing, you devil you. *That's* why you were hounding the McDevitts for pictures of Dorsey."

"That's right, sunshine."

I nodded and gently lifted the photograph by one corner, holding it up to catch the light. Dorsey had been wearing a summer dress when she died. A sweet little thing with dainty pearl buttons running down the bodice, over a pattern of pretty flowers. The dress had a scoop neck and spaghetti straps, just as Beatrice McDevitt described. The left strap was burned off what remained of her left shoulder, but there was no faux diamond, pearl, and gold brooch in sight.

"Poor kid," I mumbled.

When I looked up, Ike was still standing over me, staring. "What are *you* thinking?" I asked.

"I'm thinking that fires don't break noses."

"You think her nose was broken?"

"I'm agreeing with you that something's wrong with her face. That's why I want you to go to the Lincoln Center library. See if they have any pictures of her. Of any play she was in. Of —"

"Why don't I just call her agent?"

"Do you know who her agent is?"

"No. But can't we call Faith Browning and ask her? I'm sure she —"

"You can't call Faith. The court won't allow it."

I pondered this for a moment. "I suppose we could show this picture of Dorsey to the McDevitts and ask *them* if her nose had been broken." Ike looked at me as if I'd suggested that we recreationally poked out a puppy's eye, so I quickly added, "But that would cause them irreparable psychic harm and break their hearts. So maybe we don't want to do that."

He walked to the other side of the conference table and started to shuffle through folders. Meanwhile the elusive thing that had been dive-bombing my head came back with a jagged persistence.

I teased and tugged at the cortex, vortex, and multiplex of my brain. What was it anyway? What . . . what . . . what?

And all of a sudden, I had it.

"Ike," I said excitedly. "In what year was Dorsey Browning born?"

Ike tossed aside a schematic he was holding and started to dig into a stack of folders. A few seconds later he stopped, pulled out a police report, and read me her date of birth.

When I spoke again, I was thinking out loud.

"Mrs. McDevitt told us Dorsey went to Hudson University, and that she joined . . . Wait a second. Let me look at my notes." I pulled a legal pad out of my purse and skimmed my scribbles. "Gamma Phi Beta." I dropped the pad, reached across the table, and grabbed Ike's wrist. "Guess what?"

"What?"

"When I was a senior in high school, I worked for a photographer named Walter Troska, and I . . . *we* used to take pictures at sorority and fraternity houses. One of our clients was Gamma Phi Beta. We shot photos at their parties and took pictures for their yearbook. Dorsey was four years younger than I, so I was long gone by then, but I'll bet you anything that Gamma Phi Beta is still Walt's client, and that when she was a sorority sister, he took dozens of pictures of her."

Ike removed my hand from his wrist, lifted it to his lips, and kissed it. "You're brilliant," he said. "We'll give them a call, make an appointment, and ask them to show us their yearbooks."

I stared at him blankly. "Make an appointment?" I squeaked.

"Right. Absolutely, Tilly. It was your idea."

"No, it wasn't. I was going to call Walt, ask him if he keeps negatives for over two years ago, ask him if he still has any from Gamma Phi Beta, ask him if we could come over, and . . ."

Ike smiled. It was such a nice smile. He's such a nice guy.

"But I like your way better," I added eagerly. "It's much more sensible to look through their yearbooks."

"It is if they still have them."

"Oh, they'll have them. Sorority houses are great on tradition. Yearbooks and illusions are things that they never, never throw out."

chapter twenty

WHEN IKE CALLED THE HOUSEMOTHER at Gamma
Phi Beta, she told us that Labor Day weekend on campus would
be chaotic and should be avoided at all costs. So he made an appointment for the following Wednesday morning at ten o'clock.
The delay made me happy, because my desk was a mess, and that
gave me Monday and Tuesday to catch up on paperwork.

After Ike made that phone call, he put the photographs of
Dorsey in an envelope, put the envelope in a file, and I have never
looked at them again. Not ever. I've looked at hundreds of pictures
of dozens of other people who have died in fires, but none ever
wreaked havoc with my heart the way Dorsey's photograph did.
It's always much easier on the soul when a poor wretch is so badly
burned that he no longer looks like a person and just falls into the
category of "amorphous victim."

Beauty in a dead body is close to unbearable.

Enough said.

After we were finished with the pictures of Dorsey, Ike said I
should scan the police and fire department reports, and the report
written by the fire marshal, to get the gist of what they said, and
that I could go over them more thoroughly later.

I indicated stacks of medical examiner reports, weather reports, newspaper clippings, and deposition transcripts. "How about the rest of this stuff?"

"All in good time, Tilly. More photographs, first. If you think you can you handle it."

"I can handle it."

The first stack that Ike gave me were the other sixteen black-and-white pictures taken by the fire department photographer. There were nineteen in all, including the first three of Dorsey. Then he put another sixty-two color photos on the table in front of me.

I looked at them. I looked back at Ike.

"Huh?" I said.

"These were taken the day after the fire by the firm Faith Browning hired to do the fire analysis." Ike flipped over the first one. A blue sticker on the back said: "VECTOR INCORPORATED. ELECTRICAL ENGINEERS SPECIALIZING IN FIRE, ARSON, AND EXPLOSIONS." When he turned the photograph over again, I looked down and grimaced. Ike nudged it off the pile. "These clowns wouldn't know a burn pattern from a dress pattern, but they sure do take pretty pictures."

It was a wide-angle shot of Dorsey's bedroom, and like all rooms after a fire, it looked like an archaeological dig.

"Hercules Electric was put on notice of the lawsuit the day after Faith's experts took these pictures," Ike said.

"Was that before or after the funeral?"

"The fire was on Tuesday. The lawsuit was filed on Thursday. Dorsey Browning was buried on Friday. "

"Ike, that's sick."

"Tilly, that's America."

"I don't want to think about it. Show me more pictures."

First, I went through the fire department's black-and-whites. I noted in the handful of exteriors that even though the front of the house was pretty much untouched by fire, there had been a lot of smoke damage outside Dorsey's bedroom in the back; the third floor, the cupola, and the roof had been so badly chewed up and spit out that they looked like houses I'd seen in World War II pictures of London after the Blitz.

I guess a residential fire is its own kind of a blitz.

The rest of the fire department pictures were of the house's interior. One, taken at the entrance to Dorsey's bedroom, focused on a smear on the doorjamb; others were of the bedroom itself, including a four-drawer night table next to a platform bed. There were a telephone, a few books, and a Hercules clock radio on top of the night table. The phone looked like a marshmallow that had been charred at a campfire; the front and back edges of the books were singed; the clock radio was an electronic nightmare in which bits and pieces of capacitors, resistors, wires, and circuit boards could be seen through an ugly black plastic crust. The night table itself was burned most intensely on the right side, the side closest to the bed. Although there was some burning under the clock radio, by far the worst damage was at floor level, where the fire had been so hot, whole chunks of the cabinet had burned off.

Also interesting was a hole where an intense attack of flames had burned through the floor and baseboard between the night table and the bed. The hole was about six inches long and three inches wide, and in one photograph, where the night table had been pushed out of the way, it looked like a crater, and I could see in it to the floor joist below.

In this same picture, the clock radio's electric cord visibly extends over the hole to a dual outlet behind the bed. Some of this cord's sheath is melted, and the rest is so badly burned that only a double strand of wire remains as evidence that it once conveyed electricity.

In other disconcerting photographs, heavy char extends along the floor from the hole in the baseboard to another jagged hole about the size of a pie plate, located halfway between the head and the foot of the bed. The wood trim on the bed above this second hole is badly charred and exhibits the same alligator-like burn pattern as on the wood surrounding the hole. Through this hole more joists are visible below the partially carbonized floor.

Two holes in the floor.

Two places where fire burned down, the way fire does *not* naturally burn, instead of up and out, the way it does.

The last picture in the stack was the real grief maker. It showed that the fire in the middle of the bed was so hot, it gutted the mattress and bedding, leaving behind a burn pattern that corresponded exactly with the areas of Dorsey's body that had been most severely burned: her left shoulder, her left hand, and her left foot.

I pushed the photos aside, stood up, and stretched. Then, without thinking about it first, I reached for the fire department's sixteen black-and-whites with one hand and for Vector Incorporated's sixty-two color photos with the other, and I plopped down on the floor between Ike's conference table and his desk. Instinctively, almost as if I were playing solitaire, I began to organize the photographs around me.

I arranged them not by who took them but by what they'd been taken of. Exteriors in two piles: front of the house and back. Close-ups of the clock radio. Wide shots of the bedroom. Smoke stains on the ceiling. Discarded upholstery in the bushes behind the house. Tight shots of Dorsey's bedroom. I dealt my photos into

neat stacks as if I were putting a jack under a queen or a two under a three, interspersing the black-and-whites with the colors so
that all of the baseboard photos were together, regardless of who
had taken them. The same applied to shots of the dual outlet, the
bed, the holes in the floor, and so on.

Since Dorsey's body had been removed to the morgue and her
bed had been thrown out before Faith Browning's experts arrived,
it was only because of the dedication and obstinacy of one fireman, Captain Burchfield, that we even knew about the burn patterns in the mattress. Otherwise that evidence would have been
gone forever.

Two and a half hours after I started sorting through the photographs, I was beginning to get an idea of what Dorsey's room
looked like immediately after the fire. In some ways, it was like
staring at a satellite photo. You have to study it and study it, almost *willing* amorphous blobs to take on form and meaning until,
Snap! All of a sudden you see it, and it makes sense. It's a hemisphere. The Northern Hemisphere. There's Canada. There's Alaska.
And there's the rest of it . . . the good old USA. That's what it was
like when I finally figured out that the right side of Dorsey's bed
had been up against the east wall of the room — the wall that separated her bedroom from the corridor.

Her bed pillows had been up against the north wall, overlooking the backyard. Also on the north wall was the dual outlet,
which, before the bed was removed, would have been hidden by
the mattress and the box spring. Two electric cords were plugged
into this outlet: one for the clock radio, the other for a floor lamp.
The deep burn pattern in the baseboard and flooring was between
the night table and the bed. To the left of the night table were two
closed windows. There was a radiator under each and a dresser in
between.

Along the west wall of the room, opposite Dorsey's bed, were another two closed windows, a small round table, a table lamp, a wicker trunk, a reading chair, and an ottoman. An oval hooked rug in front of the ottoman was far enough away from Dorsey's bed that it hadn't burned.

The south and last wall in the bedroom had one door leading to Dorsey's private bathroom, the other to the hall, and no interesting burn patterns.

That was what I had figured out by the time I'd separated all of the photographs into distinct piles. Then, with the layout of the room clear in my mind, I proceeded to organize the piles into a semblance of order, going from the area of least burning to the area of most burning, the way Ike photodocuments an *entire* structure when he walks around a building in the real world.

I started with exterior pictures of the front and back of the house. Under them, I put the interior photos of the second-floor hallway outside Dorsey's bedroom. Then interiors of her bedroom, beginning at the east wall, where her bed had been. Next, I put close-ups of burn patterns inside the bed, followed by pictures of the burned night table taken from all angles (more than three-quarters of the photos taken by Vector Incorporated were of the radio and the night table, so it was clear what their priorities were). I continued with close-ups of the burn patterns in the base-board, in the floor, and so on.

My objective was to create a logical photographic progression from the widest shot of the outside of the house to the tightest shot of char in the wood that rimmed the smallest hole in the floor of Dorsey's bedroom, with all eighty-one pictures, black-and-white and color, assembled in one heap.

It was four o'clock in the afternoon when I finished.

Ike must have sensed I was done, because I heard his chair creak, and when I raised my head, I saw him standing over me with his hand held out. I gave him the whole stack, and he carried it back to his desk. Starting with the photo on top, he looked at every single picture, in the order that I'd put them, until he got to the very last shot of the incinerated clock radio adjacent to an unburned prototype. I didn't know where to put that one, so I put it at the end.

I was still in the same position I'd been in for the past two hours when Ike looked over at me, and as soon as I saw the serious expression on his face, I got scared to death. Oh, please, I implored the gods who guided my destiny, please don't let this be another Antoine de Saint-Exupéry/Margaret Bourke-White experience. Please. Please. Please. For once, let me have done something right.

Ike carefully positioned my stack of photographs dead center on his desk. Then he stood up.

"Sunshine," he said.

Uh-oh.

"Sunshine, in all the years I've been investigating fires, I've never seen anyone do what you just did."

What? What had I done?

"The way you took pictures from different sources, mixed them together, put them in a logical order, and made sense of the whole thing. Tilly, this is pretty damn impressive."

It's a good thing I was still sitting on the floor, or I would have fallen over.

"You did a great job of photo-analysis, Fritillary Quilter, and I'm as proud of you as I would be if you were my own daughter."

Ike smiled.

What a smile. What-a . . . what-a . . . what-a . . . what-a smile. Instantaneously, I was deliriously happy. I was ecstatic. I was a lump of euphoria sitting on a coarse, oatmeal-colored rug.

"You mean I did good?"

"Better than good," Ike said, reaching into his back pocket and pulling out another of his inexhaustible supply of handkerchiefs. Then he walked over to me, crouched down, put one hand under my chin, tilted up my face, and again began to dab at my tears.

"Why," he asked, but he was still smiling, "do I get the feeling that we've sung this song before?"

chapter twenty-one

MONDAY WAS LABOR DAY. Since we weren't scheduled to go to Gamma Phi Beta until Wednesday, Ike suggested that I use Tuesday to locate the people Dorsey had mentioned in her letters to Beatrice McDevitt. Ike said it wouldn't take me more than an hour.

Yeah. Right.

I was supposed to find Daniel Burroughs, who'd played the stage manager; Lillian Mayhugh, who'd been Emily's mother; Beth Meyers, who'd played George's mother; and Arthur Dawes, who had been George Gibbs.

When I asked Ike what *he* would be doing while I was engaged in this grueling labor, he repeated the same two words that, thus far, I had found so evocative, mysterious, intriguing, and despite his earlier attempt to explain it to me, still incomprehensible: balloon construction.

Cha cha cha.

"How am I supposed to find these people?" I asked huffily.

"Open the *Our Town Playbill* to the last page. Call the producers' office, and tell the person who answers the phone that you're looking for cast members. Ask for their agents' phone numbers."

"Will it work?"

"Is the pope a Catholic?"

That's not exactly what I considered a definitive response, and I knew that what Ike called "case development" was what anyone else would call "scut work", but I was looking forward to it anyway. I have a logical mind, and there's something in me that delights in burrowing through mountains of paperwork to find what others have missed, to categorize it, and to put it exactly where it belongs.

When I was in high school, I had a history teacher named Mr. Bone who, appropriately, was an archaeology buff. He told us a story about Richard Leakey, the Kenyan paleoanthropologist who discovered Homo erectus. Mr. Bone said he'd read somewhere that Leakey's second wife, also a paleoanthropologist, had an extraordinary aptitude for organizing the bits and pieces she found in the muck and reconstructing them into skeletons. When asked how she had developed such a skill, she answered that she'd always had it, and when she was a little girl, it was so easy for her to do jigsaw puzzles that she had to turn all the pieces blind side up for there to be any challenge in it at all.

The image of her working with the blank side of a puzzle has never left me, and whenever I anguish over solutions to difficult problems or try to integrate the variables of a particularly perplexing claim, I think of Richard Leakey's wife, and I get inspired by the kind of a mind that would look at apparent chaos as a challenge instead of a crime.

I, Fritillary Quilter, am not inherently brilliant. I know that. But I've always figured that brains can be honed like knives, and that it's my job to sharpen my own. If a piece of a puzzle doesn't fit, I have to keep rooting around in the pile until I find the one that does fit. And if what I'm looking for isn't *in* that pile, I have to look in another one.

It's that hard. And it's that simple.

Tuesday morning, before I had the chance to do anything else, my boss called me into his office for an update on the Browning case. Ollie's main contribution to the conversation was to tell me that the power cord on the Hercules Electric clock radio had been manufactured by Strand Electric, and that Faith Browning was suing them, too. Ollie and I discussed this new development for a few minutes and tried to figure out how it would affect our case. Eventually, we decided that it probably wouldn't, and I went back to my desk to make my calls.

I got through to the office of the producers of *Our Town* with little difficulty, and a very nice woman, a temp who probably didn't know that she wasn't supposed to do so, read me the agents' names off a Rolodex on the real secretary's desk. I would have asked for information on the actors, too, but some instinct told me not to push. I did, however, take another shot at getting a picture of Dorsey. The temp to whom I was speaking was more than cooperative. She was positively effusive.

"Poor Dorsey," she said with chatty compassion. "Isn't it just *too* tragic how she died?"

I agreed that it was tragic.

"I saw *Our Town* five times, and I can tell you with absolute certainty that Dorsey Browning was a *real* beauty. Those brown eyes of hers were so *big*, it was like you could *jump* right into them."

I agreed that Dorsey had big eyes, even though I had seen only one picture of them opened, in which they were hidden in shadow, and three pictures of them closed, after she was dead.

But I didn't tell the temp that.

"I've seen *ever* so many actresses play Emily, but *none* of them had *half* Dorsey's talent or spirit."

I agreed that Dorsey had been a great talent. Then I gently reminded the temp that I needed a photograph of Dorsey, as well as her agent's telephone number and address.

She obligingly searched the desk.

"I'm sorry," she finally said, and she sounded as if she really was sorry. "When somebody is dead . . . I mean *deceased* . . . I guess they remove the files and put them someplace else."

Case development. Scut work.

Nobody had promised me that it was going to be easy. Not even Ike.

I thanked the temp, put my notes in order, and started to dial up talent agents. I had little confidence in my script: I was going to introduce myself to whoever answered the phone, say I was working for Dorsey Browning's insurance company, and explain that I had some questions about events preceding her death, and that I hoped members of the cast or crew might answer them for me.

I shouldn't have worried. At the mere mention of Dorsey's name, all doors, hearts, and minds opened to me. At first, I was surprised that simple phone calls could evoke such generous responses, but after a few minutes, I think I figured out why. Death makes us feel powerless. Other than sending a sympathy card or a flower arrangement, there's not a whole lot we can do to make ourselves feel better, and doing nothing is as frustrating as trying to pick up a penny with a baseball mitt.

Which is where I came in. Even though Dorsey's friends didn't know exactly who I was or what I was doing, I seemed to be a person of goodwill, so they were eager to help me do it, whatever "it" was, if for no other reason than that helping *me* was a positive course of action. No, they couldn't actually give me their talents' telephone numbers, since that would violate their privacy, but they would be happy to contact the actor or actress I was seeking, give him or her *my* telephone number, and ask them to call me back.

Would that be agreeable to me?

Damn right, it would.

Despite the eagerness of all four agents to help me, it turned out that both Daniel Burroughs and Beth Meyers were out of town. Burroughs was starring in *Design for Living* in Minneapolis, and Meyers was playing the mother in *You Can't Take It with You* in Albuquerque. Lillian Mayhugh and Arthur Dawes, however, were in town and would be notified of my request right away.

By two o'clock that afternoon, I'd already heard from Arthur Dawes. I set up an appointment with him for the following day; then I called Isaac Blessing so that we could synchronize our calendars.

Busy day. Busy day. Busy, busy day.

Ike said he would pick me up outside my York Avenue apartment at six o'clock on Wednesday morning. First we'd make the two-and-a-half-hour drive upstate to the Gamma Phi Beta Sorority House at Hudson University. Then we'd come back to the city to meet Arthur Dawes at the Gray Squirrel Coffee Shop in Greenwich Village. Last, we would return to Ike's office, so that he could show me Dorsey's autopsy report, which he explained, was pivotal to understanding what we would do next on the case.

chapter
twenty-two

THE GUARDIAN OF THE GATES at Gamma Phi Beta was so perfectly suited to her job, she confirmed my belief that, regardless of society's current refusal to categorize people, lest we offend someone's delicate sensibility, stereotypes do, indeed, exist. Everything about the woman who had agreed to meet us was, and no doubt continues to be, "essence of housemother," from her rabbity, pushed-in face, to her pink, party balloon complexion, to her pleasantly pear-shaped body, to her size eleven sensible shoes.

Her name is Frances Black.

The girls at Gamma Phi Beta call her *Mrs.* Black.

Ike and I did, too.

Mrs. Frances Black is a tall, sixtyish woman who, on the day we visited, looked pleasant and matronly in a pale purple knockoff Chanel suit. Even though her impeccably clean light brown hair had been styled in a way that fell in two unfortunate flops over her ears and exponentially increased her resemblance to Peter Cottontail, she exuded Authority with a capital A while at the same time projecting an air of maternal warmth.

"Do you remember Dorsey Browning?" Ike asked, after Mrs.

Black told us that she had been housemother at Hudson University for thirty years, and at Gamma Phi Beta for over half of them.

"Nobody could forget Dorsey."

"Why?"

She paused for a moment, seeming to give a lot of consideration to what I thought had been an easy question.

"When Dorsey arrived at Gamma Phi Beta her sophomore year," Mrs. Black said, the expression on her pink face reflective, "she was a well-spoken child, but somewhat solitary, and extremely intense. Over the next three years, she became friendlier, more relaxed, less rigid, and extraordinarily beautiful. Seeing her grow was like watching a flower respond to sunlight. Each day a petal would unfold. Then another petal. Then another after that. That's how I remember Dorsey."

"Was she a loner?"

"No, not really, although she never fully participated in our activities. You see, Dorsey's entire life was dedicated to her art. Even at dinner, she would hunch over a script. The girls used to joke that the only way you could tell Dorsey was alive was that her lips moved when she was memorizing lines. But they liked her anyway."

"Did she have a roommate or a best friend? Any one girl she hung out with more than with the rest?"

"No. No one. But . . ." Mrs. Black's face dissolved into a poignant smile. "She used to come into my office on occasion. She liked to talk to me about her dreams."

"Dreams?"

"Of being a successful actress. Of accomplishing great things. As a rule, sororities are places where it's inadvisable to stand out. Appearances, of course, are important. Social standing, less so.

Conformity is the order of the day. Dorsey broke all the rules. She stood out. She didn't conform. And she was in school for one reason and one reason only. She wanted to learn how to act. The theater was everything to her. Would you like to hear how she came costumed to one of our Halloween parties?"

"Tell us."

"She hopped around on one foot for three hours, explaining that, in honor of the macabre nature of the holiday, she had decided to come as Sarah Bernhardt *after* her leg had been amputated."

I laughed. Then, not sure if I was supposed to, I said, "Was she joking?"

Mrs. Black turned her rabbity, kind face to me, and she smiled. "Yes, dear. She was joking. Dorsey was a happy girl. Driven, but very much in love with life. She was all business on the subject of her art, but the rest of the time, she was as likely as not to be pulling my leg. I think her sense of humor was why the other girls accepted her, even though she was superior to them in so many ways."

"Looks and talent," Ike said. "Speaking of which, were you able to find any of the pictures that we talked about on the phone?"

"I didn't have to find them. I knew exactly where they were."

She leaned down and opened a large tapestry bag at her feet. Then, one by one, she withdrew a series of photographs and laid them out on her desk.

The first was a snapshot of five girls in various stages of undress, sprawled over two twin beds. There were boxes of pizza, empty soda cans, paper plates, and plastic utensils strewn everywhere. All the girls were smiling into the camera, and if ever a picture cried out for a caption, this one cried out for the words "college coeds."

"It was taken mid-semester, at one of the few parties Dorsey attended her sophomore year. As you can see, it was a pajama party." Mrs. Black pointed to a girl sitting at the foot of one bed. "This is Dorsey. Her hair was long that year, and she often wore it in a braid. She was a lovely creature, wasn't she?"

Without waiting for an answer, Mrs. Black covered the first picture with a second one, in which the housemother and the sorority girl were standing side by side in front of a fireplace, facing the camera head-on. Dorsey was wearing a sleeveless black sheath. Her hair had been cut and fell in soft waves to just below her ears. She looked younger, but also more sophisticated than she had in the first snapshot.

"This was taken her junior year. Not a flattering picture of me, I'm afraid. I was a good deal heavier then. I always make a point of getting at least one photograph taken with each of my girls. I call them my mother-daughter shots. Didn't she have an engaging smile?"

For a few long seconds, Mrs. Black contemplated Dorsey's smile. Then she covered it with an eight-by-ten of Dorsey costumed in a pert little 1950s style suit, standing alone in the center of a stage.

"This was taken during a curtain call the year she starred in the school's production of *My Sister Eileen*. She was a wonderful comedian. Did you know that it takes a smart girl to play a dumb blonde?"

Before Ike or I could answer, Mrs. Black was rummaging around in her tapestry bag again. She stayed down there for about sixty seconds, and didn't pop up until she had a large silver frame in her hands. She held it out toward Ike but didn't release it.

"This is my personal copy of Dorsey's senior year photo. I thought you would prefer it to the small picture in the yearbook."

I reached out to take it from Frances Black, but before my fingers could touch the frame, she jerked it back and began to study it herself. I'm good at reading upside down, so I had no trouble deciphering the words scrawled in turquoise ink across the bottom of the picture.

> Dear Mrs. Black — Thank you for being
> a font of wisdom, a bottomless well of encouragement,
> and a dear friend.
> I will remember you always.
> Love, Dorsey Browning

Just as I was making out the last of the inverted letters, I heard a sniff. Then another. And another. After the fourth sniff, I realized that Gamma Phi Beta's housemother was crying.

And crying. And crying.

Gone was the air of authority. Gone the benevolent dictator. All that remained was a nice, middle-aged woman, mourning the death of a girl she had once genuinely admired and loved. She sniffed one last time, handed me the picture frame, and this time let me keep it.

In the lower left-hand corner of Dorsey's photo were the initials WT. Proof, if I'd needed it, that the photographer had indeed been my old boss Walt. And it was a typical Walter Troska product, with the composition just right, the contrast perfect, and the focus keen enough to make out each individual eyelash.

"She really was a dear and lovely girl," Mrs. Black said sadly.

Dorsey Browning, then aged twenty, had smiled into the camera as if she expected it to burst into applause. The expression in her large brown eyes was mischievous and joyful, her glossy, dark hair was cut in a short pixie that emphasized the remarkable structure of her austere bones; the upward tilt of her lips was hugely appealing, and she looked as if she had just been told that she would live forever and was thinking, "Aren't I unbelievably lucky to have been born me!"

And then . . . there was Dorsey's nose.

Not a small nose, thank heavens. No cheerleader nose for Dorsey Browning. It was long, elegant, and flawlessly straight. It was, in fact, exactly the nose I had expected to be on her vital, captivating, and truly beautiful face.

I looked at Ike. He was still studying the photograph.

When he looked up again, it wasn't at me. It was at the housemother.

"Can I borrow this for a few weeks?"

Mrs. Black made that funny, gulping noise everybody makes at the tail end of a good cry.

"Will you bring it back?"

"Yes. I will."

"Why do you want it? Is there something funny about Dorsey's death?"

"Mrs. Black," Ike said somberly. "There is nothing in the least bit funny about it at all."

chapter
twenty-three

NEITHER ONE OF US SPOKE after we got back to the car, even though a part of me wanted to erupt with questions. But the rest of me was content just to cogitate upon what we had learned until the meaning of it settled into the appropriate substrata of my brain.

Two things, however, already stood out loud and clear.

The first was that Ike and I were right. Yes, the twenty-one year old woman we'd seen in those postmortem fire department photographs *was* beautiful, but she was not *as* beautiful as she should have been.

A broken nose will do that.

The second was that someone or something had broken it.

"Ike," I said. "Did you know all along about the broken nose?"

"Yes, sunshine. I knew."

"How?"

"I've investigated more than my share of DOAs."

"Dead on arrival, right?"

"Dead on *my* arrival. I know how dead people look at a fire scene. I know how they're supposed to look. After a while, you get an instinct about these things."

"If you were so sure about her nose, why did we need her picture?"

"My instincts don't constitute proof."

"Proof," I repeated thoughtfully. "Now that we have the proof, Ike, it's sad, isn't it?"

"It's very sad, Tilly."

"Are you getting a sense of her yet? Of what kind of a person Dorsey was when she was alive?"

Ike didn't answer immediately. Then he said, "I'm starting to, sunshine. How about you?"

I nodded. "That's why it's so sad."

chapter
twenty-four

WE LUCKED OUT and found a parking space on West Twelfth
Street, half a block from the Gray Squirrel Coffee Shop. As we
walked toward the door, I reminded myself that Alistair McDevitt
had described the man we were about to meet as a twenty-first-
century Huckleberry Finn.

As soon as we were inside, though, I realized that Arthur
Dawes was no easygoing Huckleberry anything. He had been sitting in the back booth and staring at the door with fervid, expec-
tant eyes. When he saw us, he jumped up, his red hair so bright he
looked like a yarn doll of Raggedy Andy. Not a very nice one, either. On first impression, I didn't like him. I didn't like the way he
looked at us; I didn't like his loose-limbed, slump-shouldered
walk, a March to Bataan from the back of the coffee shop. He
stopped about three feet away from me, and when our eyes met,
or almost met, he looked weird. As if either he were taking drugs
or *should* be taking them.

"Miss Quilter?" he said to me.

His eyes were a baby blanket pale blue, but they didn't look at
me. Instead they darted all over the place. Up. Down. To the left.
To the right.

"Yoo-hoo. Here I am. Fritillary Quilter. Call me Tillary. This is Ike Blessing."

Arthur cast a furtive look at Ike. Then he said, "You want to talk about Dorsey, right?"

And despite his frenetic manner, he said it in a deep, smooth, appealing baritone. Granted, I couldn't imagine how this freckle-faced creature from the Land of Jitter and Twitch could have appealed to Dorsey Browning, but there was no denying that Arthur Dawes had an irresistible bedroom voice.

I affirmed that we had, indeed, come to talk about Dorsey.

"Good, because that's what I want to do. My friends are tired of hearing me talk about her. But I can't stop. It's a sickness. Being in love with a dead woman. I thought love stopped when the other person died, and I hate it. I hate everything about it."

Love. Death. Hate.

Hmmm.

Trying to keep my voice level, despite my *extreme* prejudice against hysterical men, I said, "Hate everything about what?"

"About Dorsey being dead. It isn't right. It's not the way life is supposed to be. It's not how the world is supposed to work."

Ike took a step forward so that Arthur had to acknowledge his existence, and he said, reasonably, "Accidents happen."

Arthur Dawes's eyes stopped jittering long enough to glare at the fire investigator. "You think it was an accident?"

Ike said nothing.

"Well, it wasn't an *accident*." Arthur's voice became louder and more aggressive. "It was a *tragedy*. It was —"

Ike put a hand on Arthur's arm. "Let's sit down," he said, and he led Arthur to the booth where he had been sitting when we came in.

The table in the booth was empty, except for a mug of coffee.

"Did you eat?" Ike asked.

"Eat?" Arthur said, as though he were repeating a word from a foreign language. His face had displayed an entire kaleidoscope of emotions from agitation to confusion to anger to depression in less than a minute. Now, it was completely blank.

"That's right," Ike said. "Eat. As in food. Bacon and eggs. Hot dogs. Roast beef. Lasagna. Potato chips."

"Potato chips," Arthur echoed tonelessly and looked down into his coffee mug. He was thin. Way too thin.

I knew a dancer once. A guy I went to high school with who wanted to be our generation's Fred Astaire. His name was Donald Gorney. We were in the same English class for two years, and I had always admired his ambition and easy sense of humor. After we graduated, we lost touch, and I didn't see him again until four years later, when I caught a glimpse of him across the street on Lexington Avenue. Don was going north and I was going south, but I called out to him anyway.

He turned when he heard my voice, and our eyes met. I *know* that he recognized me, but instead of stopping, he rushed away. There had been a look of absolute despair in his eyes, so unmistakable that it screamed at me over the tumult of the traffic. And, like Arthur Dawes, Don was thin. Much too thin.

A year later, a friend told me that Don had been a chorus boy in a Broadway show and had married the leading lady. Shortly after their six-month anniversary, she dumped him. The time I'd seen him on Lexington Avenue was a week or two after he had been dumped. Two months later, a different friend told me that Don had been found in his apartment. Dead of unknown causes.

Whether Arthur Dawes couldn't afford to eat or had simply forgotten to unwrap the turkey sandwich in his refrigerator, he was starting to get that "unknown causes" look about him, too.

"You're having lunch with us," Isaac C. Blessing said, and he motioned the waitress over.

Ike ordered triple everything from the breakfast menu for the emaciated actor, including pancakes, sausages, and waffles.

"Flapjacks cure depression," he said offhandedly to the waitress, who had probably lost her curiosity about actors, depression, and flapjacks thirty years ago.

As soon as she left, I tried to look deeply into Arthur Dawes's shallow blue eyes. I hunched over the table and said in a whispery, conspiratorial voice, "Do you believe that Dorsey Browning was murdered?"

Arthur's jaw dropped.

His lips began to tremble, and the eyes that avoided mine over the Formica tabletop once again became agitated and confused.

"Murdered! You think that I *murdered* her. Oh, my God. This is terrible. Awful. You think . . . how could you think that I . . . Oh, my God. Oh, my God . . ."

I really, *really* shouldn't have said that to Arthur.

Before we drove to the coffee shop, Ike had made me promise that I would sit with my hands clasped in my lap and my mouth shut until he had eased Arthur into questions about the play, the cast, and his relationship with Dorsey. It was all supposed to be gradual. Subtle. Unobtrusive.

I, however, had broken my promise and committed a heavy-duty, major boo-boo. I looked at Ike. He raised an eyebrow in my direction, but he didn't have to say anything, because we both knew that I'd blown it big-time.

In a moment of insanity, I had decided to cut to the chase.

Why?

Because I was curious. Because I thought I could shock Arthur into telling me the truth. Because I was twenty-five years old, and gave in to an irresponsible impulse to flick my brain at a man who was already off balance and watch him disappear into a bubbling caldron of hysteria.

Because I was stupid, that's why.

"I loved Dorsey," Arthur said, and I have to admit that, despite my cruel and inexcusable bias against weak men, I was starting to feel sorry for the guy. "She was a wonderful person. Wonderful." He was beginning to look and sound like a half-wit. Suddenly, he reached across the table and clutched at both of my hands. "You did know Dorsey, didn't you?"

"No, Arthur," I said, gently extricating my ten fingers. "I never had the pleasure."

Arthur turned to Ike. "You? Did you ever meet my fiancée?"

Fiancée? What was this? Nobody had ever told us anything about Dorsey and Arthur being engaged.

But Arthur didn't wait for Ike to answer before he embarked upon another disquisition of mad utterings. Ike leaned forward. He put both hands, fingers spread wide, on top of the table. They were big, rough, man's hands. I'd never noticed them before.

"Arthur" — he carefully enunciated each syllable, as if he was trying to communicate with someone deaf, dumb, and from outer space — "we did not come here to accuse you of murdering Dorsey Browning. We do not think that you murdered her. Do you understand what I'm saying?"

Arthur stared at dust motes. At light waves. At air.

"Look at me," Ike demanded. "Take a deep breath, and look at me. Look."

The actor moved his eyes to those of Ike.

Miracle of miracles, they stopped skittering, came into focus, and actually stayed put.

"I am the director," Ike said, sounding like Cecil B. DeMille's

God in *The Ten Commandments.* "We are in a theater, Arthur. This is not real life. Inhale deeply. Now, exhale. Do it again. And again. Do you feel yourself calming down?" Ike didn't wait for an answer, and he didn't release Arthur's eyes. "We're going do a little Method acting this afternoon. You've been cast in a play. Your name is Arthur Dawes, and you're a hungry young actor whose role requires him to eat his way through the first act. It doesn't matter if you're hungry or not, because a professional does what he has to do to make himself credible. When your lunch comes, you are going to eat it slowly. You are not going to think about anything, and we're not going to talk until you've cleaned your plate. Do you understand me? Nod if you understand what I'm saying."

The red-haired man nodded.

Lunch was served.

Twenty minutes later, Arthur had eaten everything on all three of his plates. He'd also calmed down, and lost the madman-on-the-brink glint in his eyes. He looked healthier, stronger, and less pathetic. For the first time, I could believe there might be a backbone hidden somewhere under that quivering mass of nerves. Nerves I had no further intention of prodding. I may have behaved foolishly, but I'd done it only once. I knew that my job, from that point forward, was just to sit back, watch, and learn.

"More coffee," Ike told the waitress. Then he turned to Arthur. "You said nobody wants to listen to you talk about Dorsey. We do. We want you to tell us all about her."

Arthur Dawes crisscrossed his knife and fork neatly on his empty plate, wiped his hands on a napkin, and looked Ike right in the eye. This was an altogether different man from the one we'd encountered when we walked in.

"I don't know who you are or what you want from me, but this is the first time I've felt sane and human since Dorsey died. Thank you, whoever you are and regardless of your motivation. How did you do it?"

Ike smiled. It was a guy smile. Different from the way he smiles at women. More with the mouth. Less with the eyes. He smiled and repeated what he had said earlier. "Flapjacks. They cure depression."

Then, much to my surprise, Arthur Dawes smiled back, and for the first time, I could see a certain distant resemblance to Mark Twain's fictional Mr. Finn. He stacked his plates and pushed them off to one side.

"What do you want me to tell you?"

"What do you want to tell us?"

Ike leaned back in the booth, poured himself a cup of coffee, and looked infinitely relaxed. Clearly, this was going to be more conversation than interrogation.

"I want to tell you that I loved her. That I miss her. That Dorsey was more than just a beautiful woman with talent and brains. She was like . . . like a blueprint for the rest of us. A lesson plan on what being human is all about."

"Tell me more," Ike said.

The young actor looked up at the ceiling, as if he might find cue cards to his thoughts written there. When he started to talk again, his voice was dramatic and compelling, and I could see why he'd already achieved a modest degree of success upon the stage. "Every once in a while," Arthur began, almost dreamily, "life does something perfect. Like make a Fifth Avenue, or change the leaves to gold in the autumn, or invent a Steinway piano, or come up with a Tchaikovsky's First. That's what life did when it created Dorsey. It's as if everybody else was just a first draft, but Dorsey was the real thing. The finished product. She was the human being that all of the rest of us were meant to be." He looked down at his hands. Long, thin fingers — an artist's hands — and he shook his head. "I'm not making any sense, am I?"

"I think you are," Ike said firmly, exhibiting such a gift for listening, if there is such a thing, that I was ready to tell him about my love life, and I didn't even have one.

"Go on," Ike urged. "You said that you loved her."

Arthur shook his head. "I loved her, but that isn't the point. The point is that she *deserved* to be loved. Dorsey was . . . Dorsey was *luminous*."

What a wonderful thing for a man to say about a woman.

Luminous.

I would have to remember it.

The waitress brought us more coffee. Arthur gulped down two cups, and then began to talk and talk and talk. About *Our Town*. About how he and Dorsey met. About their first rehearsal. About the gradual merging of their offstage personalities with the characters they were portraying in the play. And everything he said confirmed what Dorsey had written in her letters to Beatrice McDevitt, and Beatrice's impression that, despite their love for each other, he and Dorsey had never been lovers. At least not in the physical sense.

Three cups of coffee later, Arthur revealed something even more surprising.

"I was going to propose to her," he murmured into his cup.

I had to lean over to hear this, and I said to myself, Aha! So you *weren't* engaged. At least not yet.

He seemed to waver on this point.

"I planned it meticulously, because I wanted everything to be perfect. The closing notice for the play had already been posted, so I decided to wait until after our last performance. I would walk into Dorsey's dressing room with the ring. Did I tell you that I bought a ring? I still have it. Why did I keep it? What do I do with it now? And I was going to say, 'A beautiful ending and a new beginning. Will you marry me?' But, of course, those were four words I never got to say."

Of course? What was "of course" about it?

I didn't have a clue. Neither did Ike.

"Excuse me," he said. "I missed something. Maybe you want to tell us why you didn't propose."

The actor's eyes started to dart back and forth, and his mouth began to quiver.

"Don't go there again," Ike demanded sternly. "Stay with me, fellow."

Arthur nodded, steadied himself, and took a deep breath. But he had to lift his hand and blot at the tears in his eyes with the back of his clenched fist. It was such a childlike gesture that I almost reached out to pat his shoulder.

That I didn't was just as well, because the next thing he said was "Buck Fitzgerald."

Buck Fitzgerald?

Why would he bring up the name of a Madison Avenue bigwig in an intimate conversation about the woman he loved?

"What about Buck Fitzgerald?"

"A week before we closed, a week before I was going to propose to Dorsey, he came to the show."

"Buck?"

"Yes, the son of a bitch."

The skin beneath Arthur's freckles reddened, and his baby blue eyes became hard and squinty. No, he didn't revert to being the semi-lunatic he'd just been, but instead of the actor across from us being an amiable, semi-employed, all-American Huck, he had suddenly become a very angry, unforgiving, and venomous young man.

"What did Buck Fitzgerald do to make you so mad?"

"What did Mr. Two-Thousand-Dollar Suits do? Not much in the grand scheme of things. He just ruined my life."

"How? Be specific."

"Be specific? All right. Fine. Specifically, after the show was over, he went backstage to her dressing room."

"Go on."

"And he fell in love with her."

"With Dorsey?"

"Yes. With Dorsey," Arthur Dawes spat out. "With my fiancée. With the woman I loved."

"The way you described her, Arthur," Ike said reasonably, "I'm sure men were falling in love with Dorsey every day."

"They were. But . . ."

"But what?"

"This time she . . . she . . ." Arthur gasped for air. At least, that's what I thought he was doing. What he was really doing was trying to hold back tears. A doomed endeavor. "She . . . Dorsey . . ." He was openly sobbing now. "She . . . she fell in love with him, too."

After that, Arthur Dawes was completely useless to us, even though Ike managed to get his address, drive him home, and walk him up to his apartment. When he got back to the car, Ike called Arthur's talent agent from his cell phone and suggested it would be a good idea for someone to look in on him, because her client was falling apart.

Meanwhile, Arthur notwithstanding, *I* was an emotional

wreck. I have a theory that there are Typhoid Marys of misery, that desperate people send out contaminated molecules of grief, and that, if we aren't careful, we get infected with misery, too. By the time Ike got off the phone, I was more than relieved to be alone with him in the car and felt as if the drawbridge had finally been pulled up over alligators in the moat and we were safe in the castle.

"What do you think?"

I expelled a sigh of relief.

Ike adjusted the rearview mirror. "I think that there's a whole new dimension to the case."

"Is Buck Fitzgerald the new dimension?"

"He is."

"What about Arthur? What do you think about him?"

"As in . . .?"

"Do you think he killed Dorsey in a jealous rage?"

"According to the McDevitts, Arthur left their party at six o'clock. Maybe he came back later. We can't prove that he did. We can't prove that he didn't. We can't be sure that the McDevitts were telling us the truth. We can't even be sure that Dorsey Browning was murdered, since there are a lot of innocent ways for people to break their noses. People bump into walls. They fall on their faces. They're hit by baseballs. Even dead people get broken noses if an ambulance driver or a morgue attendant drops them by mistake. So the fact of a broken nose tells us something, but it doesn't tell us much. What I'm really interested in is why, an hour after Arthur left the party, Buck Fitzgerald drove up in a green Jeep."

Buck Fitzgerald.

Tall. Dark. Handsome.

Buck Fitzgerald.

Rich. Famous. Successful.

A romance novel cliché.

And black. Like the man the McDevitts saw in the green Jeep.

I thought I'd read somewhere that Buck Fitzgerald was married, but maybe I'd been mistaken. He was also said to be incorruptible, brilliantly innovative, decades ahead of everybody else on Madison Avenue, and a loner. Either way, both he and his Jeep had gotten a second confirmation that put him at the fire scene, which brought us right smack up against Ike's question: Why?

"Where are we going now?" I asked as Ike took the turn onto the FDR Drive.

"To my office."

"What are we going to do there?"

"What do you think, Tilly?"

"You want me to read the autopsy report?"

"That, and there are a few calls I have to make."

chapter
twenty-five

RIGHT OFF, I'm ready to admit that autopsy reports are *not* my favorite reading material. When I first started at Precaution Property and Liability, I became involved with a homicide, which I immodestly admit I helped to solve. One of our insured's children fell out a window and died. Accidentally. Or so the grieving mama said. The file landed up on my desk, and as was our right as the insurer, I went to the policyholder's house to investigate the claim.

Somehow, from the minute the case was called in, the facts didn't sit right with me.

The mother pulled out all the stops when she launched into her teary tale of woe, and she managed to project so much grief that I could *almost* forgive the police for doing such a slipshod job. Almost, but not quite, because they just wouldn't let go of their mistaken notion that women don't kill their own children.

Every police officer I've ever met *knows* this isn't true, they know filicide is as much a fact of life as is a winter cold or the flu. They know it with their brains, but their guts rebel against the knowledge, and given anything resembling a plausible opportunity to exonerate a grieving mother, they will do so with undue haste.

I, however, have never put mothers or motherhood on a pedestal, even though my own mother belongs on one. Consequently, I was able to view the baby-out-the-window case with an appropriately jaundiced eye. First, I initiated a search of our own records to see if Mrs. Baby Killer had put in any previous claims for a child's death. When I didn't find anything there, I made a few calls to friends at other insurance companies who also had friends, and so on. One of these friends has a police officer brother in Brooklyn who got interested in the case, and with his help, I was able to accumulate solid proof, including copies of insurance polices and death certificates, that Mother Hubbard had filed accidental death claims on no less than five previous infants, all of whom had "accidentally" lost their lives when they fell down the stairs, or out a window, or in front of a bus, and so on.

Fifteen days later, when I presented this evidence to the detective in charge of our case, her initial response was to regard what I was saying with total disbelief. As she continued to read through the documents, disbelief turned into embarrassment, because after all, I'd done what had really been her job. By the time she got to the last death certificate for the last victim, the only emotions she had left were rage at the mother and gratitude toward me.

Which brings me back to the subject of autopsies.

I guess she thought that she was honoring me or doing me a favor when, after she got an exhumation order for baby number six from the district attorney, she invited me to come along with her to the morgue and observe the procedure.

I said to her then what I will always say to such warmhearted inclusiveness: "Thanks, but no thanks. I don't *do* dead people."

Yes, I am tenacious when it comes to unraveling the whos, whens, whys, and wherefores of dubious claims. But as soon as my research results in an actual corpus delicti, i.e., in someone who can no longer eat an egg salad sandwich, my policy is "Hands off."

And so I approached Dorsey Browning's autopsy report with great trepidation, hoping it wouldn't be accompanied by photographs of Y-incisions, liver sections, or spleens.

I shouldn't have worried.

Not only were there no pictures, there was almost no report. I held two thin sheets of paper up in the air, waved them toward Ike, and said, "Huh?"

Ike asked, "Did you read it?"

"I read what there is of it."

"What do you understand so far?"

"Not much."

"Remember, Tilly. Dorsey Browning died on the Fourth of July."

"And?"

"And someone at the medical examiner's office was asleep at the switch and did a sloppy job."

Again, I undulated the air with the autopsy report.

"Translate this into English for me, Ike."

He took the pages out of my hand, tossed them on the conference table, and said, "After the photo unit was finished with her, Dorsey was brought to Beth Israel Hospital and pronounced dead. From there her body was taken to the morgue."

"When?"

"At four-thirty in the morning. But no autopsy was ever performed at the morgue."

"That doesn't sound right."

"It isn't right."

"Well, what did they do there?"

"Dr. Morton Boyle performed an external postmortem examination on the body beginning at eleven-fifteen A.M."

"Go on."

"He was finished at eleven-twenty A.M. The entire procedure took five minutes."

"You're kidding. Right?"

"No, Tilly. I'm not kidding." Ike reached for the two discarded pages from the medical examiner's office. "It says here —"

"Never mind that. I believe you. Tell me more."

"The external postmortem examination demonstrated that the nares —"

"What are nares?"

"Openings in the nose . . . that the nares were not burned. It also revealed that there was no soot in the nose or throat of the deceased."

"That doesn't sound right either."

"No, it doesn't. Add this to the mix, Tilly. Blood samples were taken from Dorsey during the postmortem, before the body was released to the funeral home."

"And?"

"And a toxicological examination of the blood samples performed seven days later, on July twelfth, determined that there was no carbon monoxide or cyanide in the blood."

"I always thought when someone dies in a fire, there *had* to be carbon monoxide in the blood."

"Carbon monoxide *and* cyanide."

"But you're saying none of that was present."

"Not me, Tilly. I'm quoting from the external postmortem, which also states that the deceased's face was asymmetrical upon arrival at the morgue, and that her nose had been broken."

I looked over at the two sheets in Ike's hand.

"It said all that?"

"In different words, but yes. It's all there."

"And didn't I read somewhere in that poor excuse for an autopsy report that Dorsey's cause of death was smoke inhalation?"

"That's what you read."

"Well, how can someone die of smoke inhalation without . . . without . . ."

"Without inhaling smoke? Without their nares being burned? Without soot being found in the nose and throat? They can't."

It took me a few seconds to process this, but finally, I looked him in the eye and said, "What you're telling me is that, based on no autopsy, no burning at the opening to the nose, no evidence of smoke in the nose or throat, and no carbon monoxide or cyanide in the blood, the medical examiner's office has concluded that the cause of death was smoke inhalation."

"That's right. And don't forget the broken nose."

"Ike, I could *never* forget the broken nose."

I pushed aside a pile of papers, dropped my head exhaustedly on my arms, and groaned, "This is giving me a headache." Then I looked up at Ike and asked, "So how *did* Dorsey die?"

"I don't know. What I do know is that even before the fire started, she was already dead."

chapter twenty-six

A FEW MINUTES LATER, while I was forcing myself to reread the medical examiner's report, the telephone rang. At first I paid no attention to Ike's end of the conversation. But when I heard the name Buck Fitzgerald mentioned and then mentioned again, I put down the report and listened.

"... I know, and I'm not asking you to betray a friend. Just toll Buck Fitzgerald what I told you, and let him decide for himself.... Hey, I don't tell you everything either ... but they were having an affair.... That's right, I still want to talk to him.... Anytime. Anywhere. He sets the rules. You tell him that, and tell him anything else he wants to know, including my shirt size and blood type. Just remember that if he's as innocent as you say he is, this whole murder angle is going to let him in for a hell of a shock.... Right. Here. At home. In the car. You have all of my phone numbers.... If you say so, Cecil.... That's right, buddy. Thanks."

Ike hung up and looked at me.

"That was Cecil Lamb. He's the manager of the arson and fraud unit at Empire Insurance Company. Twenty years ago, we were firemen together, and when you had your fire, Tilly, it was Cecil who assigned it to me. He gave me my first private job. I still do work for him."

I nodded. "And Cecil's connection is?"

"His sister is married to Buck Fitzgerald's brother. Cecil met Buck at the wedding, and they've been playing racquetball together once a week ever since. I asked Cecil to tell Buck that we want to talk to him."

"Will he do it?"

"Cecil will do anything that I ask."

"I mean Buck. Will a big, Madison Avenue superstar like Buck Fitzgerald let us grill him about our case?"

"I'm not going to *grill* anybody, Tilly. And I'll talk to him myself."

"What do you want me to do while you're having all the fun?"

"If you have the time, I'd like you to go to the library to research Buck's background. Maybe you can dig up something that will explain —"

The telephone rang.

"I bet that's Buck Fitzgerald now," I said.

But it wasn't. The call had been forwarded from my office, and it was for me. Ike handed me the receiver.

A beautiful voice with a British accent asked, "Is this Fritillary Quilter?"

"It is," I answered. "Are you Lillian Mayhugh?"

"Yes, darling. My agent, with whom I am currently on the outs, told me that you want to ask me some questions about Dorsey. Was that arguably competent and unbearably unctuous son of a bitch lying to me again, or is it true?"

"It's true."

"Exactly what is your relationship with Dorsey, if one may be so bold as to inquire?"

"I'm the claims representative at the company that insures her house. Her family has insurance policies with us covering the residence as well as their personal property."

"I see. And why, specifically, do you want to talk to me?"

"I and my colleague —"

"Whom, exactly, might that be?"

"Isaac Blessing. He's the fire investigator."

"Which is what?"

"A fire investigator is an expert hired by insurance companies or attorneys when they want someone to determine where a fire started and what caused it."

"I see. Again, I must ask, what do you want from me?"

"To tell you the truth, Miss Mayhugh —"

"It's *Mrs.* Mayhugh. My husband, sadly, is dead, but like a deposed monarch, I prefer to retain all of the trappings of my lost crown."

"I'm sorry."

"So am I. Unlike Dorsey, he had no insurance, and is worth very little to me in his current position."

"I forgot where I was."

"You were telling me why you want to talk to me about Dorsey."

"Oh. Right. We want . . . I . . . well, I'm not exactly sure *what* we want from you or what we think that you can tell us. We're trying to put together a time line of the events that preceded the fire. We want to get a picture of what Dorsey's life was like in the weeks and months before she died. And we're —"

"But *why*, Miss Quilter. You still haven't told me *why*."

I looked over at Ike, who was following my end of the conversation as avidly as I'd been eavesdropping on his. When he nodded, I considered it a silent consent to say much more than I had originally been planning to say, because if Lillian Mayhugh was going to be lured into a conversation, most of our speculations were going to have to come out.

I sighed audibly into the telephone.

"We aren't a hundred percent satisfied with Dorsey Browning's cause of death, Mrs. Mayhugh," I finally admitted.

I heard a sharp snort of satisfaction. Then the actress uttered a stagy "Ha" before adding, "I've been waiting two months to hear somebody say that, even though your timing is perfectly appalling. I have to catch a plane to Heathrow from Newark Airport at nine o'clock. Do you have a car?"

"No, Mrs. Mayhugh, but Mr. Blessing does."

"Excellent. Pick me up in exactly forty-five minutes. My doorman will buzz you in, and you can help me with my luggage. There's a dreary coffee shop at the airport where we can talk. If we don't get caught in traffic, we should have an hour to discuss Dorsey before my flight."

chapter
twenty-seven

I SAID EARLIER that I believe in stereotypes. What I didn't say was that all my favorite stereotypes are British. In fact, I grew up believing, or wanting to believe, that just about every Englishman was a handsome, big-nosed, redheaded archenemy of illiteracy, like Professor Higgins. Or, to be more accurate, like Leslie Howard *playing* Professor Higgins in *Pygmalion*. As far as *women* go, there's always been only one Englishwoman for me. Mrs. Miniver, from the movie of the same name. Tall, lean, graceful, and gracious, with angular features, a creamy complexion, style, humor, and like Professor Higgins, bright red hair.

Even though I had seen Lillian Mayhugh many times on television, I hadn't connected the name with the face until she opened the door. Then my mind snapped its fingers and said, "Aha!" Double "Aha!" because, with her striking bone structure, the aristocratic arch to her eyebrows, her bold green eyes, slim, expressive lips, and that quicksilver smile, she was in every way but one (she was *not* gracious) a perfect fit for my stereotype as well.

Lillian Mayhugh is one of those women I've always admired but never had the nerve to aspire to be. Perfect hair. Perfect makeup. Perfect nails. Lush and seductive eyes. The self-confidence of a queen. The minute she commanded me to pick up her cosmetics bag — "And don't jumble it, darling, or I'll come out looking like Madam Defarge" — it was a foregone conclusion that I would like her. I couldn't help myself. I'm an unrepentant sucker for people who, for good or ill, are unapologetically larger than life.

In the car on the way to Newark, we exchanged unpleasantries — "No, darlings. I loathe London in the summer" — and gave the nitty-gritty of why we were there a wide berth. It wasn't until we were drinking coffee at the airport bar that I broached the dual subjects of Dorsey Browning and love, and how they related to Buck Fitzgerald.

"Love," the actress intoned, imbuing love with the resonance of a five-syllable word. "As actresses, we try to catch love as if it's a butterfly," she continued, ignoring any reference I had made to real human beings or a real-life situation. "We emulate lovers. We study their gestures, their jealousies, their insecurities, their euphoria, and their pain. We swoon as they swoon, tremble as they tremble, and if we think it will look good across the footlights, we tear at our hair in frustration, beat our breasts, laugh, or cry. We play Juliet to Romeo, Penelope to Odysseus, Beatrice to Dante, and for those with more modest cultural aspirations, Minnie to Mickey Mouse. Being consummate professionals, we become experts at imitating every nuance and subtlety of love, until we could convince an audience of cynics that the actor playing opposite us, whom we detest, is actually the love of our life. We are clinically analytical and expertly adept at *portraying* love." Lillian Mayhugh smiled coolly and treated us to a flash of perfect teeth. "But . . . my darlings, our constant exposure to love *dramatized* numbs us before the altar of love *realized*, and over the years, we forget what love is really supposed to be."

By the time she had stopped talking . . . orating . . . performing, I forgot why we wanted to interview her in the first place, and if I had remembered, I doubt I would have cared. I was enthralled by her self-assurance, self-importance, and personality. Ike, who was sitting across from her, seemed less impressed. I couldn't even begin to imagine why. I couldn't tell *what* he was thinking.

Ike reached for the coffee urn, refilled both cups, and said bluntly, as though she were a barmaid, "Lillian, what's your point?"

"Point?" She raised one of those perfectly arched eyebrows. "Need I have one?"

"Your plane is boarding in less than an hour, so it wouldn't hurt."

She looked carefully at Ike. Studied him, really. Ike seemed to be studying Lillian, too, and I swear I could see a sliver of something dangerous in his eye. Then he turned his wrist over and tapped the face of his watch. Lillian gave him one of those catch-as-catch-can smiles and in a more businesslike tone said, "I agreed to meet you tonight for one reason." She took a sip of her coffee, which for what it's worth, was black. "A dear friend of mine is dead. We played mother and daughter for over a year on the stage. In the theater, that can either mean nothing or everything. It meant a great deal to me."

"Were the two of you close?"

Lillian held up her right hand with the first and second fingers pressed tightly together.

"How about Buck Fitzgerald. Was he close to Dorsey, too?"

"Alas, handsome stranger. Buck and Dorsey were madly in love, which was the point of my opening oratory. That despite the ostensive callousness of those of us who emote for a living, even we on occasion can appreciate genuine emotion when it dares to flaunt itself in our face."

"By which you mean . . ."

"That despite my initial antipathy to Buck Fitzgerald, he turned out to be a prince."

"So, he made a bad first impression?"

"I feared that he would be a typical stage-door Johnny."

"But he wasn't?"

"No, darling. He wasn't."

"Did you know who he was when you met him?"

"Anybody who's ever picked up a newspaper knows who Buck Fitzgerald is. But I had no idea what his motives might be. Saint or satyr? Gallant or gross? Hence, I remained in Dorsey's dressing room to protect her from inappropriate behavior."

"How do you define inappropriate behavior?"

"Offensive language. Bad jokes. Cheap jewelry."

"Was he?" I interjected. "Inappropriate, that is."

"No, darling. He was a perfect gentleman."

"I don't get it," I continued. "One day, Dorsey is in love with Arthur Dawes, and next thing you know, Buck Fitzgerald is on the scene. How —"

Lillian lifted a single, well-manicured finger to her lips.

I stopped talking.

She looked at her wristwatch again. "Darlings, the bewitching hour is upon us, so I'll get to the point. Buck Fitzgerald, who is incorrigibly handsome and impossibly rich, told us that he'd come to see *Our Town* because he had always admired the play. Halfway through Act One, he realized that the actress playing Emily would be perfect for an advertising campaign he was planning for a new cosmetics account, and he came backstage to offer Dorsey a job. Personally, I think he was a goner before she'd finished her first scene."

"A goner?"

"Yes, darling. One rarely sees it in real life, although I've done it time and again on the stage."

"Done what?"

"Played someone dumbstruck by love, which is exactly what happened to our Mr. Fitzgerald. His lips stopped forming words. Sounds stopped resonating from his throat. He stopped moving. He stood in that dressing room like a statue, and he simply stared."

"At Dorsey?"

"Yes, indeed. Simultaneously, I might add, the same thing was happening to her."

"What was happening?"

Lillian Mayhugh looked speculatively, first at Ike, then at me, and she nailed me with those iridescent, deep green eyes. "How about you, Insurance Girl? Do you believe in love at first sight?"

I scrunched up my face and thought for a minute. I knew that I wanted to believe in it, but . . .

"Honestly, Mrs. Mayhugh, I just plain don't know."

She turned to Ike. His face was impervious and impassive.

I thought he was acting like a shit.

"Not saying, are you?" she taunted. "Or not admitting anything is more likely. You look like the falls hard and falls fast type to me." She dropped her eyes and reached for her coffee. "Alas, I'm more of a killjoy, myself. I readily admit that until I witnessed what was happening in that small dressing room in front of me, I had never believed in it myself."

"You're saying that they fell in love." Ike snapped his fingers. "Like that."

"Like that." She snapped her fingers, too.

I leaned forward, fascinated. "What was it like?"

"Intoxicating. Disconcerting. I certainly never felt that way about my husband. In fact, I never really loved him at all. I just loved the way that he was madly in love with me. But with Buck and Dorsey —" she snapped her fingers again — "signed, sealed, and delivered. He's a black man, you know."

I nodded. A black man in a green Jeep.

"And she . . . Dorsey . . . had very pale skin. It would have been easy to compare them to Othello and Desdemona, but Buck wasn't the jealous type. He was far too sure of himself for that."

"Did they have a love affair?"

"Yes, darling. They did."

"What about Arthur Dawes?"

"Poor dear." Lillian rubbed at a speck on an artfully polished fingernail. "Arthur is such a lovable schmo."

I tilted my head to one side. "If Arthur Dawes loved Dorsey, and Buck Fitzgerald loved Dorsey, who didn't love her?"

"We all loved her, darling. Buck just loved her in a different way. Like a prince loves a princess in a fairy tale."

"If that were true," I tried to reason it out, "then how did their relationship go bad so fast?"

"What makes you think that it went bad?"

"People who are happy in love don't have nervous break-downs."

Lillian Mayhugh sighed. "Alas. That's also true." She looked at her watch and then cast a brief, sidelong glance at Ike, who looked about as approachable as an ice pick, so she turned back to me.

"Almost a month before Dorsey's breakdown, her father died. She gave up her apartment in Manhattan and moved back to Riverdale."

"We know that. And we know she was still living at home on the night of the fire. What we don't know is why, if she was falling apart emotionally, she moved in with her sister instead of moving in with Buck."

Lillian did a palms-up gesture with her hands. "Because, darlings, it wasn't her father's death that caused Dorsey's breakdown, it was Buck."

"Huh?" I said. Not my most articulate response.

"They fell in love shortly before the show closed. That was in January. Buck ended the affair in April."

"*Buck* ended it?"

"That's right. When his wife came back to him, and   "

"Buck Fitzgerald is married?"

"More or less."

Ike shifted in his seat. "You're losing us here, Lillian."

She batted her exquisite eyelashes at him. "Pay attention, darling. It really isn't all that complicated. Buck was married to a model named Chloe, a beautiful and vile bitch with collagen-enhanced lips and a heart as cold as a polar bear's tit. He believed in marriage, for better or for worse, so even though our pestilent Chloe consumed vast quantities of alcohol and drugs and was sleeping with her photographer, her hairstylist, and the entire outfield of the New York Mets, Buck stayed with her for the sake of the children."

"Children?" I gasped. "Plural? How many are there?"

"Two girls. Ten and five."

"So," I repeated, trying to keep everything straight. "Buck is married and faithful, and Chloe is a drug-addicted slut. What happened next?"

"Next," Lillian continued, her voice beautiful, her tale tacky, "Chloe, in a cocaine-induced stupor, abandoned Buck and the girls."

"Then what?"

"Then nothing for about thirteen months, at which time Buck waltzed into Dorsey's dressing room and fell in love. As soon as Chloe found out that Dorsey wanted Buck, she decided to get him back. She entered a fashionable rehab, invested a few weeks in breast-beating, and learned how to play the 'I'll never do it again, please forgive me' game. Buck, credulous baby, decided that, for the sake of his daughters, he should give Chloe another chance."

"So he dumped Dorsey?"

"I wouldn't put it quite so crudely, but yes. He and Dorsey went their separate ways."

"And that's when she fell apart?"

Lillian Mayhugh narrowed her eyes at me. "Dorsey's breakdown was" — she flicked her fingers at the air — "Nothing. We want something. We lose it. Our hearts break. We recover. It happens all the time. It happened to Dorsey. No big deal. She was young, talented, and beautiful. If I'd had a daughter, a revolting thought in and of itself, I would have wanted her to be like Dorsey. I expected Dorsey to live forever. And she would have. She should have. There was something about that girl of the eternal flame."

"Arthur Dawes said that she was luminous."

"Luminous describes her very well."

Ike pointed to his watch again.

"Yes, darling?" Lillian said.

"What can you tell us about the night Dorsey died?"

"What do you have in mind?"

"Did you know she saw Buck that night?"

Lillian's mouth curved into a bitter frown.

"No, I did not know. Exactly where and when did this occur?"

"At the house in Riverdale, during the Fourth of July party."

"I know Arthur went to that party," Lillian said firmly. "And I seriously doubt that Dorsey would have invited Buck to the same party at the same time."

"Arthur came first and left first," Ike said. "Which brings us to question number two. Do you have any idea why Arthur went to the party?"

"To gaze adoringly at Dorsey, one would surmise."

"Do you think he intended to harm her?"

"Arthur?" Lillian's eyes opened widely in disbelief. "Darlings, Arthur was as harmless as an argyle sock."

"Could he have had any other reason for going to the party? Return a book he's borrowed? Steal the silverware?"

"Yes, darling. But nothing sinister. Arthur had just been cast in a soap opera, and as the director wanted Dorsey to play opposite him, I'm sure his motive in going to that horrible party was to be the bearer of good news."

"*Was* it good news," I asked, "to go from a starring role on Broadway to a small part on daytime TV?"

Lillian's answer was very much the same as Beatrice McDevitt's had been when I'd asked her essentially the same question.

"In this business, Insurance Girl, a walk-on in a spray starch commercial is good news. Speaking of which, at what time did Buck arrive at the party?"

"An hour or so after Arthur left. And he didn't actually go to the party, he and Dorsey just sat in his Jeep for about fifteen minutes."

"One wonders what they did in the Jeep for so long."

"According to witnesses, they talked."

Lillian tapped a perfectly manicured finger against her lips. "That means they were back together," she mused.

"Did you expect it?"

"Not per se, but I didn't not expect it, either. Buck went back to his wife because he'd felt compelled to go through the motions of saving what couldn't and shouldn't have been saved. In the long run, he would have divorced Chloe." Lillian flipped open her purse and took out a tube of lipstick. "I'm as sure of that as I am that I'm about to miss my plane."

"One more question," Ike said in that same cranky, non-Ike-like tone.

"I doubt it will only be one," Lillian said pleasantly. "But go ahead."

"Did you go to the funeral?"

"Certainly."

"Was Buck there?"

"Yes. In the back of the room. He didn't say a word to anyone, and he looked ghastly. His skin was gray, as if half of his blood had been drained away."

"Who else was at the funeral?"

"I thought I saw his wife, Chloe, but I may have been mistaken. Chloe is crazy, but I doubt if even she is that crazy. Dan Burroughs and Beth Meyers flew in from Albuquerque and Minneapolis. Both of our producers and the director were there. The entire cast and crew showed up, and of course, there was Dorsey's sister, Faith."

"What do you think of Faith?"

"I only met her twice, but I don't like her."

"Why not?'"

"Because she obviously doesn't like me. On both occasions, she went out of her way to snub me. I don't expect people to grovel after me, darling, but after all, I *am* a star!"

She put away her lipstick, pulled a small compact out of her purse, and began to dab powder on her nose. "Before I go, darling" — Lillian looked directly at Ike—"*I* have a question."

"Shoot," Ike responded.

"How do *you* think Dorsey died? And before you answer, keep in mind that over this past hour I have surrendered to you a large part of my rarely cooperative, sometimes belligerent, and always private soul. So don't bullshit me."

"Okay," Ike said. "No bullshit. I don't think that Dorsey died as a result of injuries sustained in fire."

"That's lawyerspeak. Tell me in English. How did she die?"

"I don't know."

"Life is short and time is fleeting. When *will* you know?"

"We're working on it."

"Do you believe that Dorsey was murdered?"

"It's a possibility."

"Who did it?"

"I don't know yet."

"Neither do I," I piped in, as if either of them cared about what I thought. Nevertheless, I persisted. "If Dorsey *was* the victim of a homicide, I'd like to hear your opinion, Mrs. Mayhugh. Who do *you* think the murderer could be?"

Lillian snapped her compact shut. "That's obvious."

She picked up her purse, and rose to her feet. "Buck Fitzgerald was an exceptionally attractive man. I told you that there were two females in the dressing room the day he came backstage. We know that one of them, Dorsey, fell in love with him. Fait accompli.

But what about the second woman in that small room? Think about her for a minute, and consider the possibility that she fell madly in love with Buck, too."

Lillian started to walk away. Then she stopped, turned, and the right side of her mouth twitched into a fleeting smile. She looked right at Ike, which wasn't fair, since *I* had asked the question, and added, "If I were you, darling, I'd put your money on me."

chapter
twenty-eight

ON THE WAY BACK from Newark Airport, I accused Ike of being what I call an anti-flirt. An anti-flirt is someone who is so afraid of engaging in lighthearted sexual banter that he becomes more or less a belligerent prick.

He laughed, the first laugh I'd gotten out of him all day, and said that, as much as he liked the concept, it didn't apply to him because he just plain didn't like Lillian Mayhugh.

"How could you not like her? She's . . . wonderful!"

Ike shook his big, stubborn head. "Your actress friend is coldhearted, superficial, and vain."

"Coldhearted!" I gasped. "Oh. No, Ike. That's just an act. Sensitive and brilliant people do it all the time. To protect themselves."

"You don't do it," Ike said reasonably.

"I'm not sensitive. I'm shallow."

"Sure, Tilly. That's why you cry all the time."

"I don't cry *all* the time. Anyway, really sensitive people don't cry. They go on the attack and say heartless, cruel, and self-damning things. It's a psychological shield for them. A defense mechanism."

"Go on," Ike said. "I like fairy tales."

"It isn't a fairy tale. I have a very sensitive and decent sister who does it. Her name is Frederica . . . we call her Freddy . . . and she's a research scientist."

"What does she research?"

"Parkinson's disease. Alzheimer's. Heavy-duty, deadly stuff. She's always telling me that she kills little babies and analyzes their body parts to manufacture synthetic medications for her lab. She's very graphic and horrible about it, and makes up long, gory stories about sneaking into hospital nurseries in the dead of night to snatch infants from their cribs. But it's a lie. She talks like that because she's so battered and bruised from the maniacs who call her terrible names because she works with fetal tissue. Her defense mechanism is to attack herself before anyone else can do it. She pretends to be worse than anyone can accuse her of being, because joking about it helps her to defuse their vicious attacks. It's a protective device. That's all."

Ike looked at me pityingly.

"You don't believe me," I said. Hurt.

"I don't think your sister is a baby killer, if that's what you mean."

"But you *do* believe that Lillian Mayhugh murdered Dorsey Browning."

"I didn't say that."

"Ike, she only told you that to throw you off base. To punish you for being so mean to her."

"Mean to her? How was I mean?"

"When she flirted with you, you didn't flirt back."

Ike looked at me. Genuinely astonished. Then he took a deep breath and let out a weary sigh. I was about to say something else.

In retrospect, probably something stupid, but when I saw the look on his face, I realized that even tough old birds with diamond eyes could get tired.

"What I believe, Tilly," he said finally, "is that it's been a long day."

chapter
twenty-nine

IKE WAS RIGHT. In less than sixteen hours, we'd gone to Hudson University to interview Dorsey's housemother and driven back to the city to plunge a red-hot poker into Arthur Dawes's heart. We went to Ike's office to discredit the medical examiner's Duh-I-didn't-even-*do*-an-autopsy report; then we rushed into Manhattan to pick up Lillian Mayhugh and drive her to Newark Airport, where we discussed many Dorsey-related issues before she made her grand exit and boarded the plane.

A typical Wednesday, I supposed, in the life of Isaac C. Blessing. Horrendous.

At around midnight, Ike dropped me off at my apartment but didn't say anything first about getting together again to talk about the case, and that left me feeling as if the Lone Ranger had ridden out of town without giving Tonto his forwarding address.

Next morning, in my office, my IN box looked like the Leaning Tower of Unprocessed Claims, and there was a note taped to the receiver of my telephone:

Dear Tillary:
Come into my office when you get here.

Why aren't you in yet?
Oliver Wicks

Okay. Okay. I know that I should have dialed the office the night before, punched in the numbers for Ollie's voice mail, and said, "I worked very late tonight. I'll fill you in tomorrow. Don't expect me until after ten." But as soon as I got back to my apartment, I collapsed on my bed and fell asleep.

I rapped my knuckles against the jamb of Ollie's opened office door. "Hi, boss."

"Come in, Tillary. Sit down."

I studied Ollie's face. His mustaches weren't quivering. A good sign. His eyes were tired but not avoiding mine. Even better. His hands were idle, and he wasn't nervously shredding napkins. Best of all.

I sat. "What's up?"

Ollie pointed to a box on the floor that was big enough to contain four large gorilla heads.

"It was delivered an hour ago."

Dead center on the box, under a sticker that said PRIORITY OVERNIGHT, was a label from Isaac C. Blessing Associates, Inc. Printed on the label were the words ATTENTION—FRITILLARY QUILTER,

"I don't suppose it's candy," I surmised. "Or flowers. Or the complete works of Edgar Rice Burroughs."

Ollie stood up. "I'll carry it to your desk."

I jumped to my feet. "Why don't we just leave it where it is, and then *you* can read what's inside?" But Ollie pushed me aside, hoisted up the carton, and marched out of his office. Before I could say "eye strain," he had deposited it on the floor beside *my* desk.

I lifted one flap of the box and peeked inside. "What do you think it is?" I whispered.

"We don't have to speculate." Ollie handed me a sheet of Ike's letterhead. The words "Table of Contents" were written above a long list of documents.

I scanned it. "It's going to take me a *year* to read this stuff!"

Ollie lifted the Leaning Tower of Paperwork out of my IN box. "I'll get Marlene to help you with these." He added in his boss voice, "I hate to do this to you, Tillary, but the home office called this morning."

I gave him the evil eye. "And?" I drawled out facetiously.

"And we only have until Friday the fifteenth to wrap up the Browning case."

I dropped into my chair, flipped open my calendar, and started to count on my fingers, as we who are not mathematically inclined are wont to do.

"Shit, Ollie. That only gives us eight more days."

"I know. I know. I tried to get more time, but you know how the home office is."

He was right. I knew. Ten years ago, on a different case, a different home office at a different insurance company had wanted to subrogate against my parents for the infamous Borkin fire that *I* had set.

But Ike had stopped that.

Now Ike was responsible for sending me a huge carton that was not filled with gorilla heads or other things that would make me smile.

"Exactly what *is* the home office threatening to do in eight days? Fire me?"

"No, Tillary. Worse. Pay the claim."

I leaped to my feet. "They can't do that! Faith Browning is a psycho pack rat. She's stashed tons of furniture and God knows what else somewhere, and damned if I'm going to let her get one cent of our money in payment of a fraudulent claim!"

Three or four people at nearby desks began to hoot appreciatively and applaud. I slumped back in my chair and glared, first at the Offending Carton and then at my boss.

"*Now* what do I do?"

Ollie, forced by the situation to be more assertive than he liked, pointed to the box and whispered into my ear, "Read everything in that carton."

I groaned.

Then with assertiveness apparently growing on him, he took a step backward and added in a normal voice, "Find out what happened to Faith Browning's possessions, Tillary, and *solve the case!*"

No one was scheduled to use the conference room for the rest of the day, so I dragged Ike's box down the hall, kicked it inside, and spread the documents out on the Panama Canal-sized table.

After I'd laid it all out, I realized that Ike had sent over much more than he had listed on his table of contents, that all of it was fundamental to a fire case, and that investigating a fire involves a whole lot of variables that had never occurred to me before. I'd told Ike that I wanted to *be* him. To follow in the footsteps of the master, so to speak; the carton he had sent over was my punishment. Or my reward.

I picked up the first document: "Burbank Electric Wire Company—Fire Report."

I flipped to the first page.

". . . the short-circuit current of the source at 127 volts was about 800 amperes."

Then, to no one in particular, I sighed and said, "Dostoevsky, it ain't."

chapter thirty

WHEN IKE CALLED MY OFFICE that afternoon, I was *not* in a good mood.

"All day," I grumbled, "I've been reading, analyzing, organizing, and extrapolating information from material that, if stacked, one document on top of the other, would go back and forth to the moon *twice*."

I was exaggerating, of course, but my eyes were tired, my back was sore from hunching over small print, my fingers hurt from pulling out staples, and I was cranky.

Ike laughed, which pleased me not at all, and elicited from me the response "Boring. Boring. Boring."

"Where do you want to start?" he asked, ignoring my complaints.

"Do I have a choice?"

"Sure you do."

"All right. Let's talk about Dorsey's will."

"Choose again. We haven't found a will."

"So what? Speculating about it has to be a thousand times more interesting than the dry-balls stuff you made me read."

"Tilly, do you want to investigate fires or don't you?"

"Yes, Sahib. I do."

"Then stop whining. Pick something."

"Okay. The Burbank Electric Wire Company Report."

"Good. Summarize the contents, and tell me what you think."

"Is this a test?"

"Yes."

I made one of those humph noises and said, "The Burbank Electric Wire Company Report includes ten pages of charts and diagrams I don't understand, as well as cross sections of flexible electrical cord magnified twenty times that looks exactly like fried eggs. It also contains test results of the heat resistance of the cord when current passes through the conductors."

"Very good, Tilly."

"It was prepared by Dr. Bertram Wolensky, who is an electrical engineer for the Burbank Electric Wire Company and a defense expert. That means he's working on our side. Right?"

"Right. Tell me the purpose of the report."

"To test what was left of the electric wire that connected your client's clock radio to the outlet behind Dorsey's bed."

"Why was the test performed?"

"Faith Browning is suing the manufacturer of the electrical cord, saying that it was defective and therefore caused her sister's death. Can she do that, Ike? Initiate a smorgasbord of lawsuits against everybody in sight?"

"She *is* doing it, sunshine. So I guess she can. What else did you get out of the Wolensky report?"

"He disagrees with the plaintiff's allegation."

"What does the plaintiff say in the lawsuit?"

"That because there was a bead on the wire —"

"What's a bead, Tilly?"

"A sort of a melted clot of metal on the tip of an electric wire where an arc occurred."

"What's an arc?"

"A short circuit, a large tourist attraction in St. Louis, or a place where you can buy hamburgers. In this case, a short circuit."

"How big is a bead?"

"About twice as wide as the wire itself. On a conventional lamp cord, it would be approximately the size of a small pearl, which is probably why it's called a bead."

"What does a bead on a wire mean, sweetheart?"

"Well, plaintiffs' experts, whom I like to refer to as the bad guys, say that because the wire was defective, it overheated, resulting in an arc, which in turn resulted in a fire, and that the bead on the wire is evidence the arc occurred. In other words, they're saying that the very existence of the bead proves the wire was defective. But Dr. Wolensky says that, after having conducted thousands of experiments, he can prove that a live electric wire will form a bead in just about any fire, whether it's the cause of the fire or the effect, because when heat destroys the insulation between the hot wire and the neutral wire, carbon is produced, the carbon acts as a sort of a semiconductor between the wires, and an arc can occur."

"So, did the Burbank wire that was connected to the clock radio cause the fire that killed Dorsey Browning?"

"According to Wolensky, it did not. He says that all it takes for a live wire to create a bead is it being in the vicinity of the fire."

"What else?"

"That the cord was almost new, and that, based on his examination of the cord remnants, there was no evidence of a manufacturing defect, and the point of origin of the fire was probably a few feet *away* from where the arcing on the electric cord occurred."

"Excellent, Tilly."

"Don't think I kept this all in my head, Ike. I made notes."

"I make notes, too."

"I know. I recognized your chicken scrawl all over the report."

"Only problem is, sunshine, I can't read my own handwriting."

"Neither could I. What's next?"

"Let's talk about the report on the Hercules Electric clock radio. Can you find it?"

"It's on my lap. By Harlan Proctor, Ph.D., P.E., Consulting Engineer. Inspection photographs taken in White Plains, New York. Photo numbers one and two are of the top of the Hercules radio. Photo number three is a printed circuit board. Photo number four is a close-up of electrical components, and except for the black goo draped over them, they don't look like they're in very bad shape at all."

"The black goo is plastic."

"Right. Photo numbers five and six show the burned plastic housing."

"Keep going, Tilly. It gets better."

"Photo number six is a view of the radio showing its bottom side. Photo numbers seven and eight are close-ups of stickers on the bottom of the radio, and . . . well, what do you know, Ike. I can make out everything. The embossed warnings about preventing fire and electric shock: 'TO PREVENT ELECTRIC SHOCK, DO NOT EXPOSE THIS PRODUCT' and so on. And most of the paper label is unburned, too. 'REFER INQUIRIES OF ANY NATURE TO OUR AUTHORIZED HERCULES ELECTRIC FACILITY' and the address. If Faith was looking for someone to sue, she must have considered that the equivalent of an engraved invitation, except . . ."

"Except?"

"Except, you'd think that if the fire had started *inside* the clock radio and burned downward from there to the night table and through the night table to the flooring . . ."

"Go on."

"You'd think that to get to the surface of the table, it would have to burn through itself first."

"You're on the witness stand, Tilly, but the jury looks confused. Can you explain yourself a little better?"

"Sure, Your Honor. If the fire had started in the area of the electronical components and the circuit board, which by the way, were *not* burned, and then communicated to the table, it would first have had to burn *through* the bottom of the clock radio, including the embossed warning label and the paper label. Since both are virtually intact, this obviously didn't happen."

"Meaning?"

"Meaning, Your Honor, that the fire could *not* have started inside the radio itself."

"How about the burned plastic housing? What caused that?"

"External heat."

"Does Dr. Proctor's report tell us anything else?"

"Well, there are some good photographs of beads on wires, but we already figured out what they mean. Photo numbers thirteen and fourteen are of the plug. There's a little deterioration there, but nothing to make your heart skip a beat. A few photos show melted plastic sheathing on some sections of the electrical wire, and there are a bunch of pictures of the nightstand, the box the radio came in, a lamp, and what looks like a sink faucet."

"What were Dr. Proctor's conclusions?"

"That the bus didn't stop here."

"Tilly. You're an expert witness. What you say has to be comprehensible to a jury."

"Dr. Proctor's report on the Hercules clock radio concludes

that no fault could be found in the power circuits, and that the electrical components of the radio which had a potential for fire ignition were relatively unburned. Is that enough, Your Honor? I'm starting to get a headache. Can we talk about something else, please? Like Buck Fitzgerald?"

"Not yet. Find the Oxford Chemical Lab report."

"Here it is. Under my half-empty bottle of aspirin."

"What does the report say?"

"Don't you want to know *why* my aspirin bottle is half empty?"

"I bet this report took you by surprise, Tilly."

There was obviously no deflecting Ike once any part of his brain was engaged with fire, which reminded me of ugly Milton Beasley, who lived behind us in Conversation, New York. Milton always insisted on showing me every last grasshopper, beetle, and praying mantis in his bug collection. I could never get away from Milton Beasley, either.

I sighed. "You're right, Ike. The Oxford Chemical report came out of left field."

"What do you think, sunshine?"

"I think that Faith Browning is demented. I mean, how many people . . . Scratch that. How many companies can she accuse of having set one crummy fire?"

"Faith's experts aren't saying that the mattress on Dorsey's bed caused the fire, Tilly. They're saying that the by-product of its combustion was toxic chemicals that, after she inhaled them, killed her. They're also saying that the burn patterns on the floor beneath the bed were caused by the Styrofoam mattress, and that after the mattress caught fire, it liquefied, melted, and burned through the flooring, which was the cause of those two holes we found in the floor."

"So, let's take this one step at a time, Ike. When did Faith decide to sue . . . let me see, what are they called? The Logan Valley Mattress Company?"

"A month ago. I found out about it last week. The report you're looking at contains photographs of the simulated burning of a mattress the same make and model as the one that burned in the fire."

"There's a lot of fire, here, Ike. The mattress was clearly flammable."

"Correct. Now, look at the photographs on the last page."

"Found them."

"What do you see?"

"Well, the fire's out."

"Yes."

"And the edge of the platform bed has the alligator burn pattern you're always talking about."

"How about the floor under the edge of the bed?"

"It's got a bunch of burned up crud on it, and some charred areas."

"Any indication that the foam mattress melted?"

"No. It looks like it crumpled up and shrunk when it burned. The way a plastic bag does."

"Anywhere the mattress turned to liquid and melted onto the floor?"

"Not that I can see. But, Ike, that part about the toxic chemicals. . . . Isn't Styrofoam a petroleum by-product, and don't petroleum by-products like plastic, vinyl, fiberglass, and Styrofoam produce toxic fumes when they burn?"

"They do."

"Then this lawsuit has some legitimacy. Or credibility. Or . . ."

"Think it through, Tilly. What did the toxicology on Dorsey's blood say?"

"That there was no carbon monoxide or cyanide in the blood."

"And what was the conclusion of the external postmortem with regard to —"

"I get it, Ike," I cut him off. "No soot in the nose or throat. Nares of the nose not burned, which means that she was dead at the time of the fire. Ergo, it doesn't matter if the mattress was filled with poison gas or Chanel No. 5, because you can't kill someone who's already dead."

"Very good, Tilly. How's that headache?"

"Did you ever see *The Blob?*"

"Not that I remember."

"Great movie. It's about this blob that invades from outer space. It starts out small but rapidly takes over the diner, the street, and then the whole town. That's my headache. It just filled up all the seats at Madison Square Garden."

"Maybe we should stop now."

"Oh, no. Gee, Ike. Can't I please read aloud to you from the first ten chapters of *Cromptom's Five Volume Encyclopedia of Unpronounceable German Chemical Names?*"

Ike laughed.

"You're a good kid, Tilly. Go to the library tomorrow and research Buck Fitzgerald. Take good notes, and call me when you're finished. I'll make a fire marshal out of you yet."

chapter thirty-one

I LOVE GOING TO THE MAIN BRANCH of the New York Public Library. I like to climb the wide marble staircases and march past the ponderous paintings on the walls to get to the research rooms, or periodicals section, or the stacks. It's fun for me, because I'm the best research assistant I know. I'm inordinately curious, and I get a big kick out of the way irrelevant details sometimes throw their arms around the neck of the subject I'm researching and just plain won't let go.

And that makes me wonder. Are they really irrelevant or aren't they?

There was quite a lot of material on Buck Fitzgerald, and I made copious notes on what interested me. I photocopied dozens of articles, researched the Internet, bought a pair of gold earrings at the library store, and all in all had a thoroughly enjoyable day.

Since I was in Manhattan the whole time, I wasn't able (nor had I been invited) to attend Ike Blessing's actual session with the man whose privacy I was invading. I say "session" because what went on between them certainly wasn't an interview, and if it was, it wasn't clear who was interviewing who . . . or whom.

Ike called me at work at about 4:00 P.M., after I'd returned from the library, to tell me how it went. He said that he had been sitting at his desk in his office when he heard a knock at the door to his office itself. Not the lobby door. He opened it and immediately recognized Buck Fitzgerald.

"What does he look like?" I asked.

"He looks like his pictures in the newspaper, but younger. Thinner. Darker. More intense."

"Tell me more."

"He's got hazel eyes. Lots of gold speckles in with the green. Very short hair. A little gray at the temples."

"Premature gray, Ike. He's only thirty-five, and . . ."

I gave Ike the index card version of what I'd learned in the library. Buck Fitzgerald was born in Highwood, Illinois, at the Great Lakes Naval Base. His father had retired from the navy as a chief petty officer and opened a small electronics repair shop. Instead of being a navy brat brought up all over the world, Buck grew up where he was born.

His real name is Sylvester Lionel Fitzgerald. He was nicknamed Buck by his friends, because he worked so hard and saved every dollar he made. Buck did well in high school and once told an interviewer that he had always wanted to *know* things, because that would help him to *do* things, and he intended to *do* them better than anybody else.

If you had asked him during his freshman year of high school what he wanted to be when he grew up, he wouldn't have known. Three years later, Buck had mapped out the rest of his life. The catalyst for this change was his first part-time job, in the printing plant of a small advertising agency in the nearby suburb of Highland Park.

Buck had been on the job only one month before he'd taught himself to type; six weeks later, he was promoted to the editorial department. A few weeks after that, he was designing ads. By the time he had graduated from high school, Buck could do everything at the agency. His boss offered him a partnership if he would stay, but he had other plans. He knew he still had some growing up left to do and believed that the military was the place to do it, so Buck joined the Marines.

The New York City Public Library has very little in its files about Buck's two tours in the marines, other than that he served in the Gulf War, that his rank when he quit was sergeant, and that he's still in the Marine Corps reserves. He was twenty-four years old when he moved to Manhattan "to become an advertising czar," or so he was quoted as saying in an interview.

Without either a college education or a diploma from a prestigious school such as the Fashion Institute of Technology, Buck couldn't get a foot in the door of a good advertising agency, despite his impressive entry-level résumé. So, knowing his assets (he was fabulously handsome), he had a portfolio of head shots made and took them to the biggest model agency in town. Less than six months later, his strong, handsome features had appeared on four magazine covers, including a *New York Times* fashion insert and *GQ*. Bankrolled by his success as a model, Buck bought into a small, failing photo studio. Once there, he told prospective clients that he would create advertisements for them gratis in exchange for photo assignments. They would pay for the photographs, but the ideas for the ad campaigns would be free.

Buck's approach to advertising was deceptively simple. He believed that most consumers are intelligent, and that what they ultimately respond to is the promise of a desired result, coupled with the truth. He was the first to come up with the sure-it-tastes-terrible-but-it-works approach to advertising. The ads he designed were attractive. They were innovative. They sold the product. And his clients came back. The second time through the door, however, they had to pay. Two years after he started, Buck sold his interest in the photo studio at a huge profit and was doing the art direction, copywriting, copyediting, set design, set direction, and self-promotion for a new advertising agency bearing his name. Within two more years, the only thing he still did unassisted was self-promotion, and at that he excelled.

Buck Fitzgerald was tall, handsome, rich, successful, and black. It had taken him exactly ten years to turn himself into something that Madison Avenue didn't quite know what to do with and had never seen before. He was an extravagantly successful entrepreneur who graciously consented to go to the best parties, attend the most exclusive openings, and be available for the occasional interview about fashion and marketing trends. But he never seemed to need anybody or to be particularly appreciative to anybody for what he had attained.

Despite his visibility at New York City social events and his marriage to a one-name jet-set model with whom he was rarely seen, Buck gave out very, very little of himself; he was extremely self-contained. The nature of a free-enterprise economy is such that the scarcer the supply of a commodity, the greater its demand. So, of course, everybody wanted more of him.

"What was he wearing, Ike?" I asked.

"A navy turtleneck. Khaki pants."

"Jewelry?"

"Just a watch."

"Rolex? Cartier? Something showy?"

"Swiss Army."

"Tell me about his face."

"Narrow. High forehead. Very strong jaw and chin. No question he's a handsome guy. Intelligent face. Eyes like a lie detector machine, Tilly. They latch on to you and never let up."

"So, he knocked on the door and you let him in. Then what?"

————

Ike had been reading a deposition on an unrelated case when he heard a loud knock at the door. He opened it before he'd thought to say, "Who's there?" and was staring into Buck Fitzgerald's anguished eyes before his brain had a chance to catch up. Right out there in the hallway, without waiting to be acknowledged or invited inside, Buck said, "I don't know you from Adam, but Cecil Lamb called me last night. He told me you're investigating a claim involving Dorsey, and that I could trust you with my life. Cecil also said you have evidence that Dorsey was murdered. Apparently, you know I had a relationship with her. If she was murdered, I want her killer found and punished. Ask me what you have to ask me. Nothing is off limits. You be the judge of what's relevant. There's nothing you can say that will embarrass or anger me. As of this minute, I have one purpose and one purpose only, and that's to help you find out what happened to the only woman I have ever loved."

Buck stopped talking as abruptly as he'd started, and in the silence that followed, he and Ike stared at each other like a couple of battle-savvy stags.

Finally, Ike stuck out his hand. "Ike Blessing."

The man in the hall responded. "Buck Fitzgerald. But you know that."

Buck reached out to grasp Ike's hand, and their handshake sealed the conditions that Buck had set.

Isaac C. Blessing and Buck Fitzgerald spent over two hours together that Friday afternoon. They started out in Ike's office, but after thirty minutes Buck said, "I'm jumping out of my skin. Let's get out of here," and they spent the next hour and a half talking as they walked up and down the Brooklyn Heights Promenade.

Ike asked Buck to begin at the beginning, so Buck told him

how he'd bought tickets to see *Our Town* and, halfway through the performance, realized that the actress playing Emily had the right "look" for his new ad campaign. All very much the way Lillian Mayhugh told us, including the moment in Dorsey's dressing room when their eyes met and, "freeze-frame," as Buck described it, "the outside world ceased to exist."

"What happened after you left the theater?"

"I'm a coffee addict. I stopped smoking a couple of years ago, and coffee's my cigarette now. We went back to Dorsey's apartment. We talked the whole night. Talked and drank coffee. And, no. I can see you wanting to ask the question, so I'll answer it upfront. We didn't make love. Not then. Not for a couple of weeks. I don't suppose you'd understand, but what we were feeling was . . . it was too big. It wasn't like being at the start of a love affair. It was riskier than that. More like making a commitment to stop breathing air and take a chance on some rarefied chemical that you just hope will sustain life."

"Scary?" Ike asked.

"It was scary all right. Like giving up your mortality, or becoming twice as mortal." He shook his head. "Either way, it was a big leap."

"But eventually, you became lovers."

"Yes."

"Did you know that one of the cast members in her play was also in love with Dorsey?"

"Arthur Dawes. He hated my guts, but I felt sorry for the guy."

"Did Dorsey still have feelings for him?"

"I'm sure she did. She wasn't in love with him, though. She was in love with me."

"Are you aware that on July the fourth, Arthur Dawes saw Dorsey in Riverdale about an hour before you did?"

Buck Fitzgerald shook his head. "No. I didn't know that."

"Is it meaningful to you that he visited her?"

"Should it be?"

Ike changed the subject. "Tell me about Dorsey."

Buck's penetrating hazel eyes rested on Ike's for a few long seconds. "I'd really like to do that. I just don't know what to tell. Only since she died have I realized how little of a substantive nature I know about her. Or ever knew. Had she been a Girl Scout? Who was her eighth-grade English teacher? Did she like to cook? What was her favorite movie? Did she know how to waltz, play the piano, or play bridge? Did she like to eat fudge or taffy apples? Did she hate mustard? Could she ride a horse? There are so many . . . too many things that I never found out."

Buck rubbed his eyes with two long fingers; then he looked directly at Ike.

"I do know a few things, though. Some funny. Some sad. Some sweet. Like that both Dorsey and her father could wiggle their ears, and that Dorsey could touch the tip of her nose with her tongue. I know that her acting and her career meant more to her than anything in the world except me, and that meaning so much to another person is a frightening . . . no, not frightening, more of a religious thing, and it's a terrible, terrible responsibility. I thought my shoulders were broad enough to handle it," Buck said dolefully. "But they weren't."

He went on to tell Ike things we already knew about Buck's marriage and his separation from his wife.

"You don't screw around with people's souls," he said, his tone painfully self-critical. "Not the way I did with Dorsey. At the time, I thought I was doing the right thing. My two girls are little bits of things, and when their mother left us, it hurt them big-time. We handled it, though, my daughters and I. We were the Three Musketeers. I thought that my love for them came first, and that if they wanted their mother back, I would have to want her back, too. But I was wrong. It would be an act of great generosity to say that I was only a fool."

Ike asked Buck if he remembered any of the dates when things with Dorsey had happened, not really expecting a lot. Much to his surprise, Buck had total recall and was able to map out a comprehensive sequence of events.

On Tuesday, January 4, he and Dorsey met

Our Town closed the following Sunday.

Dortimer Browning died on Wednesday, March 1.

"How did he die?"

"He had a massive stroke."

"Did you know Dorsey's father?"

"Yes. I'd been to the house in Riverdale a number of times."

"For what? Birthdays? Special occasions?"

"Sunday brunch."

"Then you met Dorsey's sister, Faith?"

"I know Faith."

"Do you like her?"

"Do I like Faith?" Buck Fitzgerald stopped and walked over to the railing separating the promenade from a deadly drop onto the Brooklyn-Queens Expressway below. He stared out at the harbor and repeated, "Do I like Faith?" Then he turned back to Ike and said, "That's a good question. I'd have to answer that I don't know. I didn't know how to react to her when I met her, and even now, after all that's happened, I still don't know."

"Do you have any opinion at all about Faith?"

Buck frowned. "Yes. I feel sorry for her."

This was a new one.

"Why?"

Buck opened his hands, palms up in a helpless gesture.

"The few times that I did see her, she seemed determined that I should like her and pathetically eager to please me. I don't like people who need or want my approval. It's a character defect I'm not proud of, but it seems to describe why I never responded more positively to Faith."

Eager to please?

Yet another facet of Faith Browning's personality to add to all of the rest.

"Give me some examples," Ike said.

Buck's eyes tracked a tanker moving onerously under the Brooklyn Bridge.

"From the minute we arrived at the house," he said, "Faith could never do enough for me. Was the coffee too cold? Did I want her to open the window or to close the Venetian blinds? Could she get me more muffins? Would I rather have raspberry jam or marmalade? Was the music too loud? Maybe it wasn't loud enough? She was like that whenever I saw her."

"Was she flirting with you?"

"Possibly. I'm not sure."

"What was Dorsey's attitude toward her sister?"

"Indulgent. Careful. Never cold, but not particularly warm. I don't think Dorsey liked it when her sister ordered her around. Particularly in front of me. But she never made an issue of it. On several occasions, I noticed Faith trying to one-up Dorsey, but Dorsey never took the bait. She wouldn't compete."

"Do you think Faith resented Dorsey?"

"You mean country mouse and city mouse? The stay-at-home sister and the Broadway star? I wondered about that. She might have resented her, but I honestly don't know."

"Was Faith short-tempered with Dorsey? Did she ever get mad?"

"Some subtle put-downs. 'Have another croissant, Dorsey, you're too thin' or 'Do you really think that color's good for you?' Things like that. Otherwise Faith seemed pretty tightly wrapped."

"How about Dortimer Browning?"

"Dorsey's father? A great guy. If I were half as good a father, I'd be patting myself on the back."

"What were his daughters' attitudes toward him?"

"Dorsey was crazy about him. I don't know what Faith thought or felt, but she was always pleasant enough to her father when I was there, even if I considered her . . . Let me think how to describe it. Smothering. Mothering and smothering. She obviously doted on him. Too much for my taste. It would have driven me crazy. No man wants to be babied. Sometimes, I'd catch Dortimer's eye, and the look in it was 'She's my daughter, and I love her. What can I do?' I don't think Dortimer was good at saying no to his daughters. I guess I can identify with that."

Ike took Buck through the rest of his relationship with Dorsey, from the day her sister called to tell her about their father's stroke, through their midnight ride to the hospital, to the horrible realization that Dortimer was dead. Buck described the funeral and Dorsey's ongoing grief, spiked with the humorous stories she often told of Dortimer's antics when she was growing up. He finished off with Dorsey's decision not to take time away from her acting to work on his cosmetic client's campaign, a decision with which Buck agreed.

"We were together," he summed it up, "for two months before Dortimer died, and two months after he died. Four months. That's all."

"How did Dorsey take the news that you were going back to your wife?" Ike asked.

Buck closed his eyes for a long moment before he answered,

and when he reopened them, his voice was so low, Ike had to stare at his lips to make out what he was saying.

"There are no words to describe her character, grace, and nobility," he said, and then he took a sad and ragged breath.

"No scenes?" Ike asked. "No hysterics? No tears?"

"Oh, there were plenty of tears. For both of us. Tears are outside our control. But no raised voices. No hysteria. No scenes. The only thing Dorsey asked," he continued, his voice still low and a terrible expression of strain on his face, "was that I never attempt to see her, to write to her, or to call her again."

"You agreed to that?"

"Yes. I mean, no. I promised that if I ever contacted her, it would be for keeps, and that I would be begging her forgiveness for having made an unforgivable mistake."

"How did she respond to that?"

"She didn't."

"When did this conversation occur?"

"On Sunday, April 16."

"Do you know that, shortly after that, she had an emotional breakdown?"

Buck's head snapped away from the harbor, and he glared at Ike. His skin turned gray, and he suddenly looked stricken. "I had no idea. Tell me. I have to know."

And so Ike Blessing told Buck Fitzgerald everything he knew about that period after Dorsey went to live on Labyrinth Lane. Alistair McDevitt said she had come home on Good Friday, April 21, which would be five days after Buck made his riding-into-the-sunset speech. Ike told him about Dorsey's depression, her solitary walks around the property, her absorption in repairing the miniature garden relics of her childhood, Faith's solicitousness, Dorsey's gradual recovery, and the return of her health and sense of joy.

That brought Ike to the Fourth of July.

"A black man in a green Jeep was seen that night on Labyrinth Lane. That was you, Buck. Wasn't it?"

"Yes. That was me."

"Did Dorsey know you were coming?"

"No. She'd told me not to contact her. So I didn't. That's why I hadn't known about her breakdown. I didn't even know she gave up her apartment until I went there, and the doorman told me that she moved. I drove to Riverdale that night, but I didn't call first, and she didn't know that I was coming. Nobody knew."

"What happened after you got there?"

"Dorsey saw my car from the neighbors' backyard and walked over. We got into the front seat, and I spoke first. I didn't give her a chance to say anything. I don't know what I said or what words I used, but I can tell you why I went to see her, I can tell you what my purpose was."

"What was it?"

"To apologize. To propose. I asked Dorsey to marry me."

"How did she respond?"

"She said yes. She would."

chapter thirty-two

I GOT OFF THE TELEPHONE with Ike at about 5:30 P.M., and I was shutting up my desk for the night when Ollie came out of his office and walked in my direction.

Thud.

That was the sound of a large Priority Mail envelope being dropped onto my desk, amplified by the double thud of my plans for the weekend hitting the dust.

"What's this?" I asked my boss.

"It's from Faith Browning. It was mailed to Bosley over in the legal department."

"I'm the claims representative on this case. Why didn't Faith just send it to me?"

Ollie's left eye started to twitch.

Sometimes when I ask him the same question, year after year, without even varying the sentence structure, it does that. Twitch, I mean.

"Tillary," he said with unreasonable patience, "you know how it is once lawyers get involved."

I tilted my head at the envelope.

"Did she finally send us a proof of loss?"

"No." He let out a disillusioned sigh. "Faith Browning never seems to do anything the easy way."

"Well, what *is* it?"

"Invoices and copies of receipts."

"*Now?*" I said skeptically. "During her deposition, she gave every excuse except 'the dog ate my homework' for why she didn't have a single cash register receipt, credit card statement, order confirmation, or —"

"The deposition you attended was for her personal property claim. The one we're denying. These are the receipts for the structural property claim, which we are paying. They cover the expenses incurred so far on repairs for the house."

I gingerly lifted the flap of the envelope, not wanting to deal with what was inside.

"Have *you* looked at this yet, Ollie?"

"I scanned the cover letter."

"What do you expect me to do with it?"

Ollie lowered his head guiltily and looked up at me from under his eyebrows. "Maybe you could read it?"

"Come on, boss. It's Friday night. It's the *weekend*, for God's sake. I'm tired, and I want to go home."

"Can't you take it home with you?" he asked, looking really, really pathetic. "I know you've already put in a lot of overtime on this, but if we don't come up with some hard evidence of fraud by next week, the home office is —"

"I know. I know. The home office is going to pay the full value of the claim, and probably throw in a trip to Paris, a face-lift, and a lifetime supply of panty hose."

"Two hundred and fifty thousand dollars for structural repairs," Ollie continued, apparently not satisfied that I was depressed enough. "And the personal property claim could go as high as five hundred thousand dollars. That's close to a million dollars, Tillary."

"Hey, wait a minute." I sat bolt upright. "Her personal property policy was for two hundred and fifty thousand dollars. How do we suddenly get twice that amount?"

"Replacement value."

"Oh, right. Those heirloom Ralph Lauren guest towels." I hit my forehead with the heel of my palm. "How could I *be* so stupid!"

Ollie patted me on the shoulder. It was his now-now pat. Then he turned and walked back to his office.

I dropped the entire four-pound package into my purse, having made room for it by taking out the Gutenberg Bible, and I tried to throw it over my shoulder for the cab ride home, but it was too bulky; I had to drag it by the straps instead.

I slept late the next morning, and it wasn't until Saturday at noon that I flopped down on my living room floor with a legal pad in my lap, a pencil behind my ear, and a yellow highlighter in my hand, prepared to go through every receipt Faith Browning had submitted and, one at a time, to actually *read* the damn things.

Trust me on this, it was worse than reading *War and Peace*. At least with Tolstoy's masterpiece, I could read every other word, paragraph, or (when it really got tedious) every third page.

Professional contentiousness prevented me from taking such a lax attitude on the Browning claim.

Fortunately.

There were 417 pages in all. Each receipt had been photocopied onto an eight-and-a-half by eleven-inch sheet of paper. Many were borderline illegible. The amounts on dozens of purchases were small enough to be considered petty cash, such as:

July 25	Itkowitz Hardware	Thumbtacks	0.65
July 26	Wilson Housewares	Sandpaper	0.96

Other receipts were so complex and involved, I felt I would never be able to understand them without a home contractor's degree:

August 1	Cobleskill Builders Supply	
	Truckload Price. Non-returnable	
	12 — TW20310WHP Tiltwash Windows	
	@$183.33 each	$2,199.96
	12 — White Screen for TW20310W	
	@$18.00 each	216.00
August 13	Van Ness Flooring	
	600 ft. sq. Antibes Red Terra Cotta	
	12x19 — 540 ft. @2.75	$1,650.00
	Flextile Terra Cotta 679	200.00
	Thinset	250.00
	40 Sheet DuraRock Subfloor @11.00	440.00
	10 Bottles Gnd Sealer @9.95	99.50

What in the world is a truckload price?

What is thinset?

What is Gnd Sealer?

And who cares?

I cudgeled my brain to figure out the relationships between the items Faith Browning had bought and what part they would eventually play in the repair of a Victorian house; when I wasn't exactly sure of the relevance of what had been charged, i.e., "Scoville Electronics. 1 wl sw @$6.15," I gave the insured the benefit of the doubt, guessed that it was a "wall switch" not a "wild swimmer," and hoped for the best.

Frankly, I had expected to find dozens of invoices for illegitimate purchases, but by the time I arrived at the two hundred and thirteenth receipt, I had identified only four of a questionable nature. One was for the purchase of a car floor mat. Car floor. House floor. Hey, anyone can make a mistake. Another was for limo service to a bookstore.

Maybe she was picking up a book on how to install a closet shelf? A third was for the videotape of the movie *Mr. Blandings Builds His Dream House*, which I admit, although it takes an imaginative leap, does have lopsided credibility for someone who is repairing a house. The fourth invoice was for a flagpole. There had not been a flagpole outside the original house, so I figured that this was a definite charge of the let's-see-if-we-can-slip-it-through variety.

And so, because of the apparent legitimacy of most of the invoices I had reviewed, my suspicions had been lulled and my wits dimmed by the time I got to the receipt from the Eagle Warehouse for rental of one storage unit, ten feet by thirteen feet, at $270 per month.

I had scanned it, flipped past it, and read six more invoices before my brain said, "Whoa! Slow down there. What *is* this?"

What indeed!

There was a telephone number on the invoice.

I quickly picked up the phone and dialed it. "Hello. Is this the Eagle Warehouse?"

"It would be if the Eagle Warehouse could talk. But it's just your humble servant, Jimmy Kelly."

"Hi, there, Jimmy. Are you the man in charge?"

"That I am. Chief nook and cranny stuffer. What can I do for you, lass?"

"I'm investigating a dubious insurance claim, and I have a receipt from your warehouse that I'd like to talk to you about."

"Are you pretty?"

"Who's your favorite actress, Jimmy?"

"Oh, she's long gone now, but when I was a lad, there was no one who could hold a candle to Rita Hayworth."

"I look exactly like her."

"I always had a soft spot for Lana Turner, too."

"I have Lana Turner's chin. When can I come over?"

"Oh, about an hour or two would do."

"Thanks, Jimmy. Do you like milk in your coffee?"

"Yes, lass. Milk, with a chocolate doughnut on the side."

I put on my tap shoes and my feather boa, picked up the appropriate refreshments at the corner coffee shop, hailed a cab, and rode the hour it took to get to the warehouse in the Bronx, where I was becoming increasingly convinced that Faith Browning had stored her things.

There's an expression I particularly hate associated with the work I do, and it is: "I sold it to the insurance company."

Individuals, by whom I mean creeps, who utter those seven words are always out to defraud. Some are out-and-out criminals. Some are "respectable" citizens. Most are never caught. They burn their own cars, steal their own jewelry, report it to the police, and complain that they were burglarized or robbed. Then they hide the items they *say* were burned or stolen, and put in an insurance claim.

The implied "joke" is that to make false statements to Aetna, State Farm, Federated, Travelers, or Precaution Property and Liability isn't really a theft or a crime, since — what the hell — insurance companies are big, insensitive, stupid capitalist pigs who have taken our money for years, so they *deserve* to be cheated, bled, stolen from, and defrauded.

I won't go on here and now about how repelled I am by such

a skewed code of morality, but I will say that my concern to locate Faith Browning's property, if it did in fact exist *and* if it had been transported intact from her house in Riverdale, had in it a big element of righteous indignation.

I hate cheats.

I arrived at the entrance to the Eagle Warehouse at 3:15 P.M. The taxi driver took my money and left me outside an enormous door made of what looked like medieval floorboards held together with wrought-iron hinges, thunderbolts, and the blood of martyrs. The only things missing were the alligators and the moat. This huge portal was set into the stonework of what resembled the castle in which Dr. Frankenstein had constructed you know who, and I admit that I did feel a shiver of apprehension when I pressed the buzzer over a modern-day speaker installed next to the massive entryway.

"Hello? Who is it?" I heard what was unmistakably Jimmy Kelly's voice.

"Rita Hayworth."

I expected the buzzer to buzz me right in, but nothing happened for about three minutes, so I began to fantasize that, instead of Jimmy, the door would be flung open by a limping hunchback carrying a lighted candelabrum, who probably wouldn't answer to the name Jeeves.

After another minute or two, the door opened quietly — no clinking chains or bloodcurdling shrieks — and a tall, silver-haired man appeared. He had a high forehead, a long jaw, twinkly gray eyes, and a pipe chomped between his teeth.

"It's illegal to smoke inside the building," he said. "But I won't tell if you don't. Rita, is it?"

I stuck out my hand. "My name is Fritillary Quilter, but I think Rita does more to capture the essential me."

The man, no doubt, was Jimmy. He bent down a little to study my face and said, "I don't remember your having so many freckles in 1940, but age does funny things to people. Did you bring the coffee?"

"I sure did."

"I've got a microwave oven in my office. My granddaughter gave it to me. We can heat it up there. Did you bring me a doughnut?"

"I brought you half a dozen, so you can really go to hell with yourself."

Jimmy stopped for a second to beam at me. "Ah, beloved lassie," he said with such great affection that I suddenly realized you *can* buy love, and we proceeded down the hall.

Down the long, long, long hall.

Or should I say dungeon?

No. I'm only kidding. It wasn't really a dungeon. It just looked like one.

The architecture of the Eagle Warehouse isn't really relevant to my investigation of the Browning claim, but it's not every day you get to walk down the halls of what looks like a Transylvanian castle, so it behooves me to explain that it had once been an armory for the National Guard.

For those of us unfamiliar with its history, the National Guard evolved out of our own United States militia, and has been around since 1792. For a whole lot of those years, it stored weapons, vehicles, and other equipment in gorgeous old armories like the one I'm describing. Most were constructed from thick blocks of quarried stone, with towers, battlements, and small windows covered by iron grilles; they are fortresses impregnable to bows and arrows, birdshot, and probably cannonballs. They are not, however, invulnerable to rising heating costs and escalating electric bills.

My guess is that the cost of maintaining these armories became a nightmare, and updating the heating and plumbing about as economical as raising the *Titanic*.

So there they were. Big buildings with wide-open spaces, vast halls, and corridors off of which were literally hundreds of empty rooms.

For what purpose could such an outdated but indestructible edifice be put to use?

An amusement park? A film studio? A parking lot?

Someone who wasn't asleep at the switch came up with just the right answer, realizing that, with relative ease, an armory could be converted into *a self-storage facility*. The vast spaces where military units once drilled could be subdivided into row on row of spooky, long corridors, and the overly large storage rooms could be chopped up into units of more rentable size.

A good idea, and doable.

In the last fifty years, almost all of the old armories in New York City's five boroughs have been sold to private industry, and most have been converted for just that use.

Over coffee and doughnuts, Jimmy Kelly explained the inner workings of the Eagle Warehouse; afterward he took me to the loading dock on Bishop Road and showed me two freight elevators big enough to lift armored tanks. Next to the elevators were padded dollies, a forklift, and hand trucks as wide as minivans, onto which clients could unload their refrigerators, file cabinets, beds, and whatever else they valued, push them onto the elevators, and then pull them down the halls to the individual units they had rented, where they could safely, securely, and privately store their possessions for a monthly fee.

Other than the office area where Jimmy worked (alone on weekends but with his boss, a secretary, and the company's drivers on

Monday through Friday), the building was unheated and had no plumbing. There was a weird, unfinished bathroom outside Jimmy's work area, with bare stone walls and a two-story ceiling, but the rest of the office was nice enough, with an air conditioner, file cabinets, and a new gray carpet on the floor. To the right of Jimmy's desk were nine video monitors; one was pointed at the loading bay, the other eight were focused on different lengths of hallway throughout the premises, and all the way at the back of the office was a small, modern kitchen, with Jimmy's granddaughter's microwave oven prominently on display.

Other than the anachronistic bathroom, all of the interior halls were brightly lighted and wide, and to all intents and purposes, the Eagle Warehouse was perfectly safe.

Safe, but . . .

Creepy.

Too many long, empty corridors.

Too many small, sealed rooms, filled with . . . who knows what?

Monday through Saturday, the storage facility was open from eight o'clock in the morning until seven o'clock at night. On Sunday, its hours were 10:00 A.M. until 4:00 P.M.

"How do people get their possessions here from their homes or apartments?" I asked Jimmy Kelly.

"We give them the use of a truck and a driver, free for the first two hours. It's twenty-five dollars for each half hour after that."

"Does the driver help the client load and unload the truck?"

"Not as part of the agreement they sign with us, and not as part of their bill. If they want to, they can make separate arrangements with one of our men."

"How about the lock on the door, Jimmy? Does the warehouse have the key?"

"No, lass. There's a metal hasp on the door to each storage

room. It's the renter's responsibility to provide his own lock, but we sell them here, if they want to buy one of ours."

"A padlock, right?"

"That's right."

"Do you get a duplicate key?"

"No. Nobody is allowed inside except for the owner."

"What if there's a flood or a ceiling leak?"

"We telephone the person who's rented the space and tell him to get his ass down here right away."

"So you never, never go inside a storage room?"

"Our contract permits it only if the tenant hasn't paid his rent. Then we break the lock, go inside, and after a few months, we auction off the goods."

"Speaking of rent," I said, and I held out the Eagle Warehouse invoice I had found among Faith Browning's receipts. "Can you tell me anything about this?"

Jimmy puffed thoughtfully on his pipe.

"Technically," he said, "I can't tell you anything, since you aren't the renter of record. But it isn't often that a man of my advanced years gets to spend a few hours alone with Rita Hayworth, not to mention Lana Turner's chin, so hand me another doughnut, lassie, and let me see that receipt."

Jimmy swiveled his chair around until he was facing a computer, where he keyed in a few numbers, entered this, and scrolled down to that. Then he hunched forward the same way he had when he'd remarked on my freckles, but this time he was looking at the computer screen.

"Storage Room W-7410," he said. "It was rented to Faith Browning on July eleventh of this year. This is one of our larger rooms, ten feet wide by thirteen feet deep. That particular space rents for $270.00 per month."

Jimmy pressed another series of keys. "She's current on her rent." He swiveled his chair around again and asked, "What else do you want to know?"

I frowned and bit my lower lip.

The warehouse manager said brightly, "Now, lassie. There's no cause to scowl."

I shook my head. "It's not that I'm ungrateful, Jimmy. I just need to know what's in that ten-by-thirteen space, and it looks like there's no legal way for me to get inside."

Jimmy removed his pipe from between his teeth and laid it down on his desk. "There's one thing here that needs clarification," he said.

"What?" I asked glumly.

"Do you have to actually get inside Room W-7410, or do you just have to know what's inside?"

I lifted up my head and peered at Jimmy.

"What are you saying?"

"I'm saying, lass, that I know what's inside the room."

"You're kidding, right?"

"That I'm not."

"But why? How?"

"When the lady in question called and described the job she had, we knew it would take more than one man. Ramón Santiago was the driver. He fixed it up with the client to bring along his two cousins, and they helped him load the van. But when they drove up to the dock here, I had to send Ramón out on another job, so it was I who helped the two Santiago boys to unload."

"You called her 'the lady in question' as though you didn't particularly like her."

Jimmy smiled. "Well, lass. She wasn't overflowing with the milk of human kindness."

"What do you remember about the stuff you unpacked?"

"Everything."

I jerked back my head.

"That's right. I said everything. I have a photographic memory."

"You're kidding."

"Hardly, lass. Write this down. Into Storage Room W-7410 the woman moved one green velvet settee with two matching arm-chairs. There were embroidered curlicues and flowers on the backs of all three pieces. There was an antique wood desk with a brass-studded leather top, a center drawer, and four smaller drawers on each side; there was a mahogany dining room table with six matching chairs upholstered in dark green silk; a brass music stand; a dictionary table; four cast-iron registers in the pattern of a fleur-de-lis; one large framed painting wrapped in brown paper; three smaller paintings, also paper wrapped; an upright grand piano, and the moving of it almost broke my back; a small oak lady's desk, a . . ."

And on and on and on. Jimmy dictated for fifteen minutes, and I wrote down everything he said, including the lily-patterned Tiffany-style lamp, and the green-and-gold area rug, which he somehow knew was of a William Morris design.

After he was finished, I stared down at my notes and couldn't stop myself from shaking my head. Maybe my doing so caused Jimmy to conclude that I hadn't believed him, but what I was really thinking was how did I get so lucky?

Nevertheless, he added, as if to convince me of the accuracy of his memory, "Faith Browning, as it says here on the contract, and I admit that her name had slipped my memory, is in her early to mid thirties. She has dark, shoulder-length hair, and doesn't wear much in the way of makeup. She has a small nose, a generous bosom, and if she'd had a better attitude, I would have said that she was a fine-looking woman. Is that she?"

I started to smile. Then my face broke out in a huge, guess-who-just-swallowed-the-canary grin. If this case ever got to court, the Rita Hayworth Fan Club was going to bowl them over when he testified from the witness stand.

"Mr. Kelly," I said. "You're a genius."

Jimmy picked up his pipe, tamped in some tobacco, lighted it up, puffed a few times, and leaned back in his swivel chair. Then he put his feet up on the desk and, his eyes once again twinkling, said, "Ah, lassie. Why, oh why, did you marry Orson Welles all those years ago when, even though I was still in knee pants, you could have married me?"

chapter
thirty-three

THE FIRST THING I DID when I got back to my apartment was grab the telephone and call Isaac C. Blessing Associates. Since it was Saturday, I knew Ike's office would be closed, but the news was positively bursting out of me, and I couldn't wait. My plan was to leave a long, incoherent message on his answering machine and not care if I was really talking to myself.

Never in a million years did I actually expect anyone to pick up.

Ring. Ring. Clicking noise.

"This is Isaac C. Blessing Associates. At the sound of the beep, leave as long a message as you like, and I'll get back to you."

Another click. A beep. And I was on.

"Hi, Ike. This is Tillary Quilter. You won't believe what I just did! I —"

Another click.

"Hang on, Tilly. I need a towel. . . . Okay. I just got out of the shower."

"You take showers at your office?"

"I have call forwarding to my apartment. Hold on another second or two. Have to get my robe. Okay. Got it. What's up?"

"What's up? What's up? *I'm* up, Ike. I solved our case. I want to talk to you. But in person. No more phones. When can we get together? Do you want me to come to Brooklyn, or do you want to come here? Maybe we could meet halfway in between. I guess I *could* tell you on the phone if I had to, and I probably should have typed this all out first and turned it into a memo, but —"

"Tilly."

"What, Ike? What? What?"

"Calm down."

"No. Yes. Whatever you say."

"I'll get dressed and drive right over. I can be outside your building in half an hour. Tell me everything over dinner."

"I'm too excited to go out to dinner."

"I'll bring sandwiches. If I find a parking space near your apartment, you can buzz me in. If not, we'll eat and talk in my car."

Forty-five minutes later I was sitting in the passenger seat of Ike's car and, between gulps, chews, and swallows, telling him everything I'd learned from the moment I looked at the first receipt in Faith's four-pound pile to my discoveries at the Eagle Warehouse.

"So you see," I finished gleefully, "I've solved our case!"

Ike put what was left of his sandwich into a bag on the dashboard and took a small pad and pencil out of his jacket pocket.

"Tilly." He shifted to face me. "I want you to repeat all the items that were stored in Faith Browning's unit. Start from the top."

I pulled a folded sheet of paper out of my purse and waved in it front of his nose.

"I made you a copy of the list."

"Thank you. Read it out loud and give it to me later. I want to think while I'm listening to you."

So, I began. "One green velvet settee with two matching armchairs; one antique wood desk . . . ," and so on.

When I was done, Ike said somberly, "Sunshine, you did it. Not only have you got your proof of fraud, you've also given me what I need to explain the fire."

"Damn right I have! Only thing I haven't figure out yet is *why*."

"Why what?"

"Why did Faith include the Eagle Warehouse receipt with all the legitimate expenses on the repair of her house?"

Ike rubbed his jaw with the fingers of his left hand. It was prickly. I guess my phone call caught him before he'd had the chance to shave.

"Insurance frauds always think that cops, lawyers, claims reps, and everyone else involved in investigating a claim is stupid," he said. "I saw it hundreds of times when I was a fire marshal. If they get away with x, they think they can get away with y too. Enough is never enough for them. They're greedy, and they make mistakes."

"So you think it was greed? That Faith risked the whole kit and caboodle just to push through a $270 a month warehouse rental fee?"

Ike shrugged. "Sure. Why not?"

"I like it." I chortled gleefully. "I like her stupidity and arrogance . . . and I *love* her greed. First thing Monday morning, Ollie and I are going to turn everything over to the legal department so that Bosley Kellogg can call the police. What do you think of that?"

Instead of answering, Ike asked, "Did Faith Browning send those receipts to you through the mail?"

"Yes indeedy. In the upper-right hand corner of the envelope is a big, fat United States Postal Service Priority Mail stamp."

"Then you've got mail fraud, too, Tilly. And that's a federal offense."

I clapped my hands. "Terrific. We can deny the claim, Faith can go to jail, and we can close the case."

I continued to applaud myself enthusiastically and barely noticed that Ike didn't seem as excited about the case being solved as I was. Maybe catching bad guys wasn't a big deal for him, and catching Faith meant even less. Maybe the insurance fraud aspect of a fire case bored him. Or maybe he just didn't like being dragged out of the shower on a Saturday afternoon.

Maybe. Maybe. Maybe.

Of course, I was wrong about all of my maybes, because . . .

"Tilly, I hate to do this to you."

I stopped handing myself bouquets.

I stopped fidgeting around in the passenger seat of the car.

I barely managed to croak out the words "Do what?"

"Sweetheart, you did a great job at the warehouse. You got solid evidence of fraud, and you don't know it yet, but you also discovered a crucial missing link in how the fire progressed from the point of origin to the rest of house. So you have every reason to pat yourself on the back."

I ignored the compliments.

"What do you hate to do to me?"

He took a deep breath. "I hate to burst your bubble."

"What bubble?"

"Tilly, you still haven't solved the case."

"I haven't?"

"No, sweetheart, because you haven't explained the fire."

"The fire?"

"That's right. There are two aspects to this investigation. One is the fraud, and the other is the fire. We have some questions left to answer about the fire."

"We do?" My mind was a blank. "What questions?"

"Who set it?" Ike said. "When was it set? How was it set? Was Dorsey Browning an accidental victim or was she the target of a homicide? If she was murdered, who killed her? Why was she killed, and —"

"And," I finished the thought for him, "what the hell happened to her nose?"

chapter thirty-four

AFTER IKE LEFT, I dragged my poor ego back to my apartment like a kid trailing a deflated party balloon. I was not a pretty
sight. Nevertheless, I spent the rest of the weekend writing down
various scenarios of who did what to whom, because I was determined to learn how to *think* like a fire investigator.

Ike called my office just after nine o'clock on Monday morning to tell me that, at his request, Hercules Electric had petitioned
the court for permission to reenter the Browning residence so he
could remove various sections of the walls and flooring where he
believed evidence would be found to exculpate the clock radio. I
asked him what this evidence was, but he answered that if I couldn't
figure it out for myself, it wouldn't help any for him to explain it,
and I'd learn more by coming to the fire scene and watching him
do what he did.

Fine with me.

Access to the premises was granted for Wednesday, September 13, from eight o'clock in the morning until five o'clock at
night. Ike would be allowed to photograph and/or videotape his
findings, but he wouldn't be permitted to remove anything from
the house. The court also ordered that by the time the Hercules
Electric people left the premises, the house would have to be returned to its original condition, which meant that Ike needed to

bring along a carpenter to remove the walls and floorboards before he did his investigation and to replace them when he had finished.

As Precaution Property and Liability's codefendant, Ike was required to advise us about the inspection and, at some point in the future, provide us with a written or oral report of his findings. He did *not* have to invite me along, so I was extra-special happy that he did.

With a court-ordered inspection date of September 13, and with Friday, September 15 as the home office's cutoff date for paying, settling, or denying Faith Browning's personal property claim, that left Ike and me only one day to talk about the case.

Tuesday.

I took the subway to his office and arrived in time for the last cup of coffee from his morning pot. I had brought along my trusty legal pad, covered with the inky scribbles that represented two days of work.

There were no papers at all on Ike's desk.

"Don't you take notes?" I asked.

Ike tapped his head. "It's all up here."

"Good, because I have a lot of empty space up here" — I tapped *my* head — "and I've come to you for enlightenment."

Ike settled comfortably in his big leather chair. "That's not the way it works, sunshine." He crossed his arms behind his head, put his shoes up on his desk Texas-oilman style, leaned back, and added, "You're going to enlighten me."

"The Socratic method," I snapped back brightly, smiling at my hero.

"Right. Me Socrates. You Jane. Now, go for it, freckles."

So, I did.

I told Ike that I had been thinking exclusively about the fire in

Faith Browning's house for the past forty-eight hours, and that I'd concluded the fire *and* the resulting homicide could have occurred in any of four ways. I wasn't sure which, but I was certain it had to be one of the four.

I started with my personal favorite suspect: Arthur Dawes.

"We know Arthur was at the Browning house on July fourth. We also know that he was madly in love with Dorsey Browning, and that Buck Fitzgerald wasn't his favorite human being." I looked directly at Ike. "What else do we know?"

The president of Isaac C. Blessing Associates shrugged noncommittally.

I referred to my notes.

"We know that Arthur Dawes went to the McDevitts' party to drool over Dorsey and tell her that she'd been cast opposite him in a television show. Having accomplished that purpose by about six P.M., he supposedly left. But what if he didn't leave, Ike? What if . . ."

I stopped talking for a few seconds to gather my thoughts and gaze out the window. A late summer haze covered the harbor beyond the Brooklyn Heights Promenade and gave the tugboats, ferries, and skyscrapers in lower Manhattan the appearance of floating on a cloud.

". . . what if after taking the path to the front of the McDevitts' house, Arthur waited and waited and waited. What if, tormented by the loss of the woman he had loved both in the real world and in the play, he couldn't make himself leave? What if he wanted to *go* because Dorsey didn't love him anymore, but he wanted to *stay* because he still loved her? He walked to the subway, and he came back. Back and forth. Back and forth." I turned away from the window. In my mind's eye, I could see the young actor pacing up and down Labyrinth Lane. "Maybe he stood like a gargoyle in the bushes, hidden from view. Maybe he went around the block once, twice. Maybe this. Maybe that. We won't know exactly what happened unless he confesses. Either way, Arthur Dawes came back to or never left the McDevitts' property, and he was somewhere in the vicinity of their driveway at seven P.M., when Buck Fitzgerald drove in."

I gave Ike a questioning look. "What do you think so far?"

Ike's voice was unmodulated and uncritical. "I'm listening."

Encouraged, I went on.

"From where Arthur was hidden in the bushes, he watched Dorsey get in the Jeep with Buck; he continued to watch the two of them until Dorsey got out and Buck drove away. Then Arthur became enraged. He . . ."

"Wait a second." Ike interrupted. "Where does this rage come in?"

"It started when Dorsey got in Buck's car."

"What caused it?"

"Jealousy." I started to pace. "Arthur went to the party hoping for a reunion with Dorsey. Ever since he'd been cast in the same television show as she, he'd been fantasizing that he could get her to fall back in love with him. Instead, he'd had to watch the woman who had dumped, betrayed, and abandoned him throw herself into the arms of the man who had dumped, betrayed, and abandoned her. *That's* where the rage came in."

I stopped pacing and looked at Ike.

"I'm not missing a word," he assured me.

"Good." I consulted my notes and continued. "Dorsey returned to the McDevitts' party after Buck drove off, so Arthur wasn't able to confront her right away. But an hour or so later, when Faith brought Dorsey home with her Big Headache and left

her there, alone and defenseless in that big old house . . . That's
where my first big *what if* comes in."

"It has to be consistent with the facts."

"Oh, it is. *What if* Arthur followed Faith and Dorsey back to
the house, waited for Faith to leave, and sneaked into Dorsey's
bedroom? *What if* Arthur tried to argue Dorsey into falling back in
love with him? *What if* she rejected him, they fought, he inadvertently killed her, and then he set fire to the house?"

"When was all this happening, Tilly?"

"After eight-thirty."

"Aren't you forgetting something?"

I did a rapid scan of my legal pad. Ike was right. I'd forgotten
that Alistair McDevitt and Faith Browning went back to Faith's
house at around nine-thirty in search of a bottle of vermouth.

Doing a rapid reconstruction of the events in my head, I said,
"Not a problem. Instead of Arthur confronting Dorsey right away,
he broods for a while, letting his anger and his rage build and
build and build, watching Faith and Alistair come. Watching
Faith and Alistair go. Then sometime around ten P.M., he sneaks
into Dorsey's room, flips out, attacks her, and" — I snapped my
fingers, which was rapidly becoming my favorite means of self-
expression — "dead."

I resumed pacing in circles in front of Ike's desk.

"Physical evidence?" he asked, his eyes following me.

"Broken nose," I responded. "In attempting to quiet or kill
Dorsey, Arthur inadvertently or deliberately breaks it. Second
item of physical evidence: Death. Dorsey dies. The rest of the
physical evidence has to do with the fire. I'm only making an in-
ference here, but I think when Arthur realized that he had killed
Dorsey, he wanted it not to have happened, and he wanted to

make it go away. He's an actor, and he's used to making things disappear. Scene over? Go on to the next scene. Dorsey dead? Bring the curtain down on that, too. Arthur arranged Dorsey on the bed so that she'd look as if she had been overcome by fumes. I don't know if he brought matches with him, or if he found matches or a cigarette lighter somewhere in the house, but he got ahold of some sort of an ignition source, and he set fire to the room."

"Where, Tilly? How?"

"In the bedding first. Then he crumpled up some papers or tissue in the area of the clock radio. That was his second fire, and would explain the burn patterns on top of the night table. Maybe he used flammable liquid on the floor. Lighter fluid, or WD-40. That's something else he could have found lying around the house."

I scrunched my forehead and tried to picture the room where the fire had occurred.

"He *had* to use an accelerant, or we can't account for the holes in the floor. He set the fire, closed the door behind him, and left." I nodded, satisfied that I had it right. I asked Ike, "What do you think?"

Instead of answering, my imperturbable fire guru did the Socrates thing again and responded with a question. "Sweetheart, how wedded are you to this sequence of events?"

"Why? What's wrong? Didn't I get it right?"

He dropped his feet to the floor, leaned forward, and said, "Give me your second hypothesis."

I gulped back my disappointment. "Okay. In that one Buck Fitzgerald is the murderer. He's as plausible as Arthur Dawes, but I don't like to think of him as a killer."

"Why not?"

"Because Buck's a decorated Gulf War veteran, an uncommon

individual, and a self-made man. He had to break all sorts of molds to be who he is and do what he's done, and he makes me feel good about being human, so I don't want him to be the bad guy. But I'm trying to be objective, so I threw him in the pot anyway."

"Objective is always admirable."

I didn't know if Ike was making fun of me or not, so I ignored him. "Ike, if Buck killed Dorsey, then he lied to you."

"About what?"

"About Dorsey saying that she'd marry him, Buck wouldn't have killed her unless she'd turned him down. What if . . ."

"Another murderous rage?"

"Hey. A Gulf War veteran blew up the federal building in Oklahoma City, so an honorable discharge is no guarantee of stability."

I started to pace the room again, feeling very much like my eighth-grade history teacher, Mrs. Winter, who used to march up and down in front of us like a drill sergeant when she rattled off the reasons for the Civil War. "Dorsey tells Buck she would rather eat a thumbtack sandwich than marry him. Outwardly, Buck appears to be handling her rejection with equanimity and poise, but deep down inside, he's seething."

Ike watched me intently, his elbow bent, his jaw resting on a fist.

"Explain something to me, Tilly." Ike's light eyes turn dark blue when he's thinking, like those executive toys that, if you touch them, change color and conform to the shape of your fingers. "If Buck proposed to Dorsey and she turned him down, why was she in such a good mood when she got back to the party?"

I perched on the edge of Ike's desk; I was starting to enjoy this.

"That's easy," I said cheerfully. "The rejection was painful to *Buck*, but it was *liberating* for her. Dorsey had walked away from the degrading quagmire of an affair with a married man, but now it was over, and she was ecstatic with relief. On top of that, good old reliable Arthur was waiting for her in the wings, and . . . and . . . and" — I drew it out dramatically — "she'd been cast as a continuing character in a plum television show. Why was Dorsey Browning happy? Life was good. Why not?"

Ike stood up. "More coffee?"

"Sure."

I followed him to the kitchenette, but didn't stop talking. "The logistics of how Buck killed Dorsey would have been pretty much the same as they were for Arthur, except that Buck could have waited inside his car. He just had to drive it a few yards beyond the turnaround in front of Dorsey's house and it would have been invisible from where the McDevitts were sitting."

Ike measured in the coffee grounds. When he got to the sixth scoop, I said, "In deference to my nerves, please, please, *not* firehouse coffee, Ike. Just for today."

He dumped the last scoop back into the bag.

I reached in the cupboard for two mugs.

"My third suspect was going to be Chloe, Buck's wife, but I decided to make it Lillian Mayhugh instead."

Ike looked up from the percolator. "Now, you've got my attention."

"That's because you don't like her. Lillian Mayhugh," I said, repeating her name as if trying it on for size. "If Lillian murdered Dorsey and set her house on fire, there are at least three reasons why she would have gone about it differently than Arthur or Buck. One, she wasn't invited to the party; two, nobody saw her anywhere near Labyrinth Lane on the Fourth of July; and three, she had no apparent reason for being there."

Ike plugged in the coffeepot.

"What's her motive?" he asked as I trailed him back to his desk.

"That's easy. I figured out the motive when we were at Newark Airport and she was flirting with you."

"Sunshine, I thought you liked her."

"I do like her, but I'm not, deaf, dumb, and blind. Lillian Mayhugh is a flirt. She's a tease, too, which I would consider a character defect in me but not in a movie star. Lillian likes men. She liked to flirt with them, and she likes to keep them off balance. That's not a crime. Murdering somebody, though, is a crime and would definitely bump her off the list of those who deserve my unequivocal admiration."

Ike looked at me dubiously, but remained silent.

"Let's say . . ." I pulled up a chair opposite him and did a finger tattoo on top of his desk. "Let's say that in spite of her genuine affection for Dorsey, Lillian has a bit of a personality disorder, and that she was . . . was . . ." I was trying to find the right word.

"A pyromaniac?" Ike suggested.

I gave him a scornful look.

"No. An egomaniac. That's what Dorsey called her in one of her letters. An egomaniac with a heart of gold. And let's say that even though Lillian adored her little protégé, and I believe that she really did, she hated the idea of being upstaged more than she loved anybody. Even Dorsey."

"You think Lillian murdered Dorsey because Dorsey had a bigger part in the play than she did?"

"No, Ike. Of course not. She was too much of a professional to mind being upstaged *on*stage. But backstage was something else. Before she left us at the airport, she alluded to the possibility that someone else, meaning Lillian herself, might have fallen in love with Buck Fitzgerald that night in the dressing room, and that you should consider her a suspect, too. At the time, I believed she'd said that only to annoy you, but what if Lillian was telling us the truth? What if she really *had* fallen in love with Buck Fitzgerald?"

Ike scratched his ear. Then he studied his knuckles.

"Aw, come on, Ike. Hear me out."

He looked up and met my eyes. At least he was listening.

"I'm not saying that Lillian fell in love in love, the way a normal person does, but that she fell in love the way a goddess would. A high and haughty goddess who wasn't accustomed to rejection, and found it incomprehensible that she was being overshadowed by a mere slip of a thing, i.e., her stage daughter. Ego. Ego. Ego. That's why she killed Dorsey, and that's why she flirted with you."

Ike gave me a duh-I-don't-get-it look, so I added, "She flirted with you because you're a man, and because you were there."

"Are you saying Lillian Mayhugh falls in love with every man she meets?"

"No, but that she's accustomed to men responding to her. For two very good reasons, Buck did not respond. One: He fell in love with Dorsey. Two: Dorsey fell in love with Buck. A perfect circle, except that, instead of being in the center of it, Lillian Mayhugh was left out."

Ike shook his head, but I didn't care. I was on a roll.

"As long as Buck was still married," I continued, "Dorsey was safe from Lillian's wrath. But as soon as our stylish Brit realized that Buck's marriage had gone belly-up and that he was pursuing the younger woman for keeps, she —"

"Another jealous rage?"

"Exactly, Ike. Lillian drove to the house in Riverdale. She parked her car somewhere unobtrusive."

"How do we know that she has a car?"

"She waited until everybody was drunk and Dorsey was alone in the house; then she sneaked into Dorsey's bedroom and . . . you know the rest."

The coffee started to perk.

Ike leaned back again in his chair with an unconvinced expression on his face.

I, however, remained undaunted.

"I have three more suspects," I said quickly, eager to avoid his skepticism.

"Three individual suspects, or a conspiracy of three?"

"Definitely a conspiracy."

"Does it involve another jealous rage? I don't know how many more of them I can take."

"Absolutely not. No jealousy. No love. No hate. No passion. No emotions at all. Just cold, calculating greed."

"Good," Ike said. "I like greed."

"Actually, in some ways this is my favorite. I like it better than I like my Arthur Dawes scenario, because it has a certain je ne sais quoi. If I'm right about it, and I think I am, what *must* have happened is that, immediately after Faith brought Dorsey back to her bedroom, she murdered her sister and set fire to her own house."

Ike said nothing. He walked to the coffeepot and filled our cups. I tagged along beside him, unsuccessfully trying to read the expression on his face.

"To the extent that Faith communicated with us and our lawyers at all," I said hurriedly, "she was lying. She lied to the fire marshals, and she lied to the police."

Ike handed me a cup. He brought his to his desk.

"The McDevitts lied, too." I leaned against the back of my

chair. "They were up to their elbows in ashes from day one. In fact, all three of them were in on it together. Faith Browning, Beatrice McDevitt, and Alistair McDevitt."

Ike peered at me over the rim of his coffee cup. "What were they in on, Tilly?"

"A conspiracy to murder Dorsey Browning."

"Now why would they want to do that?"

"The reason isn't obvious, Ike. Not in the least. So don't feel bad about missing it. I was sidetracked, too, because there are so many intense emotions floating around in this case. Arthur Dawes is passionately in love with Dorsey Browning. Dorsey Browning is madly in love with Buck Fitzgerald. Buck is head over heads for Dorsey, but he loves his daughters more. Chloe, the always-looming ex-wife, wants Buck but loves the entire outfield of the Mets. Lillian Mayhugh adores herself and anyone who wears a jockstrap. And everybody loves the theater. Love. Love. Love. So it was easy to miss that this fire isn't about love at all, even though I should have figured it out as soon as I saw that big old house on Labyrinth Lane. What Dorsey's death and this whole case is about, Ike, is *property*."

Ike looked at me dubiously. "Which property?"

"The house and grounds that Dortimer Browning left to his daughters when he died, *and* the house and garden owned by Dr. and Mrs. McDevitt, also on Labyrinth Lane."

Ike looked at me blankly. "I don't get it."

"It's easy," I explained. "If you combined the Browning and the McDevitt lots, you'd have over three acres of land in Riverdale within spitting distance of Embassy Row. That's the equivalent of owning a square block on the boardwalk between the two top casinos in Atlantic City, which in today's market is worth millions — maybe even billions of dollars. Think of it, Ike. Millions and millions of dollars. Dortimer never would have sold the house when he was alive, because he was madly in love with it. But after he died, Faith considered it hers and believed that it was all systems go. And it might have been, if her sister hadn't had a nervous breakdown and scurried home. And when Dorsey started to repair her childhood bridges and islands, all bets were off. Dorsey was going to turn their inheritance into a shrine for her dead father, and Faith would never, never, never be able to sell her half of the house. No house sale meant no big money, and Faith wasn't going to let that happen, so she sat down with the McDevitts, and all three of them decided that Dorsey had to die."

Ike shook his head. "It doesn't work, sunshine. If the McDevitts wanted to sell, why get involved with Faith? Why not just put an ad in *The New York Times*, grab the money, and run."

"They couldn't do that, Ike."

"Why not?"

"Because of synergism. "

"What's that?"

"Synergism is the whole being greater than the sum of the parts. The Browning and McDevitt properties together were worth a fortune. Separately, they were only two old houses in the Bronx. That's why the McDevitts threw in their lot, no pun intended, with Faith. They were as greedy as she was, and almost as guilty. They lied to us about everything, Ike. There *was* no Fourth of July party. There *was* no vermouth. Nor were there fans, a brooch, and an old volume of Tennyson in the library that Alistair just *had* to get. Dorsey didn't have a headache, nobody poured champagne, and nobody toasted her new job. What really happened was that Faith killed her sister, and the charming, dignified McDevitts helped her. Smack. Smack. Thump. Thump. Burn. Burn. Everything else was just a detail."

Ike looked at me steadily. Then, sadly, sadly. Slowly, slowly, my fire guru, my Socrates, shook his head.

There was a bleak expression on his face.

Sixty very tense seconds went by with neither of us saying anything. Then very patiently, very softly, Ike said, "Tilly, are you aware of any real estate companies or conglomerates that have made any offers to buy either the Browning or the McDevitt property within the last six months?"

"No, but —"

"Has anyone told you or have you in any way been made privy to conversations between Faith Browning and Beatrice or Alistair McDevitt regarding plans to sell their homes and/or to kill Dorsey Browning?"

"No, but —"

"Can you think of any reason why, if the McDevitts were party to this arson homicide, they would be the ones to call the fire department, thereby ensuring that the room where the fire started would be preserved before the whole house was consumed by flames?"

"No, Ike. But —"

"Tilly, sweetheart, sit down."

I sat on the floor, exactly where I had been standing.

Ike walked over. Then he hunkered down next to me so that our eyes were level, and I have to admit that, under the circumstances, he was really very gentle when he said, "Sunshine, we have to have a long talk, and we may as well start it now."

"What about?" I asked weakly.

"About what constitutes evidence."

chapter thirty-five

I WILL NEVER FORGET the feelings I had the first time I saw that beautiful house on Labyrinth Lane.

In retrospect, I think my reaction had a lot to do being twenty-five years old. I hadn't been away from the intimate artifacts of my childhood for all *that* long, and it had been only seven years since I'd last played tennis in Meg Nelligan's backyard. Older, more experienced people know how to modify the highs and lows of their emotional responses; they know how to keep their evocative memories firmly in place. Not me, though. I'd just rolled over on my back, stuck my paws in the air, and let my memories rub my belly. Therefore, it was something of a shock for me to return to the big Victorian, a mere fifteen days after my first visit, and realize that most of my initial perceptions of it had been wrong, wrong, wrong.

Not about the house's structure or size. I scored an easy ten on that. I just couldn't have been further off base with regard to its mood and atmosphere. It was as if my mind had colorized a picture that had really been printed in black and white. The Browning house was *not* the Nelligan house. Maybe years and years ago, when Faith and Dorsey Browning were little girls captivated by their father's emotional munificence, it had been a happy home, but not now. And not for a very, very long time.

Ike had told me to bring along my camera, so I tucked it, a little bitty thing, into the pocket of my jeans.

He picked me up outside my apartment at seven in the morning, and having survived the implied admonitions in his rules-of-evidence speech, I was little Miss Snap, Crackle, and Pop, ego restored and eager to learn what had to be learned on a brand-new day. Ike drove and talked and asked questions and prodded me the whole time we were in the car to think about what we had learned so far on the case, and to "put all of the variables together" by myself.

"Variables," I echoed blankly. "*Which* variables?"

This was his list:

- The burn patterns, with particular emphasis on the two holes in the floor. The first hole was in the baseboard, between the night table and the bed. The second hole was in the flooring toward the center of the room, midway between the head and the foot of the bed.
  What did those burn patterns mean?

- The path of the fire
  Where did the fire go after it broke out of the bedroom?

- The condition of Dorsey's nose
  Was it broken before or after she died?

- Dorsey's death
  Was she murdered, or did she die as the result of an accident?

- The fire itself
  How and when had it started?

- Balloon construction
  Why was it relevant in this case?

"Do *you* know all of those answers?" I asked Ike.

My fire investigator nodded.

"And I suppose you already know what we're going to find when you pull up the floorboards in Dorsey's room?"

He looked at me. "If one and one still equal two and water still runs downhill, I know."

What was *that* supposed to mean? I wondered silently. I said aloud, "How about motive, Ike? If someone set the fire, do you know what his motive was?"

"You don't need motive to prove arson, Tilly. You just have to show that a fire was incendiary in nature, and that your suspect had the opportunity to set it."

I found that most unsatisfactory.

"Don't you *want* to know why?"

Ike patted me on the shoulder. "Don't worry, sunshine. You'll get your motive."

Ike and I beat the traffic and got to the Browning residence at a quarter to eight. The carpenter that Hercules Electric hired had arrived a minute or two after us. He was a taciturn fellow named Angelo, with a bulldog jowl and stubby, varnish-stained fingers that were all the same length. Angelo seemed content to sit on his toolbox and wait for someone to tell him what to do. At about five minutes to eight, two cars turned into Labyrinth Lane at the same time. One was the Hercules Electric corporate counsel, a broom handle with a law degree who never introduced himself, didn't smile back when I smiled at him, and had eyes the color of clear soup. He didn't say a word the whole time we were there and had come, I suppose, because some partner in the firm told him to baby-sit his experts. The driver of the second car was Faith Browning's attorney, one of the little teapots I'd met at the deposition.

Much to my surprise, Faith was also in the car. In the passenger seat.

I shot a look at Ike. "Did you know she was going to be here?"

Ike shook his head.

"Is it a good thing or bad?"

"I don't know, Tilly. Just don't let her hold your wallet."

When she got out of the car, I realized that in the weeks since I'd seen her, Faith Browning had changed as drastically as had my perception of her house. Both had relinquished something in the nature of gloss and allure, and neither was in as good shape as I'd expected them to be. Faith had lost a lot of weight and, instead of prancing around in designer clothes, was wearing dark slacks and a too-big denim shirt over an unremarkable tank top. She cast only one hostile glance at Ike and me, which given her usual behavior, felt as if a red carpet had been unrolled at our feet.

Faith was quiet; she was obviously unhappy. And, unlike the first time I had seen her, she didn't even try to make an entrance.

Which was beside the point. The point was: Why was she there at all? Yes, this was her house. But why not let her lawyer handle all the details? Why would she, or anyone in the middle of litigation, want to be anywhere in the vicinity of opposing counsel if she didn't have to? Unless she felt that she personally had to protect her interests from charlatans like Ike and me?

Faith unlocked the front door, and as we followed her up the porch steps, I realized that the house, although sparsely furnished, was no longer bare. There was a pale brown sofa, love seat, and ottoman combination in the living room with a small, wrought-iron coffee table in front of the sofa that was probably on loan from the backyard. I could also see the edge of what looked like a massive oak armoire in the dining room. The foyer was still empty, which didn't surprise me, since I knew that most of the original furnishings, including the upright piano, were in storage at the Eagle Warehouse.

Some famous person, maybe it was a movie director, once said that "atmosphere is everything." In spite of the promise I'd made to myself to be objective, as I climbed that flight of stairs I realized that I couldn't have agreed more. There was something unpalatably wrong with just about everything in that almost empty house, and by the time I got to the second-floor landing, I had convinced myself that everything about it — including its walls, floors, and ceilings — was steeped in grief.

I followed Ike, who was following Faith and her lawyer, and I caught a glimpse into the two bedrooms that overlooked the front driveway. One bedroom was Faith's, which, according to our court order, was totally and absolutely off limits. Court order, schmourt order. I was going to search it. It and all the other upstairs bedrooms as well.

But not yet.

First I trailed after the legal honchos to "the fire room," which in Ike Blessing lingo is where the fire started. The way Ike explained it on the phone, his plan was to take up the floorboards and subflooring in Dorsey's old bedroom because he wanted to look at the floor joists in both areas where the fire had burned through the floor. Why he wanted to pursue this esoteric forensic investigation he did not explain. I did, however, realize that, while he and the carpenter were doing that, it was the job of the rest of us to keep our mouths shut and stay out of their way.

Dorsey's room had changed since the first time I'd been there. Then it had coral walls and was empty. Now it looked like a small luxury suite in a Caribbean hotel. There was a floral chintz sofa where Dorsey's bed had been, and a white wicker desk where Dorsey had had a chest of drawers. Elsewhere in the room were armchairs, throw pillows, end tables, lamps, a bookcase, and a bureau. A hooked rug covered a small section of beautifully varnished tongue-and-groove floor in the center of the room, and the floor itself was pristine.

Humph, I thought as I considered the room's flawless planes. How the hell is Ike going to find evidence of anything at all in here, let alone evidence that there had once been a fire?

But my doubts weren't his doubts, and it took Ike and the carpenter only a few minutes to move all the furniture up against the west wall, as far away as possible from where the fire had begun.

After the furniture was moved, Ike showed Angelo where Dorsey's night table had been, and Angelo chalked off two feet along the baseboard with a tape measure. Then he looked up at the fire investigator for approval, asking, "Here?" Which I soon realized was his entire vocabulary of the spoken word.

Ike nodded and paced off six feet from the baseboard, to a point a few inches to the left of where the center of Dorsey's bed used to be. The carpenter, tape measure in hand, grunted "Here!" and opened his tool chest. He removed a claw hammer, a chisel, and a circular saw, and with an audience that was immediately reduced by one, he set to work. I was the minus one, because as soon as I heard the first grinding chords of the circular saw, I unobtrusively slipped away.

Something had been nagging at me since my first visit to the Browning house, and I was determined to find out what it was. I sneaked into the hall outside Dorsey's bedroom and stood motionless for a few minutes, waiting for the house to "talk" to me. Slowly, slowly, I started to rotate like a sunflower, not sure under which cloud the sun was hiding on an overcast day.

Talk to me, I commanded the house. Talk to me, talk to me. I knew that even though this house in which I was standing *was* an architectural duplicate of my childhood friend's home, it also *wasn't*

I paced the second-floor corridor. Up Down. Up. Down. I studied the ceiling. The walls. The floor. I tiptoed past the door to Dorsey's room and entered the smaller of the two front bedrooms. The one that was *not* occupied by Faith.

It was rectangular, unfurnished, and had been painted melon green. Being of the opinion that only lawns, money, and pistachio ice cream should be green, I was not favorably impressed. In Meg's household, this had been Mrs. Nelligan's sewing room, and as a teen I'd spent hours there attaching sequins to collars and basting stitches on sleeves and hems. If memory served me well, the tiny closet to the right of the door had not been altered and was exactly the same size, shape, and location as the one in Mrs. Nelligan's house.

I rooted myself in the middle of the room, activated my girl-photographer internal measuring device, and did a slow turn.

I concentrated. I observed.

Nothing appeared to be out of place, out of balance, or out of kilter, so I returned to the hall.

On my way past Dorsey's room, I stopped for a few seconds to peek inside. Ike was blocking my view of Faith and her lawyer, which meant that they also couldn't see me. Angelo the carpenter had run the circular saw toward the center of the room and was turning it at a right angle, so I continued quietly past the door and down the hall into Faith's bedroom.

Weird room. Not unattractive in and of itself, but more what you'd expect for a man in his sixties or seventies than for a young woman who loved beautiful things. As I looked around, I decided that it had probably once been Dortimer's bedroom, and that, other than a post-fire cleaning and fumigation, nothing since his death had been changed. A huge, ancient mahogany bed dominated the space, with spiky pineapples topping the bedposts and a thick, dark, tapestry bedspread with a unicorn motif. Across from the bed was a big chest of drawers that I think is called a chiffonier, and next to that was a davenport-type sofa. There were new silk lampshades on candlestick lamps, a brown corduroy reading chair with an aged afghan tossed over one arm, and a beautiful cherry secretary at which Faith paid her bills (I looked through the envelopes).

There were also, I noted with a great deal of resentment, a whole lot of framed family photographs on the walls, tabletops, and shelves. Lots and *lots* of photographs, which made a complete fabrication of Faith's declaration to Beatrice McDevitt that none of her pictures survived the fire.

Dorsey, too, was well represented in this gallery, with a series of photographs showing her as a toddler through high school on the wall behind Faith's bed. A final picture on Faith's night table was a medium close-up of Dorsey in her Emily costume.

There's a line in *Our Town* when Emily and George are talking to each other from their respective bedroom windows just after they realize that they've fallen in love.

Emily says to George, "— My, isn't the moonlight *terrible?*"

The look on Dorsey's face in the picture reminded me of that scene. She is gazing skyward with enormous, luminous eyes and a wistful smile on her face. Luminous. Arthur Dawes's word. Arthur Dawes's description. And as soon as I saw that photograph, saw the girl *in* that photograph, I felt as if I knew her. Knew her from the shiny crest of her soul down to the very tips of her toes.

I wasn't aware that I'd spoken aloud, but after the words came out, I heard myself say, "Hello, Dorsey. So *that's* who you were!"

And suddenly, I was very, very sad.

I did a cursory search of the rest of the room before I embarked upon my unmethodical comparison of Faith's bedroom with the one I'd grown up with, and when I was done, I took Dorsey's photograph off the wall, slipped it into my purse, and left.

No. I didn't know what I was looking for.

But I did know that I hadn't found it.

When I returned to the hall, I couldn't hear the circular saw's strident whirl, but I caught the carpentor saying, "Here?" "Here . . ." and "Here!" in an otherwise silent room. Whatever Ike and Angelo were doing was apparently absorbing the attentions of everybody inside sufficiently that I would probably be able to get away with one more search.

At least one.

I opened the door across the hallway from Dorsey's room to what, in the Nelligans' house, would have been Meg's bedroom. I used to sleep over at Meg's house a lot and was familiar with every crack in the ceiling, every loose segment of butterfly wallpaper, and every crevice in the closet where we used to stuff our chewing gum, for no reason I can think of that makes any sense.

In Faith Browning's house, Meg's bedroom had been turned into what I call a "hodgepodge room." Neither library nor den, it was a little bit of each. A place you could flop on a leather sofa, scribble in a diary, or sit with your legs flung over the arms of a comfy chair, listening to records of 1940s and '50s Broadway musicals on a stereo system as old as the shows from which they came. There were a gigantic, brown-and-beige hooked rug, a large brass telescope pointing at the floor instead of out the backyard window, and an antique rolltop desk with a multitude of pigeon-holes. An enormous, gold-framed lithograph of the solar system hung over a barrister's bookcase that contained four shelves of books on astronomy.

I was, obviously, in what had once been Dortimer Browning's study.

The first time I'd been in the house, all the rooms, even this one, had been empty. Since then, every item must have been scrupulously cleaned, restored to its original condition, and repositioned with museum-like accuracy.

I stood silent, listening to what the room had to say. Listening to the cushions on the chairs, the pens in the penholders, the drapes on the windows, and the stacks of envelopes pushed to one side of the crowded desk. Slowly, slowly, slowly, my mind attuned to any and every nuance of size, shape, and shading, I began to turn.

My eyes rested on the doorway to the hall.

Nothing there.

I studied the bedroom's south wall, knowing that the stairwell was on the other side.

Everything just right.

I looked at the old-fashioned casement windows on the room's east wall, paid for by Precaution Property and Liability and identical to the original windows that had been replaced.

Nothing fishy there.

I evaluated the framed lithograph of the solar system over the bookshelf on the north wall.

My eyes shifted slightly to . . . to . . .

Something was wrong.

Something was odd.

Something was definitely out of kilter.

I thrust my mind back to Meg Nelligan's bedroom.

I cast myself back in time.

Thinking. Thinking. Thinking.

The distance to the north wall from where I was standing should have been exactly three steps. In Meg's room, on that very same wall, there had been a pastel painting of a ballerina in a pink tutu.

Okay, here we go.

One step.

Two steps.

Two and . . .

Stop.

In Dortimer's study, no third step was possible. The room was shorter by a little over two feet. There was a door in the north wall that opened into a private bathroom. I entered the bathroom and paced it off.

It was off by a foot and a half.

I thumped my fist against the wall that separated Dortimer's hodgepodge room from the bathroom. Tap. Tap. Thump. Thump. Quiet tap taps. Quiet thump thumps. I scrutinized every joint and ripple in the wallpaper. I ran my fingers over every inch of baseboard trim. Then, hoping I might snap something free or jar something loose, I jammed my foot against a small area of trim where it jutted out an eighth of an inch from the baseboard, and before I realized it was happening, a two-foot segment of bathroom wall swung open on an invisible hinge.

My heart jumped and lodged itself in my throat like a fishbone; it started to pound wildly. Bam. Bam. Bam. I thought for sure I was going to have a massive coronary; I took a deep breath and ordered myself to get a grip. The pounding continued, so I decided to ignore it, rationalizing that twenty-five-year-olds don't have massive coronaries. At least, none that I knew.

I peered inside the dark enclosure and groped along the walls on both sides for a light switch. Then I waved a hand around in front of my face until I felt the spidery, soft string of a pull cord. I yanked. A bright overhead bulb illuminated the dark recess of a hidden closet.

Fascinating.

The closet was five feet deep by thirty inches wide. If I'd been in England, it probably would have been a historical curiosity called a priest's hole, built during one of the Reformations to hide Catholics from some pissed-off king. Since it had been added surreptitiously to a house built in the late nineteenth-century in the United States by a man who believed in UFOs, I wrote it off as another manifestation of Dortimer Browning's eccentricity.

All three walls of the closet were covered with narrow shelves, and the shelves, I quickly realized, were filled with journals. The spines of the ones along the back wall were date-stamped in gold foil: 1955, 1956, 1957, and so on, up to the year before last. I arbitrarily pulled out 1980 and perused a few lines Dortimer Browning had written about Tyrangea, its people, its planetary orbit, and its place in the general scheme of things.

Gently, respectfully, I returned it to its shelf.

I pulled out more journals from different shelves and discovered Dear Diaries in Faith Browning's schoolgirl hand and a play written by Dorsey when she was ten years old. I also found a fragile stack of faded love letters from Dortimer Browning to his new bride. I spent too long reading the love letters, and only after I'd wasted precious minutes did my eyes fall on a small black box located on a shelf very near the closet's entrance, in front of a row of leather journals that looked almost new.

On an instinct that it was going to be important, I took the camera out of my jeans pocket, focused, and snapped off two pictures. Then I pulled a tissue off a shelf in the bathroom and used it to carefully lift off the box's lid.

Bam. Bam. Bam. My heart started to do it again. Like a billy goat butting its head against a refrigerator door. Bam. Bam. Bam.

I removed the top of the box. I gently laid it aside. I looked inside.

There it was. What I hadn't known I'd been looking for, but after dozens of spins and rotations, many measurements, and much pacing, had ultimately found.

My first inclination was to pop it all, box included, into my purse and bring it back to Ike, the way a cat brings its master a dead mouse. But *stealing* isn't high on Isaac C. Blessing's list of approved activities at a fire scene, so after a millisecond's thought, I left it where it was.

I raised my camera to my eye and continued taking pictures. I used a pencil to manipulate the object and photographed it from all sides. When I was done, I put the lid back on the box and used the rest of the film to shoot the closet from every angle I could think of, each click of the camera scaring me half to death. The hardest part was waiting for the damn flash to recycle before I could take the next shot.

The whole time I was doing it, I was also dying to stop everything and look for Faith's journal, if there was one, of the incidents that had taken place over the past six months.

But I restrained myself, and click.

Wait for the flash. Click.

Do it again.

When I was finally, finally finished, I tucked my camera back in my pocket, turned off the light, and did a quick be-still-my-heart. Then I took a deep breath, or least tried to, and very, very carefully, I crept out of the room.

chapter thirty-six

NOBODY NOTICED I'd been gone.

Nobody noticed when I took up a position next to Isaac C. Blessing. Even Ike didn't seem to realize I'd returned, since he was staring at the carefully delineated boundaries of what was going to be a Big Hole.

As soon as I walked in, I felt a tactile tension in the room, as if everyone was waiting for someone or something to leap out from behind a sofa and yell, "Surprise!" The silence was as oppressive as the tension, and all eyes were tracking Ike like hungry puppies waiting for a bone.

He made no move or gesture to acknowledge that I was back, and when he spoke, it wasn't to me but to the carpenter. "Pull it up, Angelo. Then give me the hammer and move aside."

Angelo removed the last floorboard, and Ike turned to the rest of us. We were lined up like tourists peering over the edge of the Great Divide, agog with anticipation.

"We're here to find out what happened in this room," Ike said, his eyes dark with intensity. "This was not an easy fire to investigate, because this is not an ordinary house. Fifteen years ago, at the Howard Hotel in Gramercy Park, I investigated a similar fire in a similar series of rooms. Because two separate fires had broken out on two different floors, the security director tried to convince me an arsonist had set them both. I knew he was off base, because there was no forced entry, and even though there had been a potential for massive destruction, the fires were small and inconsequential.

"The first alarm went off on the seventeenth floor. The second on the nineteenth floor. Since multiple points of origin are often indicative of arson, there was reason to consider the fires suspicious. But often isn't always. What happened fifteen years ago at the Howard Hotel is relevant to what happened here on the Fourth of July, so there's a reason why I'm telling you this.

"The fire at the Howard started at a short circuit in a fluorescent light fixture hooked to the ceiling of a linen closet on the seventeenth floor. The short created a spark that ignited nearby combustibles, and the combustibles burned inside the ceiling panels above the light fixture for ten or fifteen minutes before spreading horizontally to an air conditioner duct.

"Once the fire had reached the ductwork, it was free to communicate vertically, igniting small particles of ceiling material and dust as it moved upward from floor to floor. Eventually, sparks flew out of the ductwork and landed on a panel of floor-to-ceiling draperies hanging next to the air conditioner vent on the nineteenth floor, igniting them, too. That's why, even though there were two separate fires in two separate locations, unconnected by what we call a 'burn pattern,' there was still only one point of origin — in the fluorescent light fixture in the linen closet. Nobody set the fire; it wasn't arson."

Ike paused for a few seconds to glance around the room.

"When I was called to investigate this fire, I thought I might be dealing with a similar scenario. But the room where the fire started, *this room*, had been gutted and rebuilt before I got here, so there was nothing left for me to look at."

I turned to see how to Faith Browning was taking Ike's implied criticism, and wasn't surprised to see an angry and defensive look on her face.

"Fortunately," Ike continued, "a fire department photographer took pictures of the fire scene before it was altered. We were able to show those photographs to a judge and convince him that crucial evidence might still exist. Specifically, the court approved our request to remove a six-foot-by-two-foot section of flooring and subflooring, and examine the floor joists and wall studs under this room."

Ike pulled a hammer out of his back pocket. Then he turned to me.

"Would you please get my camera?"

I did a quick search of the wicker furniture, saw his camera bag perched on a floral chintz pillow, walked over, and brought it to him.

"*You* take the pictures, Tilly."

I grimaced but not intentionally. Ike's camera, not being a point-and-shoot, is much more sophisticated than mine, and as we all know, I have this little problem with f-stops and synchronization.

"Don't worry." Ike read my mind. "Focus in the crosshairs." He showed me where they were. "Here's the focus, and here's how you advance the frame. The flash recycles immediately. It's easy. You'll do fine."

He stepped back from the hole and shooed away everybody but me. "Take some establishing shots first, Tilly. I want a record of how the area looked before I remove the wood blocks from the floor joists."

A floor joist, for those as ignorant of building construction as I was, is one of many wood beams that run parallel across a room, from one wall to the opposite wall. Their purpose is to hold up a ceiling or a floor. I took half a dozen shots of the exposed joists from every angle I could think of. Then I stepped back. Ike returned to the hole and crouched over the edge.

By now, everybody was staring at perfectly aligned, finished and unfinished, stained and unstained, sanded or rough-cut lengths of wood, utterly fascinated by bare planks, the mere thought of which would ordinarily put them to sleep. Hell, I was staring too, but it wasn't until my eyes linked up with my brain that I realized what I was looking at. Ike had told me earlier that floor joists are always two inches by six inches, two inches by eight inches, or two inches by twelve inches, but that a house as old as this would probably have been built with the larger and heavier boards. He was right. Two-by-twelves were exactly what we were looking at through the opening at our feet.

In the post-fire pictures Ike showed me at his office, I had seen a badly charred floor with big burn-through holes gouged into its surface. In rebuilding this room, Faith's contractors had first torn out the burned flooring. They had nailed new subflooring to the old floor joists, and then nailed bright, beautiful, squeaky clean tongue-and-groove oak boards on top of the new subfloors.

Per Ike's instructions that morning, Angelo the carpenter had sawed out and removed a two-foot-by-six-foot segment of the new floor and new subflooring. We were now staring into the hole he had created. As I looked down, I could see tiny bits of char in the open spaces (they're called "bays") between the floor joists. What these burned bits had been before the fire is anyone's guess. Now, they were indisputable evidence that there had once been a conflagration.

Ike flipped his hammer to the claw side and pointed to two

short, clean boards nailed to either side of a badly burned two-by-twelve joist. He inserted the claw behind one of the new boards and cautiously pried it away. Then he did the same to the second board, letting both of them drop to the ash-strewn ceiling of the den below.

Ike moved forward a few inches and blocked my view. When I leaned over to get a better look, I momentarily met Ike's eyes and gave him an encouraging smile. In return, I got a barely perceptible twitch of the left side of his upper lip.

"As soon as I saw the photographs of the burn patterns in this room," he said, shifting his body and restoring my view, "I knew that the Hercules Electric clock radio hadn't caused this fire."

I heard angry whispers behind me, turned and caught the tail end of a heated, if inaudible, exchange between Faith Browning and her lawyer. The little teapot put a schoolmarmish finger over her lips; Faith responded with a hostile glare. Then she clamped her jaw shut and seethed.

I enjoyed the performance thoroughly.

Ike didn't seem to have noticed it before he went on. "The reason I knew that my client's product didn't cause the fire was that the fire department's photographs clearly indicated flammable liquid pour patterns in at least four separate locations in this room. The first burn pattern consisted of a three-inch hole between the night table and the head of the bed, where fire had eaten through the baseboard into the floor and extended six or seven inches toward the center of the room. In one fire department photograph, I could see down through the hole to the ceiling of the den underneath."

Ike stood up and walked to the north wall of the room, where the head of Dorsey's bed had been. The toe of his right foot rested inches from the bare area that had been exposed by the carpenter after he had removed the baseboard and trim.

"Low burning is rare in an accidental fire, but we could see in the photographs that fire had violently attacked the flooring here and had incinerated a big chunk of the back and bottom of the night table. This low burning is a clear indication that flammable liquid was used.

"Flammable liquids are accelerants," Ike continued. "Which means they speed up a fire's rate of burning by making the fire burn hotter, faster, and more intensely. Accelerants are composed of hydrocarbons, and hydrocarbons can penetrate porous fibers more efficiently than water, and can infiltrate areas that water can't."

Ike knelt beside the bare area of wall where the baseboard had been. "If you pour an accelerant like gasoline, kerosene, or turpentine, it's going to soak between the floorboards before it burns away." He touched the handle of his hammer to a dark pattern etched into the floor joist. "Imagine that you're painting a window and making a messy job of it. Paint is slopping over the bottom edge of the windowsill and spilling down the side of the wall. When it dries, it looks like dribbled varnish, or stalactites, or tears. Now imagine that someone is pouring kerosene, gasoline, or turpentine on the floor of a room. Flammable liquid penetrates through the floorboards to the floor joists underneath, and when that room is set on fire, a pour pattern is going to be seared into those floor joists that looks exactly like the sloppy paint job I just described. Fire investigators call this a 'weeping' burn pattern." Ike looked up. "For obvious reasons."

When he looked down again, he pointed at a charred area on the original floor joist. Only seconds before, the black marks etched into the wood's surface had meant nothing to me. Now they had the unmistakable look of tears.

Tears.

Weeping.

Of course.

When Dorsey Browning died in this room, the room itself had wept. Ike Blessing, my mentor, my fire investigator, was teaching me that tears are more than just heartbreak; they're evidence. Solid evidence that a flammable liquid had been poured and a permanent record had been etched into the floor joists below. Solid evidence that an incendiary fire had been set, and that a woman hadn't just died but had been murdered.

I stared at the weeping burn pattern, shaking my head and thinking, Poor Dorsey. Poor, happy, sad, beloved, and betrayed Dorsey.

Ike stood up, and the abrupt motion snapped me back to reality. He returned to the hole in the floor where he had pried the two clean boards off the old joist. Now that I understood what he was looking for, I could see a similar weeping burn pattern on that old floor joist, too.

"Sometimes," Ike said, "fire investigators talk about an 'arson triangle'; there are three points in this triangle, and in the course of investigating a fire, it's our job to identify all three. The first is to prove that a crime was committed, and that we're not looking at an accidental fire. The burn patterns in this room are unequivocal. We know this was a set fire. The second point of the triangle is opportunity. We have to prove that an arsonist had access to the fire scene, and that he was there at the time of the fire. Opportunity was the dead end I kept running up against, because I didn't know the ignition source. An ignition source can be a match, an explosive, an intense concentration of heat, or a combustible combination of chemicals. Without knowing what the ignition source was, I couldn't know how the fire had been started, and without knowing how it had been started, I couldn't know who had started it."

Ike tipped an imaginary hat in my direction.

"At least, I didn't know these things until my colleague, Fritillary Quilter, provided me with a crucial piece of evidence."

Crucial piece of evidence?

Me?

The last time I looked, Ike had been admonishing me for *ignoring* the rules of evidence.

He motioned forward his little group of on-lookers, and I felt Faith sidle up behind me. Since she wasn't whispering, glaring, or fidgeting, I wondered if she'd been as gripped by Ike's explanation as I was, or if, as my mother used to say, she had "swallowed her tongue."

"Look under this charred floor joist," Ike commanded.

We followed his finger with our eyes.

"The room under here is the den. After the fire, someone nailed a wood panel about the size of a legal pad onto the ceiling of the den, right beneath this joist."

I leaned over.

Yep. I could see it.

Ike stood up and brushed off his jeans. His eyes briefly met those of Faith Browning, and I swear I heard our policyholder gasp.

"This is an old house," Isaac C. Blessing said, thankfully retrieving his camera from me. He aimed it somewhere west of his feet and clicked the shutter.

"According to Fritillary's research, it was constructed in 1885. Since then, the plumbing and electricity were modernized, but the rest of the house hasn't changed. In particular, if the heat had been turned on, the furnace that was installed about forty years ago would have been distributing warm air the same way on the Fourth of July as it did in 1885."

Ike snapped two more pictures.

"The physical evidence of this fire told me that it had started in this room, but I still couldn't figure out how any of my suspects could have gotten into Dorsey's bedroom to set it. Another big problem was why the McDevitts, who lived next door, hadn't seen flames shooting out of the back of this house until eleven-thirty at night."

Ike stepped to the other side of the hole, positioned his camera at a new angle, and took another shot.

"Even though I didn't know when and how the fire started, or who started it," he went on, "I had already put together a few two and twos and was sure about my time parameters. I believed that both of the two men who visited Dorsey Browning on July fourth had left by seven-fifteen. I also believed that, after spending time in a car with one of them, Dorsey immediately rejoined her sister and the McDevitts in their backyard.

"Witness statements added some more variables to my time line. The first was Faith Browning saying that she was hot. This occurred after Dorsey came back to the party but before a headache forced her to leave. The second was Faith going into the McDevitts' kitchen for some fans."

Ike stopped to take a breath, and in the brief pause that followed, I heard a rustle of fabric behind me and an angry exchange of words. Then Faith elbowed forward and demanded, "Exactly what are you implying, Mr. Ash-Man?"

Instead of answering, Ike directed a raised eyebrow at Miss Browning's attorney, who promptly dragged her client to the back of the room.

"The next three incidents also took place before Dorsey went to bed," Ike continued. "One. After Faith returned from the Mc-Devitts' house with the fans, a bottle of champagne was opened. Two. At around eight-fifteen, Faith proposed a toast to Dorsey's new job on a television show. Three. Within minutes of drinking the champagne, Dorsey developed an excruciating headache, and Faith had to bring her to her room and put her to bed. On the surface, all three actions look innocent, but —"

Faith broke away from her lawyer. "I don't have to listen to this!"

This time, Ike looked toward his client, the Hercules Electric attorney, who presumably was present to defend our right to be there. Mr. Personality, however, avoided Ike's eyes and said nothing. So good old Bosley Kellogg leaped into the fray.

"Miss Browning," he stated firmly, "we have a court order that permits us to examine the floor joists in this room. It does not, however, require you to remain here while we do so. You may leave at any time."

"Ridiculous!" Faith erupted. "This is *my* house. I insist that *you* leave!"

Bosley looked at Ike and shrugged, so Ike ignored them both and went on.

"Another significant event occurred at about nine-thirty, when Faith Browning and Alistair McDevitt walked across the lawn to get a bottle of vermouth from her den. Initially, I didn't think this was relevant, because Dr. McDevitt stated unequivocally that Faith was never out of sight or earshot during the less than two minutes she was in the den. The only way out of the den was through the library door, and that's where Dr. McDevitt was standing. So it seemed impossible for Faith Browning to have been the arsonist or to have set the fire in Dorsey's bedroom."

"Amen!" Faith said loudly, as though Ike had doused her with holy water.

"The times were wrong, too," he went on methodically. "If Faith had set a fire in Dorsey's room at nine-thirty P.M., and I couldn't prove that she did, how could she have kept it from being discovered for another two hours?" Ike shook his head. "No matter how I fiddled with my time line, I couldn't make it work."

He handed me his camera. Again.

I took it from him and let it drop to my side.

"An incendiary device," Ike went on, "— any incendiary device, whether it's a rope soaked in gasoline or a candle with a two-foot wick, has just one purpose, and that's to give the fire setter enough time to get away from the fire scene to establish an alibi.

"Since none of my time frames worked, the only possible conclusion I could come to was that the person who set this fire was resourceful, intelligent, and clever enough to have devised a way of delaying ignition. But when had he or she done it? Where, and how? Was the fire premeditated? Or was it set on the spur of the moment by an arsonist cool under pressure, spontaneous, and shrewd? I just didn't know."

Isaac C. Blessing stepped over the hole again. He put his arm around my shoulder and gave me an affectionate squeeze. "At least, I didn't know until this budding genius here discovered that someone had removed four cast-iron registers from this house after the fire, one of them from this very room."

I croaked out the word "Register?"

But what I was thinking was "Budding genius?"

Ike released me and hunkered down over the legal-pad-sized piece of wood he had pointed out a few minutes before.

"On the night Dorsey Browning died," he said, "there was a

register in the ceiling of the den, between these floor joists, exactly where this plywood insert is now. Directly above it, where we're now standing, was another register. They were separated only by the twelve-inch height of a floor joist. But when we took up the floorboards this morning, we didn't find a register, and if you went downstairs, you wouldn't now see a register or a hole in the ceiling of the den, because after the registers were removed, both openings were sealed up."

Bosley Kellogg, who was rapidly becoming my favorite lawyer, raised his hand, as though he were in school. "Ike. Excuse my ignorance, but exactly what is a register?"

"A register is a grille that lies flush with and fits over a hole in a floor or ceiling. It's usually made of ornamental brass or cast iron, and it's designed to allow a maximum amount of air to pass from the room below to the room above to more evenly distribute heat."

"Thanks, Ike."

"You're welcome. Anything else?"

Bosley shook his head, and Ike continued. "Once Fritillary told me about the registers, I could integrate them into my time line. I've already said that someone poured flammable liquid in this room, but other than describing one pour pattern at the base of the night table, I haven't told you where it was poured, who poured it, when, or how. The *when* was sometime around eight-twenty P.M., after Faith brought her sister home with a headache. The *how* was with kerosene. Dorsey was already either unconscious or dead at the time. Faith arranged her on the bed, got kerosene from a closet or a cupboard somewhere, and splashed it in the bedding, on the night table, and on the floor between the night table and the bed. Then she laid a trail of flammable liquid from the baseboard behind the night table to the register in the middle of the floor. Faith removed the register, splashed kerosene on the floor joists and subflooring, and put the register back. Then she shut the door to Dorsey's room, returned the kerosene to where she'd found it, and hurried back to the McDevitts' party, getting there within fifteen minutes of when she'd left and calmly reassuring her neighbors that she had tucked Dorsey safely in bed. About an hour later, Faith told her hosts that she wanted to get a bottle of vermouth, but her real purpose was to go back to the house so that she could re-enter the den and set the fire.

"And so at approximately nine-thirty on July fourth, while Alistair McDevitt was examining books on the library shelves outside the den, Faith Browning was standing on the seat of a chair she'd positioned directly under the register in the den's ceiling. It's my guess that she used a log igniter instead of a match, since there's a fireplace in the den. She flicked it on, pushed the flame through the grid of the register, and held it against the flammable-liquid-saturated joists and floorboards of Dorsey's room overhead until they caught fire a minute or two later. The same minute or two it would have taken her to find a bottle of booze."

I was stunned.

Never, never, never had I really suspected that Faith set fire to her own house. My conspiracy theory was one thing. Greed and revenge have a warm and fuzzy appeal to an admirer of nineteenth-century French novels. Faith involved in insurance fraud? Yeah. Sure. Faith would happily defraud anybody of anything, and thanks to my friend at the Eagle Warehouse, I could even *prove* that she had.

But Faith as an arsonist? Faith as a cold-blooded killer?

No, I thought. No way. What possible motive could she have? Why would she . . .

Then I remembered the hidden closet, and what I'd seen in that small, black box. I remembered what Buck Fitzgerald said about Faith's pathetic attempts to one-up Dorsey.

I remembered —

Ike interrupted my thoughts. "And that brings us to the time delay."

Again, I heard movement behind me.

I craned my neck, and . . . Well, well, well. Faith Browning, unbeknownst to her attorney, was inching toward the door. I looked anxiously at Ike, but he shook his head dismissively and kept talking.

"In the 1880s, a lot of houses were built in a construction style called 'balloon construction.' This is one of them."

Aha! I thought. The balloon construction mystery, solved at last.

"After Faith ignited the joists and floorboards under this room, the fire smoked and smoldered for a while without really taking off. Ten or twenty minutes later, it began to move between the den's ceiling and Dorsey's bedroom floor, slowly spreading horizontally to the studs on the walls that hold up the house."

Ike walked back to the north wall of the room, where the night table had been and where a small section of Sheetrock had been removed, exposing horizontal floor joists and vertical two-by-fours. These two-by-four boards, also called "wall studs," extend *up* to the attic and *down* to the cellar. Each stud is separated from its neighboring stud by sixteen inches of empty space. Like the spaces between floor joists, these are called "bays."

In a house under construction, where nothing has been erected but the infrastructure, walls studs are the vertical boards that compose the house's skeleton or frame. As the rest of the house is being finished, the interior and exterior walls will be attached to those studs.

"Nowadays," Ike said, "most houses are built of platform frame construction, which means that all the floors in every room extend beyond the interior walls to the exterior walls of the house, and the floorboards in the small space between the interior and exterior walls act as fire stops, to prevent smoke, flames, and heat from traveling up the void between the wall studs.

"But this is an old, balloon construction house, and the floorboards are nailed to the interior walls. That means there's a void between the inside and the outside walls, and no fire stops. Come here," Ike said. "I'll show you what I'm talking about." And he drew us toward the wall and told us to look down.

Sure enough, there was a four-inch gap between the inside wall of the room and the outside wall of the house, and it went around the room like a moat around a castle. As soon as I saw it, I recalled the day that Ike and I had stood in the cupola and he'd dropped a silver dollar through a crevice between the floor and the wall to demonstrate how an object could fall straight down to the cellar without hitting a single floorboard anywhere in between.

"I already mentioned that the fire in the Howard Hotel was similar in some ways to the fire in this house," Ike said. "In the hotel fire, cinders traveled vertically up an air conditioner duct and started a second fire two stories away. Here, the fire migrated horizontally under the flooring to the vertical bays between the wall studs on this north wall, where it smoldered for over an hour before bursting into flame. After the fire got going, the void between the inside and outside walls served as an air shaft or conduit and, like the air-conditioning duct at the Howard Hotel, allowed flames to travel up to the attic, the cupola, the windows, and the roof."

"When did it break through the roof?" I asked.

"At around eleven-thirty. Two hours after Faith stuck a flame through the register in the ceiling of the den."

Two hours, I thought. One hundred and twenty minutes. That was a hell of a lot of time for fire to smolder in the nooks and crannies of a house. Enough time for . . .

I made a slow circle of Dorsey's bedroom with my eyes. "Ike. Why wasn't —"

"I know, Tilly. Good question. You want to know why, if there was so much fire in the rest of the house, this room wasn't completely destroyed."

That's *exactly* what I wanted to know.

"Before the fire started, someone had closed all the windows and doors in Dorsey's bedroom. Not opening them was the only mistake the arsonist made. One confusing aspect of this fire is that it went in two different directions. You know about the fire that moved up the bays between the wall studs and took out the roof. The fire in this room was much less eventful. First, flames followed the trail of kerosene up through the register, partially consuming the floor, the baseboard, and the night table beside Dorsey's bed. The fire went on to burn her bedding, shoulder, hand, and foot before using up all of the available oxygen in the room. Without oxygen, a fire goes out, and that's what happened here. That's also why, even though the upper floors of the house were demolished by fire, this room survived relatively intact."

I dropped my pencil. When I bent down to pick it up, I realized that She Who Had Been Sneaking Out Behind Me was no longer there.

"Ike!" I blurted out in a panic.

"Not to worry," he said.

He turned to Faith's attorney. "I think your client figured out that this isn't about a lawsuit anymore."

The little teapot sniffed indignantly; then she, too, walked out of the room.

That left only the good guys. Me. Ike. The Hercules Electric attorney. And Bosley Kellogg. I moved closer to Ike and whispered, "The medical examiner's report stated that Dorsey didn't die from fire, and nobody dies of a headache. So what killed her?"

Ike dug into his pocket, pulled out a tiny, brown bottle, and gave it to me. I read the label: "Nitroglycerin tablets 0.4 mg." Dumbfounded, I handed it back.

"I found a bottle just like this one in the McDevitts' backyard."

The McDevitts' backyard! Of course. I remembered seeing Ike reach down between two pieces of slate with his handkerchief that day. I'd been going to ask him what he had picked up, but I forgot.

"When the McDevitts were taking off the furniture covers," he said, "I saw the sun glint off something next to my chair. My gut told me it might be important, so I was careful of fingerprints. The prints on the bottle I found are being identified as we speak."

"What prints?" Bosley Kellogg interjected. "What bottle?"

"The bottle Faith got when she complained to the McDevitts about the heat. She didn't really go in their house to get fans. That was a ruse so she could get nitroglycerin tablets out of the bathroom."

"*What* nitroglycerin tablets?" Bosley persisted.

"The ones she'd put there herself. Her father had angina, and Faith asked the McDevitts to keep a bottle of his heart medication in their bathroom. Just in case."

Bosley nodded. Then he shook his head.

"Dortimer Browning died months ago. Why would they still have this in their house?"

I thought back to the ancient jar of Vaseline and the long-expired bottle of aspirin I had seen in the McDevitts' medicine cabinet. "Believe me, Bosley," I said. "They never throw anything out."

Then I tapped my finger against the bottle in Ike's hand. "Ike, do you think this whole thing — the arson — the murder — do you think all of it was premeditated?"

"No. I think some catalyst that night pushed Faith over the edge, and she snapped. Whatever it was, it triggered a response that didn't interfere with her ability to coolly plan and execute a murder. Faith knew about the bottle of nitroglycerin in the medicine cabinet because she'd put it there herself. She had to think fast to steal the bottle, unscrew the cap, and when no one was looking, dump the tablets into Dorsey's glass of champagne."

I suddenly remembered a detail from our interview with Beatrice McDevitt. One that Ike had mentioned earlier. "Faith proposed a toast to Dorsey's new job."

"Right, Tilly. And the person being toasted always feels obligated to drink, so Dorsey probably drained her glass."

I considered that for a few seconds.

"Wouldn't Dorsey have seen or tasted something wrong?"

"Nitroglycerin dissolves instantly, and it's tasteless. But the side effects hit her like a Mack truck."

"The dizziness, the flush, and the headache."

"That's right. A violent headache brought on by a rapid fall in blood pressure. The low blood pressure caused Dorsey to stagger when she got to her feet. When Faith grabbed her, she didn't realize that she'd dropped this."

"This" being the small brown bottle nestled innocently in Ike's hand.

"Then what?" I prodded.

"Then Faith helped Dorsey back to the house."

"Like a good older sister?"

"Like a good older sister."

"How did she break Dorsey's nose?"

"I don't think she did. Everything about this case is typical of a murderer who wants to distance herself from the reality of her crime. A fatal dose of pills dumped into a glass doesn't require physical contact, and you don't have to touch your victim when you're pouring flammable liquid out of a bottle. Faith even set the fire from a different room, on a different floor. So I think the broken nose was an accident. A fluke. We know Dorsey was on the verge of losing consciousness after drinking the champagne. I think she stumbled and cracked her nose on the way into her bedroom. There's a smudge on a picture we have of the doorframe to Dorsey's room. I think that smudge is blood, so we may even have a photograph to prove it."

"Big sister poisons little sister," Bosley reiterated, a look of confusion still on his face. "She does it impulsively and deliberately. I get that part. What I don't get is why, if Dorsey was already dead, Faith set a fire?"

"She set the fire to destroy the evidence." Ike shook the small bottle of pills. "An autopsy wouldn't have detected an overdose of nitroglycerin, but Faith didn't know that. She panicked as soon as she realized that she really had killed Dorsey, and she decided to get rid of the body."

"Enter kerosene," I said. "Enter vermouth, alibi, and register, the last of which I so brilliantly discovered."

"That's right, Tilly."

"Where did Faith get the kerosene?"

"She already had it in the house. More than one witness told us that she used kerosene lanterns at her parties."

I started to nod, but an unresolved thought intruded. "Wait a second, Ike. Faith poisons Dorsey. Dorsey dies. Faith gets away with it. So why would she draw attention to herself by suing Hercules Electric?"

"I don't think that she planned to sue anybody, but when the fire marshal said the clock radio caused the fire, it was as if he gave her a gift of misdirection."

"I still don't get it," Bosley said before I had a chance to admit that I didn't get it either.

"Faith was thinking long range," Ike explained. "She thought if she took on the guise of an irate policyholder whose sister was the victim of a defective product, nobody would ever call the fire incendiary, and nobody would think arson or murder."

"It worked, too." I nodded my head vigorously. "I just wanted to get her for insurance fraud. Even after you proved it was arson, I didn't suspect Faith."

Ike tucked the nitroglycerin bottle into the front pocket of his jeans and took the hammer out of his back pocket. He looked like he was getting ready to leave, but I had a few more questions, so I grabbed the hammer out of his hand.

"Ike, do you think Faith is going to skip town?"

"I doubt it."

"Where did she go?"

Isaac C. Blessing smiled. "My guess? To get a criminal defense lawyer."

"Is she running scared?"

"Nope. Faith Browning is sure she's smarter than the rest of us. That's the way people like her think. She'll be smarter than us on the day she's arrested; she'll be smarter than us when the jury's deliberating the verdict; she'll be smarter than us when she's serving a life sentence for murder."

Ike took his hammer out of my hand. "And she'll be smarter than us fifty years after she's dead."

chapter thirty-seven

IN THE CAR ON THE WAY BACK to Manhattan, I asked Ike about the arson triangle. "You said that it has three points, like a real triangle. First you have to prove that there's arson."

"That the fire was incendiary in nature. That's right, Tilly."

"Second, you have to prove that the arsonist could get in to do the dirty deed."

"Opportunity, sunshine. Right again."

"So what's the third point on the arson triangle?"

"Motive."

"Ah. Motive," I said, breaking into an enormous grin. "Motive is exactly what I've been thinking about all along. What do *you* think Faith's motive was?"

Ike Blessing turned his eyes away from the road for a long moment to look at me. "Sweetheart," he said. His diamond blues were nowhere near as serious as the solemn expression on his face. He had a nice face, I noticed, not for the first time. Square jaw, blond stubble, and smooth skin. Skin the color of a perfectly baked croissant. "I'm a good fire investigator. I'm good at reading burn patterns. I'm good at interviewing witnesses, and I'm good at getting bad guys to confess. I can also change the spark plugs in a

1957 Chevrolet, and I have a great recipe for Thanksgiving stuffing. But I'm not the greatest psychologist in the world, so how about I leave the 'motive' part to you?"

Me?

Me, as in the person who'd been pawing around in Faith's possessions while he and Angelo were playing cut-and-paste in Dorsey's bedroom?

Me, as in the person who violated the court order, went places I wasn't supposed to go, looked at things I wasn't supposed to see, and found things I wasn't supposed to find?

I sighed heavily. If Ike was going to trust me to figure out an arsonist's motive, I guessed it was confession time. I told him everything I'd done, even though I hurried through most of the measuring, pacing, probing, and searching parts, until I got to where I discovered the hidden closet. Then I stopped, indulged in a long, dramatic pause, and told him about the box.

"What was in the box?"

I dug my camera out of my pocket.

"I'm not going to tell you. I'll show you."

By then, we were on the FDR Drive heading south. I told Ike to get off at the Ninety-sixth Street exit and drive down Second Avenue, because I knew there was a one-hour photo shop a few blocks from my apartment.

He pulled up at an empty meter, I dropped off the film, and while we were waiting the thirty-eight minutes it took to develop my prints, he turned to me with a very un-Ike-like expression on his face.

"Don't think of me as your friend, Tilly; think of me as a pissed-off district attorney who wants to know what you were doing at that fire scene this morning. And before you say anything, I want you to consider the legal ramifications of your answer."

I was surprised by Ike's sudden change in mood, but I didn't argue. I closed my eyes and thought back to my search of the second floor of Faith Browning's house. I remembered how I'd carefully paced off the rooms. I remembered my initial disappointment at finding nothing, my excitement at the discovery of the hidden closet in the hodgepodge room, and . . .

Then I opened my eyes. Ike still looked remote and forbidding. Even the expression in his blue, blue eyes.

So I thought about *that* for a few more seconds.

I reconsidered my answer.

I wasn't smiling, and I wasn't too sure of myself either when I said, cautiously, "I . . . I was so interested in . . . in . . . what the fire investigator was doing in Dorsey's room that I stayed there the entire time and I watched you . . . him . . . work."

Ike's voice was low and commanding. Very biblical and Judgment Day. "Are you sure?"

I felt my heart starting to do that damned billy goat bam bam bam thing again.

"Yes, sir. I'm sure."

Ike patted my knee.

He dries my tears. He pats my knee. He protects me from irate district attorneys.

Nice guy.

"Good. I don't want you getting jammed up for breaking the law."

Nag. Nag. Nag.

"A court order permitting us to investigate burn patterns under structural members in a house does *not* constitute blanket permission to search the homeowner's closets, drawers, or personal papers. Understood?"

"Yes, Ike. It's understood."

I said it, but I'd said it tentatively, as though my brain were a hand feeling its way blindly through a briar patch of moot points. Therefore, not only was I unready, but I wasn't in the *least bit ready* for Ike's next mood swing. He reached behind my neck, pulled my head forward, and gave my forehead an avuncular kiss.

My *forehead*, for God's sake.

Old men are so weird.

Then he released me and whispered into my ear, "Good work, Tilly. Don't do it again, but I'm proud of you."

I smiled. A big slice-of-watermelon smile, because no less than twice in one lifetime my beau ideal had said he was proud of me.

Proud. Proud. Proud.

Of me. Me. Me.

That was really neat.

I looked at my watch, saw that almost forty minutes had passed, and ran into the shop. A few minutes later, Ike was slipping the pictures out of the envelope and looking at the one I'd taken first, of the small black box on the shelf of the hidden closet.

"In situ," I announced, using the archaeological term for an object that is photographed in its original position.

I leaned toward Ike as he flipped through the pictures until he got to the one I took of the box with the lid off. I wanted to gauge his reaction when he saw what was inside.

It was, of course, Beatrice McDevitt's turquoise brooch, and it looked exactly as Beatrice had described it: a big blue stone surrounded by gold twists, faux pearls and diamonds. It was *the* turquoise brooch, I had no doubt, that Beatrice had pinned to Dorsey's dress the night she was murdered.

"This," I said, holding up the picture, "was the motive. This is the reason why Dorsey Browning died."

Then I sketched out for Ike the series of big or little events that I believed had built and built and built in Faith's mind until, overcome by whatever nut jobs are overcome by, she had reached into her back pocket and pulled out her homicidal maniac pill.

Later in the week, after the police got a warrant, searched her house, and read her diaries (which were later used by the prosecution to show intent and by the defense to show diminished capacity), two facets of Faith's personality were revealed that supported my theory of what had happened. The first was that she was a control freak. As long as Faith could dominate her father, fussing about what to eat, what to wear, how to spend his money, *and making him do what she told him to do,* she was as happy as a robin tugging at a big, fat worm. Even after Dortimer died, she continued to enjoy her position as head of the household, and she was in heaven after Dorsey came home a complete and total nervous wreck.

Everything was going well for Faith while Dorsey's world was crashing in around her. First Dorsey's father, the man she loved longest, had died. Then Buck Fitzgerald, the man she loved most, had abandoned her. By the time Dorsey came whimpering home, her play had closed, she had no professional identity, and she had zero self-confidence. Dorsey was exactly the delicious morsel of pathological insecurity that Faith needed to boost her own rapacious and unhealthy ego.

Older sister coddles younger sister. Older sister protects her, encourages her, feeds her, plans her day . . . *manages* every aspect of her life in the way that only one who is dominant and successful can *manage* one who is weaker and less capable of succeeding in the vast and unforgiving arena of life.

Arena, as in stage.

Stage, as in theater.

Theater, as in beautiful, talented Dorsey, toast of Broadway and long-term leaseholder on vast portions of her father's heart.

Which brings us to the second facet of Faith's personality, the one that she would deny, sputtering and protesting indignantly, to her dying day: the jealousy facet. Faith Browning was violently, vengefully, and insidiously jealous of her younger sister.

Faith was jealous of the acting roles that Dorsey got.

She was jealous of the roles Dorsey didn't get.

She was jealous when Dorsey fell in love.

She was jealous when the love affair ended in disaster.

If Dorsey had been injured in a skiing accident, or mugged, or falsely arrested for a crime that she didn't commit, Faith would have been jealous of that, too. As long as Dorsey had a will, and that will manifested itself in her gargantuan love of life, Faith Browning would continue to hate her younger sister with a smoldering jealousy so deep and so perfectly hidden from everyone, including herself, that Dorsey's only means of salvation was distance, or failure.

Dorsey was safe when she lived and worked in Manhattan, away from Faith and the house in Riverdale. She was safe after her nervous breakdown, when she was a parasite-like appendage who drifted aimlessly around their backyard. Dorsey's nervous breakdown had segued into depression. Depression implied failure, and failure was foodstuff to Faith.

And so, on the Fourth of July, Dorsey's death warrant had been written in the glow that was cast by the resurrection of her happiness, and she was killed by her own joy. Because Faith Browning could tolerate many things, but she could not, would not, and did not tolerate Dorsey regaining her magnificent sense of life and her professional success. That and all of those other many, many galling successes.

First was Arthur Dawes. Loved by Dorsey, rejected by Dorsey, and back again to offer Dorsey not only his heart but also a plum role on an award-winning television show.

Outrageous.

Then there was Buck Fitzgerald. Rich, famous, celebrated, and unavailable Buck Fitzgerald. Buck had dumped Dorsey and returned to his wife. But Buck was back, too, not only throwing himself like a mutt at Dorsey's feet but also asking her to marry him. Marry him!

Unacceptable.

And worst of all, worse than Dorsey's happiness and success, was that terrible moment when Dorsey, not content with flaunting her men and her job offers in Faith's face, had taken the one thing that had always and indisputably belonged to Faith and Faith alone: Beatrice McDevitt's devotion. Because, for whatever unfathomable reason — and Faith didn't even want to *think* about it — she'd always known that *she* and not Dorsey had been Beatrice McDevitt's *preference*.

Her favorite.

Always. Always. Always.

Faith *owned* Beatrice McDevitt's love.

Just as she "owned" the cheap turquoise brooch that Beatrice gave to Dorsey when Dorsey's strap broke on the Fourth of July.

"Anyway," I finished with something less than a flourish. "That's my theory."

"So Faith killed her sister for a pin? Is that what you're saying?"

"No. I'm saying that even though Faith kept her green-eyed monster in a cage for years and years and years, it broke out the night Dorsey got everything she'd ever wanted, which was the same night Faith felt she'd lost everything she had ever wanted to possess or control. Beatrice giving Dorsey the brooch was just the pin that pricked a balloon already filled with toxic gases. It had to, and it did, explode."

Ike grunted. He took the photograph of the brooch out of my hand and stared down at it. "Ugly," he said, a sour expression on his face.

I took it back and studied the twists of gold, the small fake diamonds, and the three or four minute faux pearls. "I think it's sort of pretty myself."

"No." Ike shook his head. "I mean Faith's soul."

chapter
thirty-eight

WITHOUT LETTING THEM KNOW where the informa-
tion had come from, Ike made sure the right people in the right
positions of power knew how to find the hidden closet in Faith
Browning's house, so that after search warrants were issued they
would be able to locate the brooch.

That small piece of jewelry, along with the McDevitts' sworn
statements about the events that transpired at their doomed
Fourth of July party, guaranteed Faith's arrest. The fire department photographs proved that no item of jewelry had been affixed
to Dorsey's dress when her body was found in the debris of the
fire. There were no pins found in what was left of the burned bed-
clothes. Nor was any jewelry listed in the personal effects the
medical examiner's office returned to Faith after the postmortem
and before Dorsey's body was released to the funeral home.

All of which meant that for the brooch to have ended up in
Faith's possession, she had to have taken it off Dorsey after Dorsey
drank the nitroglycerin-laced champagne, and before Faith set
the fire.

If there had been an innocent explanation for Faith having
taken the brooch, the brooch would have been found among

Dorsey's things in her bedroom. It wasn't. Only homicide and theft were consistent with it being hidden away in a secret closet. On top of which, Faith's fingerprints were all over the small black box, and her thumb print was on the back of the pin.

Stupid woman. Stupid, jealous woman.

Along with the diaries and the brooch, the police eventually found Dorsey's long lost will tucked between Act One and Act Two of the leather-bound edition of *Our Town* that Lillian Mayhugh had given her.

In it, Dorsey had left everything to her sister, Faith.

Her residual beneficiaries, which became important since Faith wouldn't be allowed to inherit, were Arthur Dawes, Lillian Mayhugh, and Alistair McDevitt, the estate to be divided evenly.

Just a few weeks earlier, before Ike discovered the weeping burn patterns on the floor joists in Dorsey's room, I'd mused aloud that Dorsey hadn't seemed real to me. She was real to me now. She'd been real to me from the moment I came upon her picture when I was searching Faith's room. The one of Dorsey in her Emily costume. The picture I had stolen.

I showed it to Ike when we got back to his office, because I had a romantic notion that he would hang it on his wall as a souvenir of the work we'd done on the case. But one look at those wistful doe eyes and the enraptured, joyful expression on her face, and we both knew her picture wasn't going up anywhere.

It was too sad.

I did have five copies of it made, though. I sent one to Arthur Dawes, because he'd described Dorsey as "luminous," and I thought such devotion and insight deserved a reward. I sent one to Buck Fitzgerald, because he'd told Ike that Dorsey was the only woman he had ever loved. I sent one to Dorsey's housemother,

Frances Black, because she'd compared Dorsey to a rose. I sent one to Alistair McDevitt, because he'd taught her to say, "the gaudy, blabbing, and remorseful day is crept into the bosom of the sea." And I sent one to Lillian Mayhugh, because she had been wise and frivolous enough to give Dorsey a flamingo pink feather boa, and she'd taught the young woman to cash her paychecks right away.

I charged the developing costs and the postage to the Browning file, put the original photograph into a folder, gave the folder to Ike, and closed the case.

I was sitting in Ike's big leather chair behind his desk.

It was Friday afternoon, and I knew I should go back to my office and start work on a new file, but I didn't want to. We'd just tied up the last of the loose ends on our adventure, and I had absolutely no intention of facing reality for the rest of the day.

At least, not yet.

I *liked* sitting in Ike's chair. I *liked* his big oak desk. I *liked* his office. It's a nice office. Big room. High ceiling.

Spectacular view.

Ike brought me a cup of coffee. Then he sat down opposite me in the visitor chair, where I usually sit.

I looked at him.

He looked at me.

His eyes are really quite remarkable. They're light. They're dark. They sparkle. They teach. They think.

I drank my coffee but didn't say anything.

Neither did Ike.

Isaac C. Blessing.

It had been a hell of a case, and working with him had been a hell of a ride. For three full weeks, I had envied nobody. Not the meteorologist who can tell a nimbus cloud from a stratocumulus cloud. Not the musical prodigy who can play Tchaikovsky's First. Not Antoine de Saint-Exupéry. Not Margaret Bourke-White. Not even — well, at least on some levels, not even Cyrano de Bergerac.

For the first time in my life, I felt that I was using all of the fuel in every single cylinder that fired up the engine of my brain. My brain was happy, and my happy brain was making *me* happy. I like being happy. I liked working with Ike. I wished that it didn't have to stop, and that it could go on forever. But everybody says that all good things come to an end, and who am I to contradict everybody?

So I stood up and stuck out my hand. "Isaac C. Blessing Associates," I said to Ike, "it's been a real honor."

Ike stood up, too.

The phone rang.

We looked at each other. We looked at the phone. We looked back at each other.

Ike reached for it. "Ike Blessing," he said.

He listened for a while. He said things like "Right" and "Do you have a fire report?" and "Let me look at my calendar."

He scribbled a few notes.

He hung up and said, "I have to go out on a case."

I didn't respond, but God, I felt terrible.

"It's in Coney Island."

He unlocked a drawer, took out a gun and a holster, strapped the holster to the belt of his pants, and tucked in the gun.

I wanted to cry. But I didn't. Not this time.

Ike started to walk toward the door. Then he stopped, turned, and smiled.

"You'll like Coney Island," he said.